$\mathcal{H}$armonies

of

$\mathcal{W}$ar

Ruby Fitzgerald

Soldier Bear Entertainment
Chicago, Illinois

This is a work of fiction. All characters portrayed in this book are either products of the author's imagination or are used fictionally.

HARMONIES OF WAR

Copyright © 2017 Ruby Fitzgerald
in Association with Soldier Bear Entertainment

Edited by Jaime Coates
Cover Art by Przemyslaw Urban
Concept by Soldier Bear Entertainment
Map by Ruby Fitzgerald

A Soldier Bear Entertainment Publication
Chicago, IL

www.soldierbearentertainment.com

ISBN 978-0-692-91361-1

First Published June 2017
Published in the United States

Dedication

To those few people who have stayed
by my side and in my heart through
thick and thin.

Special Thanks to

Steve O'Neill
Jaime Coates
Kat Silvia
Saphina Del
Jeremy Applebaum
Ashley Siech
Zachary Grace
John and Lorie Coates

The Nine Energies of Magic

Fire Sculptor - the ability to conjure fire and manipulate its form

Water Weaver - the ability to conjure and control water

Wind Whisperer - the ability to control weather and provide swift travel

Earth Grounder - the ability to move earth and metals

Seer - the ability to see the multiple paths of one's ever changing future

Mind Handler - the ability to see another's thoughts and manipulate them

Shape Shifter - the ability to change into another living being

Healer - the ability to heal, either themselves or others around them

Spell Spinner - the ability to cast spells

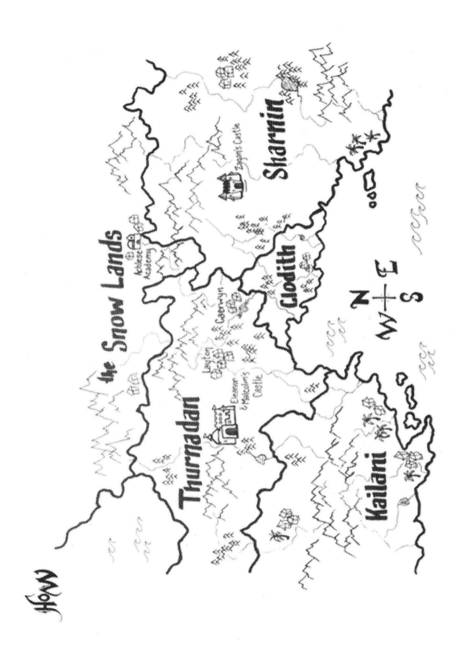

There's beauty in even the most gruesome and grotesque –
in even a shattered soul that's faced neglect
where once a body lay beaten and abandoned
flung free from lashes, steel, and speed
now grows the gentle stem of blossom brightened
beneath the earth where once buckled boots did tramp
and blood was spilt and lives were lost
a baby wolf takes a mewing breath deep'in the soil damp.

I kissed your lips, you kissed my jaw and both our hearts were lost
not to love nor each other but to let our fates crisscross
like the wise-traveled star that embraces its fiery demise
for wearily lost and wandering sought
we search for the home we were always denied
while dreaming of freedom from the strains of temperance
we're led by wind and passion and deathly deep desire
to our lonesome tears and cycling sets of ordinance.

Prologue

Twenty four hours ago the Achlese Academy was destroyed by the evil King Zagan of Sharnin. Zagan has built an army of Descendants by ensuring freedom and a land of their own once Thurnadan is defeated. By destroying the most renowned students and teachers at the Academy, there are no Descendants left to assist Thurnadan. Zagan is confident that there is no longer any that exist more powerful than he.

One

She was blue with cold, lying naked in the snow, wavering between consciousness and the afterlife. Ice began to form around her limbs. All around her the bodies of her dear friends lay still. The battle was lost.

A pain filled her body. Her charred skin, steaming in the snow. She felt the bitter cold on every inch of her skin, her back exposed to the wind. Dark gold scavenger birds beat their wings against the stormy skies in anticipation of the unusual feast before them. As the evening winds rose, howling out the sorrows of wandering souls slain in wars long past, the struggling woman desperately tried to connect to any mind in the vicinity.

Help me, she gasped with her mind into an empty space. Or so she thought. All but one of the birds had now abandoned the grounds and flown away. She stopped, sensing the only mind near her was not friend, but foe.

She watched as the indigo-eyed intruder scoured the tundra below. Circling the field of bodies the bird spotted a jagged rock and landed upon it. His golden feathers ruffled then smoothed into a thick golden cloak that brushed the snow. A man now stood where the bird had been perched. Tall and pale skinned, he stared silently at the slew of mangled bodies beneath him, eyes full of suspicion and resolve.

Help. She closed her eyes and held her breath, quieting her mind.

King Zagan of Sharnin must have ordered him to remain behind and ensure that there were no survivors. She could not risk being discovered.

She heard him step from his perch and kick at several stiff bodies. He was most likely waiting and watching for a response, but she knew he would not find a trace of life left within the waves of icy corpses. She felt his feet move on the ground, getting closer and closer to her. Out of the corner of her eye she watched as he picked up a necklace from the snow. There was a clear stone with black shards running though it hung from a silver chain. He coiled it in his hand and placed it into his pocket. He started to move quicker now. She sensed his impatience as his pauses between bodies became shorter. He must be mindful of the changing evening sky, as she had been, eager to take shelter. In flight, the impending storm would make visibility increasingly difficult, and he was probably anxious to get out of the jagged peaks before the wind whipped him into the pines like a rag doll.

How she wished she could do just that to him, but her weakness was growing.

He must be satisfied with his findings, for she heard him revert to his feathered form and beat the air with his broad, golden wings.

A sigh of relief would have escaped her if she had the energy for one. She needed all of her power to withstand the coming tempest.

The winds of the storm ensued, and cold, white flakes fell heavy, burying her alive as the night slipped into dawn. Almost all feeling had left her body by the time the weary morning sun set fire to the gleaming drifts of snow above her. The crystalline rays of light could not penetrate the thick covering, but rather set it aglow. The silence in the air was interrupted by the crackling of the icy mountain tops as they continued their slow journey down the jagged slopes.

Hope drained from her body along with her remaining strength as she reached out a third and final time. *Please. Help.*

****

A procession of a hundred soldiers guarding two gilded carriages rounded the cliff in the midst of the blizzard ridden tundra. The scout of the footsore party, head hung and eyes squinted against the glare, rode but a few paces from where the attack had occurred, yet neither he nor any other soldier noticed the dead beneath the ice.

Riding in the middle of the caravan, just ahead of the first carriage, two horsemen scanned the surroundings with the sharp eyes of veteran soldiers. Argus, the High Constable, shifted in his saddle with military precision, his expression somber but eyes alert for danger. The other rider held his dark-haired head high and proud with an undeniable air of royalty. King Malcolm, husband of Queen Eleanor and ruler of Thurnadan, was also alert, but it was not danger that pulled at his senses. His back muscles tightened, and his heavily gloved fingers stiffened on the horse's reins.

The wind drove straight through his bones. He was not used to experiencing such cold. King Malcolm looked out into the white mountains and drifts, remembering the last time he went to the Snow Lands when he was a young boy. He had not been back since. The last time had been the same task, to ask the Descendants for aid. He was just a prince then. He looked out over the harsh mountains. In the distance, he could see the rocks falling from the side. They tumbled down into the snow beneath, echoing across the ice. Before his wandering mind completely took over, something else pulled at him. A voice.

The King turned to the bulky, graying rider beside him. "Constable, call a halt." Argus raised his voice to bring the men to a standstill.

"What is it, Your Highness?" Argus asked, deep gravel in his voice. His hand instinctively went to the blade at his side, large muscles flexing in his arm, bright hazel eyes focused intently on his King. "My Lord?"

The King did not respond but rather focused on what he heard - or what he *thought* he heard. He dismounted and unsteadily walked away from his horse. His eyes searched through the wind and snow.

Help me, a voice threaded weakly through his mind, tugging at his consciousness and pleading with his heart. *Help me.*

"Do you hear that?" The King whispered. "It's a woman."

Argus dismounted and followed Malcolm. He shook his head, eyes narrowed with suspicion. "Whole 'lotta Descendants live in these parts. Think it be one of them scoundrels messin' with yer mind?"

The King fell to his knees as a wrenching sob filled his head.

"My Lord!" Argus rushed to lift his King to his feet.

Please. Find me. Help me. The voice pulled at his mind. He felt her pain, her cold.

"Dig. Find her," the King ordered, blue eyes focused with determination.

Malcolm saw the skepticism cross his constable's eyes, but Argus signaled over a dozen silver-clad soldiers to remove the snow where he'd pointed. Within moments, the bare bodies of slain victims were uncovered.

4

"They're dead, Sire. Not a single heart poundin'." Argus continued checking for signs of life... "The attacks are gettin' more violent by the day, it seems."

"And we are too late," the King added, staring at the carnage before him. "These might be those of the Achlese Academy."

King, the voice whispered so faintly Malcolm was barely sure he had heard it. His eyes darted across the bodies. *Help.* He sank to his knees and stretched out his hand to a woman with fiery red hair.

"This one – this woman here! Check her!"

As a soldier, Malcolm had killed more men than he cared to admit and had seen many suffer and die, yet he was still struck hard by the horror before him. These were not soldiers.

Malcolm's voice caught and broke as Argus felt the woman's neck. "Is she...?"

The Constable knelt beside his King while the others shook their heads at the carnage. "At least fifty-five of 'em torn limb from limb, stripped an' left for the birds an' wolves to devour. Ain't nobody coulda' done this 'cept Sharnin soldiers. King Zagan has an army of em'. He's comin', Sire. He's comin' fer certain."

"Sire!" A boy's voice burst through their shock and sorrow. "You're right! She's got a bit of breath!"

Argus called out to the carriage. "Doctor, yer assistant found someone alive!"

The doctor, Lairson, poked his head out of his carriage, skin paling and yellow-green eyes widening in disbelief.

"Impossible," he whispered. "Wounded and out in the snow? Not after this storm. This does not bode well." Nonetheless, Lairson went to the fallen woman. "Magic," he mumbled. "It reeks of magic."

5

The woman's long, scarlet locks covered her upper body but her wounds were still clearly visible. She had a multitude of bruises, burns, and a long, vicious gash that ran across her throat and up the length of her jaw to her temple. She did not move, nor was there a tremor of warmth in her body, but faintly, desperately, a flutter of breath escaped her lips. The doctor stared at her.

"This makes me more than nervous, my Lord," he told King Malcolm. "These people were mercilessly ambushed and slaughtered. I cannot help but know and voice that it's dangerous to meddle here. I think it's best we not make ourselves the next target."

Malcolm ignored the doctor's worries and had the woman covered in blankets and lifted into the doctor's carriage. Since the ground was too frozen to bury them, the rest of the slain were lain together and burned.

"We must return to the Thurnadan Castle at once," the King declared.

"For the sake of the King, do what ya can for the woman," Argus ordered Lairson as the troop slowly regrouped to continue on its way.

****

Lairson stepped back toward his carriage, grumbling with a voice muffled by his hood and shaggy chestnut hair. Once he and his young assistant were inside, the carriage immediately lurched forward and began to move. The doctor fell over. He gathered himself and pounded his hand on the roof of the carriage.

"Give a man some warning!" Lairson spat.

6

Shaking off his long robes, Lairson turned his back to the blanketed figure on his cot, muttering curses under his breath. He did not like the idea of helping this woman, but he did like the idea of keeping his head on his shoulders. He cracked his back and his hands then stretched out his arms. He turned to the woman and called on his own magic.

"Levar agora tirar a dor," he whispered.

Violet sparks danced from his fingertips then burst from his long sleeves, filling the small interior of the carriage. The sparks fell like stars onto her body. "What was that?" his assistant inquired.

"For the pain," Lairson said, grabbing for his medical bag. He reached in and pulled out a vial of pale green liquid. "Uncover her legs, arms and her heart," he instructed the boy.

The boy did as he was told, his hands shaking the whole time. Lairson uncorked the narrow vial in his hand and knelt beside the cot in order to spread the unctuous substance over the woman's heart.

"I know there's magic. And magic can't hide from me," he grunted. A sheer net of gleaming links hovered over the woman's body and softly rounded her curves, lying close along her limbs. "Just as I suspected," he gloated.

After a moment, the potion glowed and both it and the woman began to twist and seize. The air reeked of burnt vanilla and rosemary.

"What is that doing? I thought you healed her pain?" The doctor's assistant asked, extremely unnerved by the woman writhing in front of him.

"It's an Exposing Potion," Lairson uttered curtly. "The stronger a Descendant, the more violet their veins. I can see how bold her blood runs; she thinks she can hide," Lairson laughed. "The richer the blood, the richer the magic. The

7

Exposing Potion will strip her of the spell that hides her Inkings. Watch."

Once the woman relaxed again, the potion faded and seemingly disappeared into her skin. Her veins throbbed as magic roamed furiously beneath her skin. It pulsed out from her heart and up into her neck and face. Lairson smiled, he loved being right. Just as he had expected, a raven-black Inking took shape.

"Seer?!" the boy exclaimed.

Lairson's face was alight with smug triumph when he saw the twisted lines appearing along her nose and left eye, but his mouth fell open when the magic continued down her arms and into her hands. Unexpectedly the magic revealed an Inking of black flames on her left wrist accompanied by an Inking of waves on her right.

"Fire Sculptor! And Water Weaver?!" The boy became nervous. "She has three Energies?"

On her chest, the Inking of a coiled lizard began to appear.

"She's a Spell Spinner too?" Lairson's lips pulled tight and his expression hardened as the magic sliced down her torso and into her legs. Within moments, Inkings of rolling hills and billowing clouds were visible on her ankles.

"Earth Grounder and Wind Whisperer." The doctor raised a hand to cover his mouth then turned away with a mix of awe and horror.

Lairson pounded on the roof of the carriage with three strong knocks and the carriage came to a halt. The doctor grabbed a blanket, covered the woman, then shook his assistant by the shoulders. "Go!" he hissed. "Get the King. Now! We are in great peril!"

The boy sprinted out of the carriage as fast as he could. He ran through the snow, tripping over his feet several times to the snickers of the other soldiers. When he came to the King's side he panted, "My Lord, the doctor says you must come, immediately!"

Malcolm, annoyed at the unexpected delay in travel, followed the boy back to the carriage. "What is it, doctor?" he growled at Lairson as he ducked inside. The King stared transfixed at the shimmering Inking on the woman's face.

"She has the markings of a Seer." "So, she is a Descendant. Congratulations, Lairson. If that is all, we must be on our way."

"My Lord, that is not all. Look" Lairson hesitantly pulled back the blanket from her limbs. "What makes me fearful, Sire, is that she must have an immense ability for each Magical Energy. I noticed her veins when I first examined her. Purple as mulberry wine! I have never seen such potential power. I believe she is a victim of Zagan's savagery, and if I'm right then his army cannot be far from here and we are in the gravest possible danger. You know what Zagan is capable of. Who knows how he did it, but we are no match for that, Sire. We must rid ourselves of her at once!"

"All four elements. And a Seer." The King tapped a finger to his lips appearing to be lost in his own thoughts. "It is amazing, to be sure."

Lairson tripped over his words, fear harrying his speech. "Sire, with all due respect, you do not hear me. We must destroy her while she's in this weakened state. Who knows what terrors she might bring upon us when she's at full strength, assuming Sharnin soldiers don't find us first!"

"Your own talents with magic make you strong, but I do not threaten to murder you in your sleep because of them. Don't be so shortsighted, Doctor. Besides they left her for dead. Heal her and we will speak with her when she is well."

9

"But—!"

"Do not think me a fool, Lairson! With this many markings, *this* many gifts, she must be a student from the Achlese Academy, if not a professor. The Sharnins must have slaughtered these poor souls to keep them from aiding us. Think logically. We have never seen this many Inkings. She could have enough power to aid us in defeating any foe, including Zagan himself."

After straightening the white gold clasp of his cape, the King stood looming over the doctor. His stern countenance gave clear warning. "Tend to her wounds as I instructed. Her counsel may be of benefit to us, and I am certain Queen Eleanor will wish to speak with her." Malcolm turned and leapt down from the carriage.

Lairson called out, "But Sire!"

"Silence. Good doctor, you will keep her alive. We need to know why such treachery occurred."

"Sir," the assistant boy mewed up at his master, "why is her having so many markings a bad thing?"

"Get inside!" Lairson snapped. The boy tripped over his robes as he scrambled inside and Lairson shut the door behind them. With a lurch forward they were on the move again.

"She has more power than has been ever known or seen in one Descendant. That much power in one Descendant is dangerous and concealing it makes it that much more suspicious. One who hides their markings has no respect for the laws of Thurnadan. I know many others who would think the same. I have half a mind to put a rag to her mouth and finish her off myself." Lairson glowered.

"Why cover them?" the boy pressed.

"Exactly," Lairson retorted as he was engulfed in the ramifications of their situation. *Of all the foolish ways to die, taking a Sharnin arrow over some damn girl,* Lairson thought to himself as he rifled through his bag again. "Using a hiding spell is deceitful. Which is why within Thurnadan, all Descendants must show their Inkings so that they can be easily identified," Lairson sighed and reluctantly elaborated, "while some would call them gods, others would call them demons. The lucky and the cursed. In Sharnin, Descendants will immediately be enslaved. Yet some of the vilest possessors of magic are in positions of great power. Such as Zagan, the pitiless King of Sharnin, and his cold-blooded soldiers. Other Descendants hone and perfect their magic, using it to others' benefit. The Achlese Academy in the Snow Lands was full of such people. Those we just buried." Lairson laid his hands on to the woman chest. A blue light shone from his fingers and hovered over her bruises. They began to fade ever so slightly.

"You mean these were the Descendants the Queen asked us to escort from the academy to help against Zagan?"

"Yes, precisely," the doctor huffed. "Queen Eleanor is far more tolerant of the Descendants than most. She too wants the help of magic to counter the violence of the war. Of course, only if they concede to her laws." He removed his hands from her as the blue light lingered. Lairson sat back and looked out the slit window of the carriage. He could see the King riding more closely now.

****

"Argus," Malcolm suddenly turned to his High Constable "I request your counsel: what do you know of Descendants when it comes to battle?"

11

"Sire, it ain't my gray hairs that have taught me a' war," Argus half smiled. "When I were a young and eager man," Argus continued, bringing his horse alongside the King's, "I din' have respect for the simple life, so I took on the soldier's yoke." Argus spoke softly, his voice barely audible above the steps of the troop. His gaze wandered the tundra, "Fights back then were simple an' straightforward. You had a sword or a knife and a shield, and ya fought until it was yer last breath or his. Years after I joined, a terrible war broke out along the Clodith border. I'm sure my King was taught of it."

Malcolm slowly nodded, "The Battle of Clodith and Sharnin. When Zagan annihilated Clodith in just days." He remembered his teachers impressing upon him every misstep of Clodith's military leadership.

"That be the one," Argus agreed. "T'were the most gruesome battle I'ever been witness to. Villager and soldier alike fell by the thousands. Zagan had mighty powerful Descendants. People even said that they were so powerful they had to be Ancients — gods of old come back to destroy the people of Clodith. They had arrows that poisoned in seconds and tundra wolves, claws dripping with venom so strong one scratch will turn ya into a corpse. Fires that would burn 'cross our eyes... the battle was doomed it was. Clodith tried, we did, we faltered an' fell. And the Sharnins, they hadn't any mercy at all. When we who remained alive surrendered, they tied us to their wolves, dragged us along, and then forced us to watch as they destroyed our homes. When they left us to die, we were wounded to our souls. Not many lived ta' the mornin'. When the two men that was wit' me healed, they decided ta' venture home to the river's mouth in hopes that sumone'd survived. But I couldn't go back. Not there. I couldn't bear the sight of all that I held dear in kindling. I were certain that everyone I knew had been slain in that terrible battle," Argus stopped suddenly, his throat tight. "It was many years ago but I can still see that green and white Sharnin banner, a tundra wolf, dagger at its feet, taunting us as it flew o'er our brethren's' fallen bodies. The Clodith banner, with our orange mountains and arrows, lay trampled in the dirt. I wanted to kill every Descendant and Sharnin I could get my hands on."

Malcolm let a slow, thoughtful breath out before meeting Argus' eyes with his own. "And have you?" He asked.

"They're enduring creatures, Descendants, ta' be sure. Killing them don't tend ta' be an easy thing. And I may have the speech of a commoner, but I ain't a dullard. A lotta' Descendants are bonded. Somethin' mental-like, makes it so they can hear each other," Argus tapped a finger to his forehead, "even if they be miles apart. Makes death a brutal thing, I reckon. If ya know it be happening to a friend an' there ain't nothin' you can do. I watched my Captain slice 'is own throat 'cause of Descendants playin' with his mind," Argus swallowed hard, "I've taken a number of their lives, but I ain't proud of it. As I killed em', I got to seein' some o'the ones I'd slain hadn't done no harm. They was healin' my own kind and growin' food in just days for the hungry. Yet my hatred caused their deaths. I gave up my oath. Laid it away, I did. And in battles since, many a time it's been their spells an' strengths that kept me alive. They make evil enemies, Sire, but damn worthwhile allies. Sharnins on the other hand, I'll be takin as many o' them bastards as I can." He smiled grimly at his King as they rode on.

"That is the conclusion I have come to as well. We will let no harm come to the Descendent within our care. Thank you."

"In yer service, your Highness," Argus bowed in his saddle.

The King had a massive feeling of dread growing in his stomach. The methodic swaying of his horse as they rode did nothing to put his mind at ease. "Zagan appears to be not only getting more aggressive in his style of battle, but he is also getting closer and closer to our lands and people. As soon as she wakes we must inquire as to what the woman knows of Zagan and his agenda."

"It is no wonder Thurnadan's queens have repeatedly made the punishments for breaking magic laws more and more severe," Malcolm huffed. "Any kind of mutiny could result in them joining Zagan in our demise." *Or worse, another like Zagan rising in our own halls,* the King shuddered at the thought of a possible enemy within.

"Forgive me if my words be too bold, but people ain't ever been fond of being controlled. Don't be fooled by them Descendants. Makin' a Descendant feel trapped is like snarin' a wild boar an' expectin' it not to try an' maul ya."

"I know," Malcolm admitted. "We need assistance from the Descendants or we may all suffer the same fate."

Malcolm stroked his horse's mane as he tried to clear his tumble of thoughts. He suddenly felt much too tired for his age. Absent of feeling except fatigue, he noted the sky's warning of returning snow.

"We shall stop for a meal and to set up a storm guard."

Argus again bowed in his saddle, then rode to the front of the caravan, calling the halt. Soldiers began to pull to the side into the base of a nearby mountain. It was as much shelter as one could hope for in the Snow Lands.

****

14

Inside the doctor's carriage, the woman twitched in a feverish sleep. Her skin had warmed, but her breathing was still weak and her pulse was erratic.

"Look!" The boy pointed to her face. "You're Healing magic is working!"

Lairson sat on the carriage bench adjacent to the woman, transfixed by the slice across her neck that had been a deep and vicious stroke. He watched as bit by bit her wounds faded, healed, and disappeared. *There is no possible way that this is the work of MY magic,* Lairson ruminated as he witnessed her once vicious wounds heal.

Just as Lairson was recovering from his shock, the carriage slowed to a halt and the King burst in.

"How is the woman doing?" Malcolm inquired.

Lairson turned to him but said nothing.

"How — ?" The King squatted on his heels by the cot. His mouth fell agape as he ran a finger along the faint trace of a cut on her neck. A buzzing tingle ran up his arm and his skin shimmered with radiant gold spirals. Malcolm felt rapidly stronger; the fatigue from earlier drifted away without resistance. He sighed, drawing his finger away from the woman's soft skin. The glow that had encompassed him lingered for a few seconds, then it too drifted away.

"A Healer," Lairson breathed, "she is a Healer as well."

"Isn't she supposed to have the Inking also?" the assistant boy piped up.

To their surprise, the woman coughed and rolled to her side, facing away from them. "You missed one," she stated hoarsely.

Lairson and the King pulled back with a start.

She raised her hand to the back of her neck and gently pulled her hair to the side; there beneath her fingers, another Inking was revealed.

"The gleaming leaves of life do shine, to help and heal all mankind'," the assistant recited, riveted by the Inking in the woman's skin of a weave of vines curling up her neck.

Lairson touched his own Healer's Inking on the back of his neck thoughtfully.

"Healer of others and self," the woman added as she carefully pulled the blanket back around her shoulders. She coughed and then a golden shimmer covered her body and within moments she fell still in a deep healing slumber once more.

"A threat to us, Lairson? I think not," the King chuckled softly. "This is an omen, a wonderful omen. My dear fellow, don't look so pensive. This woman will be a great aide to us!"

"Sire, I must protest."

"Lairson please," the King interrupted in an almost jovial tone. "Do you really think that poorly of me?" the King raised his eyebrows. "I am not irrational." He swept his cape back, clapped the doctor on the shoulder, opened the door then leapt down from the carriage where Argus awaited his King. "We will take the northern route to avoid the Sharnin Army. That should give us a three days journey to the castle. I know it is longer than expected but my feeling is that the army will have headed back to Sharnin with any captives."

"Aye, my King," Argus nodded.

"But the southern route through Caerwyn and Layton would be faster," Lairson interjected.

"We will go north," the King commanded.

Lairson mumbled as he shut the carriage door. He sat down against the wall in a huff.

"Are you the same as her?" the doctor's assistant asked.

Lairson snorted. "No, not at all."

"But you can heal-"

"Yes," Lairson concurred, shooing his assistant away. "I was born with a tiny amount of Healing magic, but it's my medical training that's gotten me to where I am. Hard work, not luck. Her though," the doctor's face crumpled into distaste, "her type tends to be lazy, self-serving, reckless, and thinks they are above reproach. Just because someone has magic doesn't mean they deserve it."

"B-but," the boy hesitated, still confused. "My mother says the Ancients are our forefathers, and the root of all magic because the Ancients thought them worthy, and therefore gifted them with special abilities."

"Does she now?" Lairson chuckled snidely.

"Yes, sir," the boy shifted in his seat uncomfortably. "She says the Ancients' scales were shiny as glass, eyes hot as fire, bodies bigger than the house we live in, and that their minds were so open to the world around them that they could see all things, past, present, and future."

"It's a pretty tale," Lairson sneered, "but it is an old myth and a bedtime story and it doesn't change my mind. The King might think this woman is good, but I am not fooled. Too much power in the wrong hands leads to terrible things." The doctor added more to himself than to his assistant, "Mark my words, she will do us no good at all."

"Myths and bed time stories huh? Old fool. If you are so scared of me what makes you think a simple rag in my mouth would do the trick?" The woman grunted as she rolled over in her cot.

"Quiet witch!" Lairson reprimanded as he stepped out of the carriage, slamming the door. He directed his eyes to the sky. The storm brewing outside suddenly and cruelly heightened its fury. A white-out thickened the midday air. The troop of men with their rescued red-haired Descendant hunkered down for the night despite the early hour.

Two

Seventy miles southwest, Malcolm's wife, the Lady Queen of Thurnadan, was pacing impatiently in her bedchamber. She ran her delicate fingers along the velvet walls. Their violet looking almost blue in the moonlight. The castle fell dark and quiet with the cover of night. Only the flames of the torches in the hall lit the castle. Her trusted lady's maid, entered to find the Queen tucking into a dark, floor length cloak. Light from the hall spilled into the room, casting beautiful shadows on the floor as it gleamed through the wood carved furniture. Her cloak managed to nearly vanish the Queen into the shadows despite her haughty air, striking beauty, and the small, shiny braided silver crown wrapped across her forehead. She tucked her soft waves of golden hair into her cloak. She turned, her violet-blue eyes piercing in the moonlight.

"Your Highness," whispered her maid, "shall I lend a light?"

"Yes, but keep it low."

Bridget, her meek and petite lady's maid, snapped her fingers together and cooed the words of an Ancient's spell, "Dar a luz." The coiled lizard Inking on her chest vibrated as a pale glowing sphere appeared and settled in her palm.

"Be careful now," the Queen walked at a brisk pace being careful to make little sound as they glided out the door and into the cold hallway of the castle.

"You are certain of the risk you take?" Bridget squeaked.

"Yes," she retorted, her eyes hooded and shadowed. "Come, I need you to show me that passage. Do not tarry, we have no time to waste. The King is expected back soon. Should he discover us or our intentions..."

Bridget gulped audibly. "Yes, my Lady," she bobbed a quick curtsy, mousey brown curls swinging down off of her shoulders.

The two moved as shadows across the stone halls, down the grand marble staircase, through lesser used rooms, and then down the narrow servants' stairs that led to the kitchens.

The Queen remained hidden at the base of the stairs as Bridget attempted to inconspicuously enter and distract the castle's cook.

"Bridget!" the head cook bellowed. "Just what do you think yer doing? Don't be assumin' I can't see ya. What're ya doin out late like dis?"

The Queen cringed, backed against the wall trying to remain still, certain her ruse was over, but Bridget just laughed.

"Why, my dear," the maid winked mischievously at the rather large, middle-aged man, "ya know me, I'm always gittin' into trouble." She laughed again flirtatious as ever. "I just wanted to snag a lil' sumtin' to eat."

"Bird," the cook turned away from Bridget. "You knows my Seer's ability means I can tell when you ain't tellin' the truth. And don't be insultin' me by talking like that. I've been hearin' ya talk to the Queen. I knows ya ain't one o' us commoners. Go on, git. Ya hear me?"

"Your Seer ability is as about as strong as I am tall," she joked.

"Aye, I can always tell when ta' King needs more drink."

"So can I," she winks.

Bridget snagged an apple from the counter then stood on her tiptoes to give the cook a peck on the cheek.

"Out, be gone wit' cha girl!" He growled as Bridget glided away. The cook turned his back to the door and his attention back to his kitchen.

"My Lady," she whispered, back to her usual persona. She gestured to the Queen to follow her. "This way. It's clear now."

They walked down the back corridor behind the kitchen's ovens until they came to a dead end.

"I see no way down to the prisons from here," Eleanor looked suspiciously at Bridget, who looked knowingly back at her.

"There is a way, but you're standing on it," she gestured to the trap door on the floor.

"Well, you are the one with magic. Go ahead spell spin," the Queen snapped. "Get it open."

"Zamento," she twisted her fist in a half circle motion. The lock popped open.

After a bit of hassle, Bridget managed to haul open the well-hidden trapdoor to the underground passage. A wooden ladder with missing rungs propped against the wall was barely visible below them. Far below that, the end of the passage was impossible to see. A thick darkness consumed the space and seemed to rise through the air before flooding out onto the floor.

"Get me the light again," Eleanor commanded, pointing to the passage. "Let us see how far this goes."

Bridget snapped her fingers, and the glowing orb returned. She focused her energy on the light until it grew to near the size of her head then dropped it down the passage. It fell slowly, then stopped and hovered about halfway down.

The Queen sighed, resigning herself to the gloom. She pulled her cloak snug around her, then bravely turned to lower herself onto the ladder. A few rungs down, she stopped and looked back up at her maid. "I think it would be for the best if you leave me now. Close the door – I can find my way from here."

Bridget hesitated.

"Go," the Queen insisted, her smooth skin wrinkling as she frowned, "and remember our agreement."

The maid bit the inside of her plump lower lip. She straightened her shoulders and reached for the passage door.

"Good luck, my Lady," she mumbled as she let the door close.

Inside the shadowed passage, the Queen trembled. Each step caused fear to well up in her more and more, but she strode forward, determined. Her stubborn nature, and the oath made to her mother on her deathbed, forced her to continue.

When the Queen at last reached the floor beneath the ladder, her knees buckled and she collapsed in relief. Once she had staggered to her feet again, she waved away the sphere of light and blindly felt her way through the space until she found the handle to a door. She pushed on it, and the door swung inward, scraping a bit as it crossed the floor.

Eleanor peered out anxiously, searching the hallways for guards. She crept into the passage keeping her back to the wall and moving with as much speed as her courage would allow. She knew the prisoner she sought was in the deepest part of the dungeons, far from the main entrance. Eleanor pulled her hood over her head and smiled in an attempt to reassure herself. *You promised, you can do this. It is what must be done,* Eleanor thought in an attempt to steady her nerves. Unfortunately for her, as she rounded the corner of the dank and musty hall, she came face-to-chest with a prison guard.

He grabbed her by the shoulders and spun her around so her chest and head were being painfully pressed into the wall.

"Just where do ya think you're going?" the guard asked mockingly.

"It would be wise of you to remove your filthy hands from me," the Queen spat.

"Oh? And why is that?" chuckled the guard.

"Because you are likely to have your head removed from your shoulders for your transgression," the Queen seethed, shaking the hood off her head.

"My Lady," the guard gasped, dropping to his knees and lowering his forehead to the ground. "I did not recognize - Highness, forgive me!"

"Silence," the Queen growled. She closed her eyes, "Are there others stationed in this hall?" The guard snapped to attention in an inebriated state of compliance.

"Not in this one, ma'am. The next one over. I can call them if you need," he responded eager to please his Queen.

"That will not be necessary," the Queen frowned then raised an eyebrow in contemplation. She spread her fingers wide across the guard's scalp and murmured under her breath. "Thy mind is at mine own mercy." Her violet eyes shimmered as her words took hold. "You will..."

The Queen sighed, feeling a twinge of guilt for using her mind-handling magic. Yet the circumstances called for it. *You must, it is what is necessary,* she thought assuring herself. Her voice strengthened with resolve. "Forget that you have seen me. But first, you will escort me to the Shape Shifter, Donovan. And you will release him."

The guard shuddered under her touch but did not protest her orders. He turned toward the steps at the right of the passage, his feet moved his body down the stairs. The Queen followed, her eyes unwavering from their focus on the back of his head.

He grunted as they reached the solid iron cell door. The bars of his tiny cell were glowing with a rich green light. A glass box slid on the bottom of his cell where small morsels of food were placed for the prisoner every day. These measures were taken to prevent him from shifting. A combination of the spells placed onto the iron and keeping him under fed allowed weakness to prevent him from shifting.

The guard took out his keys, unlocked the nine bolts that opened the door. The Queen touched her fingers to the back of the guard's neck. "Return to your post," she whispered, "and stay there until it is time for you to head home."

The guard saluted, blurry-eyed, and stalked away. "Oh, my dear, sweet Queen," the young handsome man, golden-blond curls falling across his face. "Sometimes, Eleanor, your magical talents unnerve even me."

"Here, eat. You'll need your strength." She pulled a small loaf of bread and dried meat from the deep pocket of her cloak and tossed it to Donovan.

****

The dawn was breaking over Caerwyn, a village about four days' march east from the Thurnadanian castle. Silvia sat alone at the edge of a small green lake. Her narrow waist and warm, earthy complexion gave her a youthful appearance despite her years. She had carefully folded her midnight black hair into a braid cascading down her back. A streak in her hair wrapped perfectly from her temple down though the braid like a single silver ribbon. Although the skin around her mouth was creased with laughter lines, her blue-gray eyes belied the hard life she had lived and the horrors she had endured. It was a rare moment when she was able to slip away by herself. She watched the fish jump in the lake creating ripples of green water. Her soft white shirt billowed in the breeze. The call of the birds in the air made a pleasant song to her ears. Strangely, in this particular session of precious seclusion, she did not feel at peace. The hairs on the back of her neck stood on end. Tiny indentations on the bank and a shimmer in the grasses made her certain she was not alone. She tied the base of her braid with a single strand of leather. As she pushed the braid over her shoulder there was a crack in the shadowed trees behind her. She turned to discover her intruder, but could find no one. Nothing. She turned back to the lake, listening carefully for any signs that would confirm her suspicions. Silence.

Adjacent to her, a pace back from the lake, a man was tucked discreetly behind a large tree. Only his eyes, so pale a brown they were near beige, disrupted the flow of green cloth from his cap to his muddy boots. Invisible and motionless, he watched her.

Silvia sensed his presence. Her expression deepened with apprehension.

"Hello?" she called out. Nothing.

She began to tuck her tight brown pants into her knee-high leather boots. She took one long, sweeping glance around the lake, tightened her laces then turned towards the trees giving one last look into the darkness. Unsatisfied, she swiftly fled up the path toward the village.

She ran through the bushes and the golden fields of Caerwyn, passing workers and farmers on their way into the market, kicking up dust the whole way down the dusty path.

"Silvia! There you are! Where'd you disappear to?" inquired a grandfatherly figure, one of the elders of Caerwyn. He was a sweet and simple farmer that took it upon himself to the caretaker of the villagers.

Gingerly rubbing her temples, she croaked, "Someone was watching me. Just now."

"You saw someone? Who? What did they look like? You were the only one to go down that path for hours," questioned the old man, wrinkling his brows in confusion.

"No. No, I didn't see anyone. I felt them. I felt someone watching me. And there were signs of someone else having been down by the pond." Silvia grabbed the man by his shoulders and pleaded with him to believe her. "Something is wrong," she begged. "I don't know what or how, but I can sense there are intruders. If they are not already here, they will be shortly."

He patted Silvia's hands and gently removed them from his shoulders and anxiously told her, "Go home, Silvia, you can't always think the enemy is right around the corner, people will start to treat you different." He looked at Silvia, a little sad and worried, "Go, your mother was asking for you."

The old man slowly walked away as Silvia tilted back her head, wishing she believed she was just being silly. She ran her hand along her braid in agitation, then hurried down the street to her house. *Could it have just been paranoia?* She wondered as she opened her front door.

From the door, she could see her mother, curled up on a pile of blankets by a small fire. "Silvia? What's taken so long? What's the trouble?" she wheezed when Silvia entered. "Sit," she patted the hard-packed floor beside her, hand trembling faintly as she did so.

"Foolishness is all, mother. I have caught myself up in my own simple foolishness," Silvia replied.

"My brave and noble daughter is incapable of foolishness," her mother said half sincerely as she began to cough violently.

"Here drink," Silvia smiled sadly, holding a clay cup to her mother's lips. "Tell me what ails you. I was told you were calling for me."

She finished sipping the water and stared at Silvia with the kind of silence only a mother could. The kind of silence that let Silvia know that until she confided the events of the day, her mother would no longer speak.

"Alright," Silvia caved. "It happened again today. I believe there were remnants of spies. I know someone's been watching me, watching the village," she paused. "We are not safe." Her mother lay still, eyes closed. For a moment, Silvia's heart raced in panic, thinking her frail mother had passed. "Mother?" she whispered. She gently touched her mother's cool trembling hand.

Her mother's breathing became audible and steadied. Remaining with her eyes closed, she spoke to Silvia in an unearthly strong voice. "You must go to Ryder. He is the voice among us and a wise man despite his youth."

"Ryder is not interested in what I have to say. He never has been," Silvia protested.

"He is fearless, honest, and a proven leader. You have doubts because of his lack of formal training, but your grandmother was Kailani, do not ever forget that. They were the most intelligent of them all, with only real-world experience to train them, none of your formal education. I believe you lost in training to a full blooded Kailani did you not?"

Silvia wanted more than anything to protest her mother's seemingly cruel words, but was unable to. Despite her own feelings she knew her mother was right. Ryder had proven himself and she *had* lost to a Kailani. Her training had failed her before.

"Now, Silvia. Go to Ryder and seek his council," her mother sighed then curled to her side and fell asleep. Silvia reluctantly rose to her feet, looked down at her sleeping mother, refilled her clay cup with fresh water, then hurried out the door.

****

Down the street, to the far edge of Caerwyn, where the village's only ale house resided, Silvia moved toward it with purpose. The streets of the village were alive with the bustle of the morning market. In her swift pace, she nearly knocked into a cart, but spun out of the way with grace and agility. This caught the attention of a nearby group of children who gave a short but excited cheer. She stopped to smile at them and tossed a coin into the pouch of the vendor. She grabbed two oranges and playfully tossed them to the children. She gave them a wink and was gone back to the task at hand.

As she lifted her eyes over the crowd she finally spotted Ryder. He was tall and brawny but not bulky. He had the kind of frame that told you he knew how to handle himself but the soft presence of one for whom battle was a last resort. The scar interrupting his left eyebrow was not earned in battle but in an accident in his youth that marred his otherwise perfect features. Despite his lack of years, he was a strong voice for the people of Caerwyn and they trusted him. He was tying up his horse at the village ale house when she caught up to him.

"Ryder!" She called. "Oh, Ancients, you stink!"

"Silvia. Good morning to you as well," Ryder greeted her with as much charming sarcasm as he could muster. His sandy hair fell into his hazel eyes and the shadow of his golden wheat colored beard was short but pronounced. For a moment, she forgot her mission.

"I urgently need a moment of your time." Silvia insisted, glancing around at the men striding in from the fields.

"Of course. Come eat with me," Ryder led Silvia toward the ale house, his free hand guiding her gently by her upper arm.

"Don't you want to-," she gestured at the water basin nearby for him to at least wash up a bit.

"Yes, well, can't have you dining with a foul beast now can we," he ribbed. "I'll be in in a moment." Silvia turned to go inside, but not without bashfully catching a glimpse of Ryder as he removed his vest and shirt. He gave her a wink as he caught her staring. Silvia stormed inside, covering her flushed cheeks.

Once inside, Silvia took a seat near the window. Careful to choose the seat in the corner so as to not cause a scene with her news. After a few moments Ryder walked in through the door, still wet but much less fragrant.

"Speak your mind," Ryder said as he gestured for the barkeep to bring them two ales.

"Down by the lake..." Silvia started and stopped, uncomfortable with voicing her concerns.

"Yes?" Ryder inquired, as a barmaid set a loaf of bread and large wedge of cheese on the table. He immediately reached for it.

Silvia was annoyed and it showed in her tone, "By the lake there were subtle signs of intrusion. As though someone had been there but not wanted to leave a trail." She left her thought unfinished, fidgeting as she watched Ryder eat.

Ryder chewed slowly, swallowed, then asked, "A stranger, you think?" He ran his calloused hands through his already mussed hair. Silvia nodded solemnly. The barmaid came back and set two pints of Queen's Stout in front of them.

"What is this?" Silvia questioned, staring into her cup.

"It's the Queen' Stout. Try it, you'll like it. Vanilla and cinnamon."

"Fancy," Silvia said as she took a sip. "It's good!"

"I told you. Now what is it you were saying?"

"Last week in the Mordelan's forest I was hunting and came upon a half-eaten Falcon."

Ryder was not convinced, "I can name a thousand creatures that would dine on a Falcon."

Silvia was growing impatient. She slammed and open palm on the table and shouted, "it was half shifted!"

"Stop," Ryder interrupted, his eyes darting across the room. "Calm down."

Silvia composed herself, the gritted through her teeth, "It was half-shifted into human form with the green clothing of a Sharnin soldier. It looked like something enormous had taken it's left arm off and a huge bite out of its side. I have no idea how he got there but that is what it was."

"Is this absolutely what you saw? Do you swear on the Ancients that he was in Sharnin Soldier attire?"

"I do, I tried telling Avokki but he insisted I was seeing things and that I stop being so foolish." Silvia steadfastly held her gaze with Ryder.

"It sounds like a tundra wolf mistook him for a meal and attacked before he had the chance to shift. Silvia, I wish you had come to me sooner," Ryder spoke resolutely. "On my trade routes, there's been entire counties wiped out by magic. Whole towns nothing but ash, valleys and homes flattened by gusts of wind so strong they uprooted trees. Anyone left alive had no mind of their own, like it's been taken away, everything washed clean out of their head. Usually, the first sign of Sharnin invasion is a Shifter scoping the lands and reporting back to King Zagan. Only this one doesn't seem like he got the chance to report, which means they will send another. Which explains the signs of intrusion you saw." Goosebumps rose on his arms, "Sharnin is raiding, torturing, and killing without mercy. I've even heard rumor that Zagan is pursuing the Thurnadan castle."

"That's insane!"

"Shhh!"

"Sorry. So, what are we going to do?" Silvia urged.

"What can we do? He has an entire army of Descendants. Powerful ones. With them under his control I don't see how anyone can stand up to him. Our best bet is to hope he won't come here. I don't see why he would, there are no Descendants in this village. Maybe he sent scouts just to confirm that."

"Wait, how can he control Descendants?"

Ryder leaned in over the table and he spoke softly as it creaked under his weight, "I've heard stories that he feeds them the Indigo Venom to keep them powerless."

"Indigo Venom?!"

"Shhh."

"But I thought the Indigo Venom just stripped away your power?"

"He uses a small dose to keep them just weak enough so that he can control their minds. Zagan is a Mind Handler."

"He must be hunting Seers then. To make that much Indigo Venom would take more Seers than I thought still existed," Silvia realized. Ryder stared wide eyed at her. "What? I've heard things too," she confessed. "My grandmother was Kailani. She told me about the Indigo Venom once. You need Seer's blood to make it work. The only living Seer thought to still exist with enough power was last seen at the Academy."

"Although it's hard to tell with so many of the Descendants covering their Inkings," Ryder interjected.

"Yes."

"The Sharnin army has become unstoppable with the Descendants under Zagan's influence."

Silvia had become quite pale and seemingly feverish. Beads of sweat had formed in her hairline.

"Silvia? You okay?" Ryder reached over to check her forehead.

"I'm fine," she insisted, lightly removing his hand. "I know Zagan has no mercy, and to have that kind of power is an unimaginable force of destruction." She paused, the light draining from her eyes. "Except it's imaginable to me. It's very real to me."

"Silvia my apologies, I'd forgotten that you lived in Clodith when it fell to Sharnin."

"Yes, and it was the Battle of Clodith and Sharnin that brought me here. I couldn't fight that war. I escaped as best I could and am in no hurry to go back."

"You were a soldier?" Ryder's brows raised in disbelief.

"Yes. And this town has given me the peace I have desperately searched for."

"I would never have guessed," Ryder teased her. For a split second, a smile attempted to form on her face, then fell.

"We must make a stand against the Sharnin. They are coming. I know it."

Head turned looking out at the fields, Ryder spoke slowly, "I've kept the horror stories from the villagers because I don't want to raise a panic among them," his voice faded.

Silvia snorted and looked out the window on to the street of innocent villagers going about their day. "Cruelty does not even begin to describe the nightmares Zagan is capable of. This is the time for panic! They need to be worried." Silvia turned her head to look at Ryder, his strong figure silhouetted by the dusk light.

"Silvia," his hands clasped into fists, "they are not here. We don't even know if they are going to come here. What would they even want with us?"

"You still don't understand. I know he is coming. I can feel it."

"Oh, I didn't realize you were a Seer," Ryder jested. Silvia punched him in the arm.

"We need to act now. As quickly as we can. Night will fall soon and then it will be too late."

"Listen to yourself, preparing for a battle that may never come. Don't be foolish."

Silvia stood and she slammed her fist on the table. "It will come. I will be ready. And if you were smart you would be too!" She turned to realize the whole room has fallen quiet. She stared Ryder down for a moment, then moved quickly out the door. Ryder was left staring at her through the window as she disappeared into the bustling street.

Three

At the Thurnadanian castle, the first blue light of morning peeked into the dungeon through a small grate in the ceiling, high above the corridor. Eleanor waited with Donovan as he regained his strength.

"I am not reducing myself to the vile persona of a rat to exit this dungeon. You can escort me out in my human form with dignity," Donovan hissed, cheeks red with scorn.

"Donovan! For pity's sake!" Eleanor dismissed him. "I risked myself and my crown," she continued "and for what? You to debate me for which creature is best to shift into to escape! Besides, no one ever sees a rat coming. You have only moments before the morning changing of the guard begins, the choice is yours. Mother put you in here, she should have left you to die. I, fortunately, have never suffered a guilty conscience. I would leave you to die. Unfortunately, I promised mother I would honor her last requests."

"You are so charming, dear sister," Donovan muttered sarcastically as he patted Eleanor on the cheek.

"Half-sister," she snapped, drawing away from his touch. Donovan just laughed.

"You have always been so weak. Always one to please, to obey, and make everyone happy,"

"Stop!" the Queen demanded.

"Did mother coerce you into promising to free me with her dying breath?" He taunted with glee, stepping so close to Eleanor, she could feel his breath on her lips. "Just like mother to leave you with a mess," he taunted. "And just like you to be mother's little puppet. Even in death she has you running errands."

"How dare you!" Eleanor slapped him.

"Yes," Donovan purred clutching his cheek. Eleanor turned away from him. "And now you reign. 'The Ivory Queen'. Look at how pure her young beauty is. So sweet to take in all those Descendants, having no magic herself," Donovan teased. "Isn't that the story?"

"You know nothing," Eleanor snapped.

"Oh, but I do. If the people knew about me, I'd rule, but as it is I'm not the man you're worried about."

Eleanor turned back to him.

"That's right. I know all about King Malcolm and how he gets the adoration of your subjects. All the while your subjects forget they even have a Queen. Remind me again who rules Thurnadan?"

"I should let you rot in here."

"Yes, you should. That is why you will never be the Queen Mother was," Donovan's small nose crinkled up. He shook his head slowly, "I wonder what my father will think of all this." The steady beat of footsteps sounded down the hall, pausing Donovan mid-sentence. "My father, will find all of your little Descendants, and will enjoy controlling every single one of them, even...you."

"So, it's true?! Zagan has secured the Indigo Venom? Someone with so much hatred should not possess something so strong." Eleanor pleaded. Suddenly starting to put the pieces together, the bizarre events of the last few weeks all pointed to one thing. War. Eleanor began to feel light headed. "Zagan will never have Thurnadan."

Donovan laid a single finger on Eleanor's pursed lips. "Now now sister, the guard will hear you."

Donovan's gaze snapped to the cell door in realization the guard was about to be upon them, a smile started to pull across his face. He snorted defiantly. Donovan rolled his neck and stretched out his limbs, feeling for his magic. "It has been such a long, long time since I have become such a foreign creature," he focused intently then dropped to the floor as a medium sized rat. All but his hollow green eyes were unrecognizable. He scampered around a bit, toes tapping on the stone floor, then stood on his hind-legs and bobbed his head a few times as if assuring himself that his rat form was indeed all in one piece.

"And I wonder why my subjects are terrified of magic," Eleanor shook her head. She felt the impending sense of doom because of her choice to free her half-brother, but it was now out of her control.

Eleanor turned to creep out the cell door and down the hall. Cautiously, she made her way back to the hidden passage. She heard only her own breathing and the tap-tap-click of rat-Donovan making his own escape. As the suddenly weary Queen took one last look around the dungeons she saw the white-tip of her half-brother's tail as he disappeared into the shadows of the hall.

"Guards!" A terrified voice shouted into the darkness. "Sound the alarm! There's been an escape!"

****

The afternoon sun was beginning to fall in Caerwyn, bright red streaks flared across the horizon. Silvia stood at the threshold of her small house. It was quiet, except for her mother's coughing occasionally cutting through the air. Silvia looked down at her fingers as she absent-mindedly twisted a gilded pommeled knife between her fingers. The knife slipped, slicing her index finger. The dark red blood pooled in the cut and dripped onto the grass. She then pulled the knife away and watched as the cut vanished. She wiped away the blood, her finger was left unharmed. Her horse tied nearby was becoming unusually restless. She turned to check her mother was still breathing. Suddenly, she heard the buzz of an arrow. She looked to the sky, another, then another. The ambush she feared had begun. The Sharnins were here.

"Silvia?" A crackling whisper of a voice came from the bed by the wall.

"Mother!" Silvia gasped as she ran back in the house. She dropped to her knees by her mother's side. "I have to get you out of here. Now!"

"No," she cooed. "My healing magic has dissipated. My time has come," she smiled softly. Toothless and wrinkled, white hair mostly gone, Silvia's mother knew she was too old and weak to survive a journey. She knew that her going would only slow the others down. "Eventually love, even the strongest of us must die."

"I can't just leave you here!" Silvia begged. Once again, her eyes filled with tears. Her hand trembled as she reached to tuck the blankets more closely around her mother.

"Yes, you can. Because you must."

"Mother please!" Silvia felt her heart breaking but she knew her mother was right. She was tired of saying goodbye to those she loved. Another arrow whizzed through the sky. Silvia's mother patted her gently on the head as the clamor of battle grew in volume. Finally, Silvia found the strength to rise unsteadily to her feet. She crossed the room, to a carved, cedar chest. Silvia withdrew and dressed in the armor of her family. The blood of her father and her grandfather, fierce with the might of generations of soldiers, coursed through her veins with firm resolve. She tightened the straps of the leather vest quickly and slid her arms through the metal bracers and fingerless black gauntlets. Finally, she placed the slim breast plate over her head and tightened it. The white dragon of the Kailani emblazoned across the chest. She had not worn it in years, yet her armor still fit her well.

"Silvia?" Her mother reached out as tears began to wet her cheeks. "Ancients guide you." Silvia ran back to her mother, held her hand and kissed her on the forehead just as a flaming arrow pierced the roof of their home. The roof was quick to catch fire. "Go. You must go," she whispered.

Silvia solemnly bowed her head toward her mother, grabbed her sword and knife then strode through the door toward the sounds of battle. Another burning arrow sliced through the air and into the dry grass. She turned back, only once to see her whole house being engulfed in flames. A rage filled her as she watched orange flames leap towards the sky, setting fires along her street and lighting shadows with a hellish gleam. Silvia mounted her horse and, setting her gaze on the village, tore away to join the fray. A cold sweat settled on her skin as she leaned forward, and coerced her horse into a gallop. Loose rocks sprayed out behind her horse's hooves as she drew her sword and prepared to take revenge for everyone she had ever loved.

This time I will make it right! This time I will not run! I will make those animals pay for every life they have taken! Silvia reassured herself despite her apprehension. *Those who threaten my home, my peace, and my friends will not live to take another soul.*

She pushed away the memories of bandaging the wounds of fighters who had survived, when she had been unable to save her family. Silvia reached the far edge of town. The villagers were in a panic, the rooftops alight with flames. Screams and cries from women and children flooded the streets. Silvia spotted a young boy. Too young to fight, but old enough to help. "You there!"

The boy turned to her and looked up at her on horseback. "Me?"

"Yes, go and get the women and children together, head for the forest to the west, go toward the Thurnadan castle and seek safety there," Silvia commanded. The boy nodded his head and ran off to gather everyone he could.

Silvia turned back to the street. From the hills to the east she saw the Sharnin approaching. A small group of only a hundred or so soldiers.

Ryder stumbled out of the ale house and saw Silvia on horseback. Silvia gave him a shocked look, "Have you been in there all day?"

"I didn't have any plans. Is this really what you want to discuss right now?!" Silvia shook her head. "How many?"

"About a hundred."

Ryder moved to mount his horse. He grabbed his axe from his saddle. In one swift move, he was on his horse. "Let's go!"

They rode to meet the Sharnin soldiers at the edge of town in hopes of giving the villagers more time to flee. Behind Silvia and Ryder, a group of the Caerwyn soldiers followed them into battle. Silvia charged head long into a group of soldiers. Her sword slicing through the chin strap of the first Sharnin. Blood from his neck sprayed onto the soldier behind him, blinding him and giving Silvia enough time to reel back and thrust her blade between his chest plate and left pauldron. Her blade quickly became slick with blood.

The motions were coming back to her. Her body and sword became one as she cut a swath through the Sharnin troop.

No more! Stop them! I must stop them! Silvia repeated to herself as she redirected an oncoming Sharnin sword and plunged her own sword into the back of the soldier's neck. Her Healer ability was being pushed to its limit as arrow after arrow whipped by her, several of them grazing her exposed shoulders. She could feel the Sharnin poison being expelled from every cut before the wound could heal. Her body began to ache with the impact of defense. In the darkness, the pain, the blood and the sweat, the screams and slicing of metal rang out. Tornadoes of wind and dirt burst from the cobblestone streets as pounding rain, vicious flames, and the figures of wolves, soldiers, and Descendants moved through the morbid dance of war.

Suddenly Silvia was hit in the chest by a smoldering ball of flame. Falling out of her saddle, Silvia's back hit the ground and the air rushed from her lungs. A Sharnin soldier set the tip of his blade to her throat and grinned.

"If I had more time, I'd get a lot of satisfaction from your suffering," he sneered. Certain her death had come at last, Silvia swallowed and said nothing. The soldier's arm tightened as he prepared to thrust. His helmet suddenly shook as a great battle axe came crashing down on it. The once cocky soldier fell limply to the ground with Ryder's axe affixed to the back of his skull.

"Get up, get moving," Ryder barked at Silvia as he pushed the dying Sharnin off his axe.

Silvia sprang to her feet and met another soldier head-on. Their swords crossed, sliced, and swung until Silvia gained the advantage. She watched her blade plunge into the man's heart, and into the next man's stomach, across the next man's throat. She lost track of the number of soldiers she killed, their faces of matching agony became blurred together in her mind. Her own blood mixed with her enemies' as her injuries accumulated far more quickly than her magic could heal. She could summon no more energy to heal. Not as fast as the attacks came.

The streets around her were covered with the bodies of the fallen. The few Caerwyn people on the battle field that remained alive were greatly outnumbered. In exhaustion and grief, they lowered their blades, dismounted, and dropped to their knees in defeat. Ryder, among the soldiers that fell to his knees, looked over to Silvia with a subtle nod. Silvia sank to the ground, she kissed the hilt of her sword and closed her eyes. She knew what was now to come.

Four

Malcolm's caravan continued on its way home, through the early nightfall. The cold of the Snow Lands lingered in the King's bones, making him shiver. He pressed his legs more firmly against the sides of his mare for warmth. Northern winds, blizzards, and the rough, icy terrain had caused many delays, making the King concerned about matters he was unable to presently attend to back in Thurnadan. He pressed onward. The wind whipping through the peaks of the mountains that separated the Academy from Thurnadan made it all but impossible to hear. The snow drift hung thick in the air. The King was startled when Lairson tumbled out of the carriage in a most undignified manner. He ran to where Malcolm and Argus were riding. They chuckled at the doctor's confused expression and disheveled appearance.

"My Lord," Lairson huffed, "she wants to speak to you."

"Halt!" Argus commanded. The carriages rolled to a full stop.

The King dismounted quickly and went to the carriage. "Lairson, care to join me?" He asked as he stepped aboard.

Lairson's face pinched. "Afraid not, she dismissed me," he retorted, irately. Malcolm smiled and ducked inside. The red-haired Descendant, almost completely healed but still weak, sat up at the King's entrance. She spoke somberly without opening her eyes. Still wrapped in blankets, naked beneath the sheets, the King was inclined to view her as feeble and perhaps only loosely grasping her senses. He sat across from her.

Her eyes flashed open with a blue light glowing from her eyes. The King stumbled back a bit. Then the light faded to reveal her beautiful honey colored eyes. "Trust me," she reassured. "Do not doubt what I have to tell you. I have unsettling news that you must believe. Your Queen...Eleanor... has betrayed you." The King snorted dismissively and was about to make a flippant reply when he looked closer at her eyes. The faint hint of an indigo rim around the pools of honey entranced him. Suddenly, spirals of gold magic filled the room. In a spellbound gaze, Malcolm felt every thought and memory, worry and satisfaction he had ever experienced swell from his being and pour into the woman before him. It was as if his very soul was washed from the shore of his body, seduced and drawn out by her stunning eyes.

When he felt empty, a fragile physical shell of all that had once filled him, he sighed and felt strangely peaceful. But, with a blink, Malcolm jerked back into his previous being. He pressed his eyes shut and clutched his hands across his face. The clanging and muttering of his returning thoughts and emotions thrashed about, attempting to break free from the King's body once again. Only after the rattling ceased did he dare uncover his face and look again toward the Descendant.

"What did you do to me, woman?" Malcolm howled, rising unsteadily to his feet in self-protectiveness.

"You may call me Aurora, I did not harm you," the woman smiled comfortingly.

"What you just did-"

"I am powerful but, despite the reservations your doctor has voiced, I have no evil intentions. I am, was, a student at the Achlese Academy."

Feeling as vulnerable as an exposed nerve, the King shuddered. "Wait," he said as he held up one finger. "That feeling is familiar," he waved his hands in front of his face, unsure how to find what words he wanted. "What you just did to my mind, erasing my thoughts and then putting them back, I remember it from a very long time ago."

"My Lord, you have no magic, yet somehow I felt your presence. I knew your name and could call out to you. There are only so many ways that this is possible. Perhaps you knew one of my companions previously. All Descendants can make a mental connection if they care to, but it is delicate when connecting with humans. It can drive them mad. You see, to mind connect, you must let me in. For most humans, the connection can be disorienting. Of course, you can refuse a connection but it takes an incredibly strong mind to do so. If one's mind is not strong, one's mind is not their own."

"Are you saying that I am weak minded?"

"No. I'm saying that you are kind hearted. Not many would dig through ice and snow for a single life," she bowed her head. "I am grateful to you, King Malcolm."

"You were in my mind."

"I am a Seer. I looked through your past and into your future. Your return may not be met with glad tidings. Haste must be taken to get back to the castle. I will aid you in your travels," Aurora briefly turned away to hide her eyes. "I owe you a great debt for finding me and giving some dignity to my companions in their death. Please trust me and let me help you. Go and prepare your homesick soldiers for a quick journey, I will gather my strength, and take us into the warmth of Thurnadan sooner than imaginable."

"I am afraid I must protest your offer," Malcolm somberly replied.

"You saw the destruction Sharnin rained down on my companions and I," Aurora beseeched him. "Why would I lie?"

"Before we left Thurnadan, I received word from your Dan'te that some Descendants were willing to assist us if we returned the favor by aiding against King Zagan's Mind Handler influences. I did not want to assume you were from the Academy though. Assumptions are foolish to make," Malcolm tilted his head in acknowledgement.

"Now it's only my assistance you can get."

"Out of respect for the generosity of the Academy and the trauma you have sustained, I will hear you out. But I will be watching you," the King said as he turned and left.

"Thank you," Aurora bit her lip, knowing she would have to inform him of everything she had divined soon.

****

As a captive of Sharnin, Silvia limped along in only slightly conscious exhaustion. Her eyes were swollen, and she was covered in cuts, scrapes, and burns. Their hands tied and chains around their throats, Silvia and her companions were forced to follow a hideous tundra wolf in the midst of a rank of soldiers. She counted about thirty soldiers leading her, Ryder, and about ten of their companions. Her vision swayed with weakness; every gulp of air she took caused searing bolts of pain through her lungs. Even the cool shade of the forest at night could not sooth her beaten body.

If they did not rest soon, Silvia feared she would faint and be drug through the dirt until she was strangled to death. She could not let herself give up; she just had to give her magic more time to gain strength so she could heal. She willed herself to take one more step then one more... one more... one more...

****

"Your Majesty," Aurora called, emerging from the carriage, healed and invigorated. Clothed in men's trousers and a shirt made from tied-together blankets. Malcolm dipped his head to the Descendant with both caution and respect. "I propose we cross the miles on a breath of wind," proclaimed Aurora.

"And what might that be?" the King inquired, his suspicions rising.

"I can have us to Thurnadan castle by morning."

"What exactly are you referring to?" Lairson scoffed, coming toward Malcolm and Aurora from the back of the ranks.

Aurora grinned playfully, "I'm surprised at you, Lairson. A man trained in the magics, as I assume you have been, should be aware of the ability of a Whisperer to create flight."

"I feel a violation of many laws is about to happen," Lairson narrowed his gaze.

"Well then, it's a good thing we're still in the Snow Lands." Aurora continued, "It seems a fitting enough time to travel with all haste. With your permission, Sire," she beamed at Malcolm, "I will turn the breeze a bit and take you home."

"Do you seriously intend to carry us all?" Lairson shrieked. "No Whisperer is that strong!"

Aurora raised a playful eyebrow to Lairson and the King. She looked to Argus as he glared at her before turning away. "What my King wants will be," Argus said begrudgingly.

"Then, Aurora, make it so," the King announced.

46

"You cannot be serious about this," Lairson screeched. "We will be turned sideways and crushed by her lack of strength," the frightened doctor warbled.

"Lairson, you saw with your own two eyes just how much magic runs in my veins. You should not doubt that I can do as I say."

"That doesn't mean I trust you."

"We have never seen the Ancients of old times and yet we trust that the prophecies of our faith and fate were written by them. We have never seen where the sun goes when it passes the horizon and yet we trust that it will return in the morning. We have never,"

"I reiterate, the Ancients are just fairy tales. You are trying to get us all killed, you fool woman!" Lairson squealed.

"Well, I can leave you behind if you really don't care to rely on my magic," Aurora smirked.

The King faced Aurora and spoke simply, "I feel swiftness justifies any risk in this situation. Please assist us in any way you can."

"Right away, My Lord," Aurora nodded then gracefully raised her hands to the sky.

"But Aurora?"

"Yes, Highness?"

"Do bring Lairson along. He does come in handy on occasion," the King chuckled as did several nearby soldiers, and even a smirk came across Argus' stone face.

"Certainly," Aurora laughed. "I will ensure he arrives alongside the rest of us. Mostly intact." Eyes wide and glowing, she raised her hands and curled her fingers as if caressing the air. The palest of sparks flowed from her outstretched fingers as she turned to the troops.

"Embrace the wind," she shouted to the men. "Do not be frightened." With that a gust of cold wind blasted passed them. Snow billowed and plumed around them. Argus' horse reared but was quickly calmed. "Forward!" Aurora's eyes twinkled as her hair swayed around her face. The wind fell against the ground, hissing and swirling like a caged animal before she settled its strength beneath their feet to slowly raise them up. A call of alarm spread from horse to man but it was not long before all became accustomed to the odd, lofty position. With a flick of Aurora's wrists, they were off, gliding above the ground at a speed that awed the weary soldiers.

****

Eleanor stared at her breakfast plate. She picked absentmindedly at the hot food in front of her. *I can't believe I freed Donovan.* Eleanor thought as she got up and walked to the fireplace. Its jagged edges protruding out into the room, taunted her mind. She was torn between the outright horror and rebellious glee she felt at her actions. Eleanor traced her fingers along the stone mantel as she faded into a reflective yet self-absorbed, trance. She knew she had loved the King once when they were young. They had made love before this very fireplace. The Queen smiled at the warm memory. A crash in the hall brought her back. She shook off the thought and let her eyes fall to the cold extinguished fireplace before her.

"My Lady, my Lady," a servant panted as he came quickly into the dining hall, trying to catch his breath. "King Malcolm's party was sighted descending from the summit of Mount Thurn, but moving marvelously quick! The scout says he should be here within the hour." The Queen made no response except to raise one fair eyebrow. "My Lady, what

48

greeting shall we arrange?" the servant questioned. Eleanor heard the whispers that threaded through the now bustling halls.

"Bring me Bridget."

The servant scurried off.

She was furious that Sharnin's savagery had made her hold on her throne and on her husband so weak. Only two years had passed since her coronation, and already her reign had been corrupted. Her subjects had idolized Malcolm and her both equally when they had first come to power, but Eleanor feared with the threat of a Sharnin invasion, the people would look to Malcom to lead.

"Oh, for Ancients' sake, Bridget!" She rang a bell for assistance. Immediately her lady's maid entered the dining hall.

"Yes, my Queen," Bridget bowed.

"Have a special feast set for the returning soldiers. Make everything to the highest perfection. Nothing spared. Make sure everything is prepped for their arrival. Now go." Bridget bowed and left the dining hall with a quick pace.

Eleanor walked out into the hall of the castle. The servants stopped their furious cleaning and preparations to bow to The Ivory Queen as she looked ahead with still eyes. Each step she took, thoughts of her brother and her treachery fell from her head like petals from a wilted flower. Eleanor plotted to seduce her husband and win back his devotion; it was not long before her sole obsession was on perfecting her appearance to overwhelm Malcolm with lust.

****

The high sun shone brightly in the sky, the Queen and her entourage stood stiffly at the top of the castle's grand balcony, awaiting the King and her soldiers. The Queen was swathed in a flowing spun-silver gown with a low, off-the-shoulder neckline to accent her figure. Her hair had been finely braided then looped in a bun so that a few braids curled around her face and slid down her neck like honey. Pink rouge brightened her cheekbones and her violet-blue eyes were majestically accented by a brush of sapphire liner. A crown of the whitest silver diamonds stood atop her head.

There was no sign of them. The Queen looked out for proof of their return. A vicious wind rose and fell just as quickly. Eleanor shielded her eyes from the wind, and when she returned her eyes to the castle grounds below her, the carriage and troops stood in the center of the courtyard. King Malcolm, looking as triumphant as ever, bowed his head with a loving smile to his beautiful Queen. She returned his favor.

To Malcolm and his troops, the Queen was a visage of pure radiance. Her smile fell when she watched a young woman exit the doctor's carriage. A stunningly beautiful woman with fiery red hair. Her eyes bore right into the Queen's. Eleanor was struck with the sensation of being disapprovingly scrutinized. It made her tremble that, despite her beauty, she still somehow felt cumbersome and imperfect.

Her gown flowed behind her as she descended the marble stairs. She stepped forward to address the troops. "Tend to your horses, enjoy a bath. A feast will be waiting for you in the banquet hall." The soldiers cheered in thanks as they moved to the stalls of the castle with their horses.

"My Lord," she finally greeted Malcolm. She kissed her husband on both cheeks, then turned to Argus, "High Constable."

"My Lady," Argus bowed.

"Good Doctor, how was the journey?" She asked of Lairson.

"Eventful, my Queen," he sneered as he pushed past them and strode into the castle, his assistant boy lagging behind him.

"And who might this be?"

"May I present Aurora. She is a Descendant from the Academy," Malcolm gestured to Aurora to come forward.

"Majesty," Aurora bowed.

"Just one," the Queen demanded. "I would think there should be at least a hundred. Where are the others?"

"If I may. The Academy fell under attack of the Sharnin. I am the only to have survived," Aurora confessed. Eleanor took a moment to take in the Seer Inking around Aurora's eye.

"I am a Seer, your majesty."

"I can see that."

"My Queen," Malcom spoke but stopped short at the sight of Eleanor's glare.

"And a Whisperer," the Queen said noticing a second Inking. "That explains the haste with which you returned to me."

"Yes. And a Weaver, a Grounder, a Sculptor, a Handler and a Healer. As well as a Spinner."

The immobile Queen watched in disbelief as Aurora reveled the Inkings on her skin.

"And, Aurora, can we count you with us? Do you swear your allegiance to Thurnadan and to me?" the Queen inquired.

Aurora bowed her head. "Yes." Her gaze remaining on the ground in front of her feet.

"Then perhaps I will make an exception for you to cover your Inkings. I don't want to cause hysteria amid the castle. Surely you understand your presence will cause a stir."

"Of course, your majesty." With one sharp blink of her eyes, the Inkings disappeared.

"Now, we will prepare for a feast. We must celebrate the safe return of my husband and soldiers." The Queen twirled back toward the castle and on the arm of her King, they strode up the stairs into the castle. Argus followed, leaving Aurora a bit apprehensive at the bottom of the staircase.

****

Slinking through the shadows of the trees, Donovan had quickly shifted from a vile rat into a wolf, watching the Thurnadan castle from afar. He longed to get back into the castle as quickly as possible, except this time not as a prisoner. No, this time he must enter the castle to claim his half-sister's throne. It was rightfully his, and he should not be denied simply because he was a product of The Great Queen's infidelity. He had to devise an absolutely impenetrable plan, but something kept gnawing at his insides. There was an unsettling feeling he could not locate.

Donovan knew that magic was somehow involved in the King's arrival and that the troop's return banquet would be rich, rowdy, and full of drunken soldiers. Donovan crept through the gardens. The scent of ash floated on the humid breeze causing the flags of the turrets to ripple.

Catching his eye, Bridget slipped quietly into the outer garden a short distance from where he crouched. Donovan cocked his head to one side, smelling the lingering scent of cinnamon bread and bathing oils that came from the maid as it threaded through the misty air.

What do we have here? Donovan wondered. As she sat down gingerly on an old bridge by the stream, Donovan's eyes snapped open with glee and his wolf jaws pulled wide into a panting grin. *This will do quite nicely.* He thought to himself as a sinister plan began to take shape in his mind.

As discreetly as he could, Donovan shifted forms. From wolf to a young man, matching in age to that of the maid, he gave himself straight, brown hair, freckled skin, and an endearing smile. Shaking away the last of his wolf's identity and fixing his figure to that of a tired but caring peasant, Donovan settled his gleaming eyes on the maid's slender figure.

"Miss?" he drawled. She jumped in surprise, hastily squashed out a green light that had been in her palm. "I didn't mean to frighten you! I'm awful sorry, miss. I was just going for an afternoon walk ya see..." Donovan continued, pouty-lipped and bashful. "I just saw you there and thought something might have been amiss. There isn't though is there? Apologies if I'm intrudin'." Donovan bit his lip and rocked back and forth on his heels. Bridget continued to watch him, slightly fearful, yet mostly curious, her chin rested in one delicate hand. "I- I guess I'll be going then," Donovan went in for the emotional kill.

"It's all right, I just," her words trailed off as Donovan turned back around. "I was startled to find someone else out here. Everyone else is preparing for tonight," she finished softly.

Donovan took cautious steps toward her. The maid looked at him suspiciously as an ill-at-ease silence followed his words. "Might I sit by you, miss?" he requested. Quiet again.

"Yes," the maid relented, "you may. But only if you stop calling me 'miss.' My name is Bridget."

"Hugh," he answered without hesitation, giving a slight bow.

"Nice to meet you, Hugh," Bridget chirped, smiling openly as Donovan settled beside her. She was taken with his handsome looks. She blushed a little as he grazed her hand with his as he sat.

"It's so peaceful out here," Donovan mused.

"Yes, quite. Perfect time to be alone. But company is nice to have too." She looked up at him, sweetly. "I brought some cerea fruit, would you like to share with me?" Bridget revealed a small handkerchief with tiny round red berries. She held them out to him. "I got them from the kitchen."

"So, you work in the castle?" he asked, returning the smile.

"Yes," Bridget bobbed her head, kicking her small feet back and forth beneath her. "I'm a maid for the Queen."

"Really?" Donovan smirked as his eyes grew bright, his mind satisfied at the convenience.

"Would you like one?"

"Yes, I would." Donovan took one immediately popping it into his mouth. He was greeted with an intense sweetness as if he had eaten a spoonful of sugar. The flavor in his mouth suddenly turned tart enough to pucker his lips and make the juice run red down his chin. Bridget giggled at the sight.

Bridget moved to wipe it off his lips. She paused.

"Thank you," he softened as she touched his face. He leaned ever so slightly into her hand. Bridget pulled away, collecting her wits about her.

"I should actually be getting back to my Queen," she confessed, "but I hope we can meet again. Tomorrow perhaps?" She dipped her head so her lashes could flutter just so.

"Tomorrow," he answered. And with that she walked back toward the castle, but not without a final glance over her shoulder.

Five

"Take away some of those candles it is as bright as midday in here," the Queen ordered. When the women had done as she instructed the room looked delicately moon-lit yet still bright enough to see the outline of her dress hugging tightly to her curves. The Grand Dining Hall was filled with the warm scent of vanilla. White linens with silver stitched table runners stretched across the wood tables that lined the hall. The flags of Thurnadan descended from the ceiling. Their silver flames of purity, engulfing the crossed swords of valor and truth, shimmered on their pearlescent pointed banners. The last light of the day poured in through the magnificent stained-glass window that sat high the in back of the hall.

"Will everything be ready in time?" the Queen turned to ask of her servants.

"Yes, Your Highness," a servant girl bowed.

"Good. Then it is time for me to dress. Bridget," she called. Bridget swept in from the hall. The Queen looked at her flushed face. "Where have you been, girl? Nevermind. To my chambers."

They arrived at the Queen's dressing chamber. She promptly began to change into a sleeveless white gown with sheer fabric cascading over flowing layers of silk. She admired her figure in the mirror. "I will wear the Ivory Orchid tonight. Prepare it," Eleanor requested of Bridget.

"Yes, my Queen," Bridget bowed, knowing the significance of this piece. Bridget went to the locked dresser and emerged with an ornately carved onyx box, the Queen's Ivory Orchid sigil a bold white against the black lid, and brought it to Eleanor. Pulling a small key from her bedside table the Queen placed it into the lock, and with a click it opened. Inside the dark box, there was a single ivory pendant that was shaped like an orchid and gilded in glistening silver. A single large diamond sat in the center of the flower. Bridget placed the beautiful and delicate piece around the Queen's neck. It flowed over her collarbones and rested gently in the center of her chest. Bridget took a step back so the Queen could admire herself once more.

Outside her dressing room in the hall, Malcolm spotted Aurora who had finished dressing and had just stepped outside her chambers.

"Aurora!" the King nodded enthusiastically.

"King Malcolm," Aurora curtsied. Her crimson tresses gleamed as they waved down her back. She was in a rich sapphire gown that made her long red hair appear like a fire atop the bluest water.

"I trust the maids treated you well?" Malcolm asked, straightening his own black and silver tunic.

"Quite well, thank you. I am feeling much better," Aurora replied.

"I can see that," the King said as he took in her glowing appearance. "We are glad to have you with us." He fumbled his clasp.

"Here, allow me," Aurora chuckled at the King's fidgeting as she reached to help, but then became serious. "Your Highness, I can see you are impatient to be with your wife but I warn you: enjoy her company if you must but do not trust her. I beg you, do not trust her." Malcom bowed his head, not wanting to believe that Eleanor was capable of betrayal.

"Eleanor is just as kindhearted and levelheaded as I am. We were betrothed before our seventh birthday and have rarely quarreled. If she was up to something, I would know." Malcom sternly glared at Aurora.

"There," she finished adjusting his clasp, "all set."

"Thank you, Aurora."

The door to the Queen's chamber opened and out stepped a glowing Eleanor.

"Eleanor," Malcolm stood in awe and took an extra moment to admire the silhouette of his glowing Queen.

"Malcolm. Aurora."

"You both look marvelous. I should be going. I will see both of you at banquet. Your Majesties," Aurora bowed then hurried down the hallway.

Act with caution. Aurora urged Malcolm. He heard her in his mind but shook it off.

"I have missed you," he crooned, stepping toward Eleanor, wondering the whole time how a woman of such exquisiteness could ever be capable of treachery. Seeing his wife's youthful, loving face only made him more certain that Aurora was wrong. Eagerly, he took her hand and escorted his Queen to the banquet.

Fanfare announced the arrival of the Queen and King into the Grand Hall. All the soldiers, servants and loyal subjects stood at their entrance. The hall was filled for their welcome.

"Her Royal Highness, Queen Eleanor, and His Royal Highness, King Malcolm," the herald announced. Everyone cheered for them. They were a stunning vision of love and happiness. Something Thurnadan desperately needed right then. Continued fanfare escorted them to their high seats at the end of the center table. Argus sat to the right of the Queen, while Aurora took the seat to the left of the King.

Eleanor raised her silver goblet, "For the safe return of my King and my soldiers. And for Thurnadan!"

"Long live the Queen," the crowd echoed through the hall.

Malcolm stood and raised his stein, "Let the banquet commence!" The musicians began to fill the room with song as more servants burst though the wide doors at the end of the hall carrying ornate silver trays of meats, fruits and vegetables. Black plates with silver gilding and adorned with the Queen's signature white orchid were placed before every guest. The soldier's eyes were wide with the cornucopia of breads and cheeses coming from the kitchen. The savory scent of cloved game birds mixed with the wafting vanilla sweetness of the cinnamon breads were filling the room. The soldiers dove into the candied feast of fruit pies dusted with sugar and the spears of meat dripping with gravy. The soldiers ate ravenously as they tossed back steins and steins of the famed 'Queen's Stout', a drink that was known throughout the land. Pure vanilla beans from the Ivory Queen's garden gave the stout its smooth taste and fragrant aroma. Dusted with cinnamon, the stout was rich and balanced with spice. It was the perfect accompaniment to the celebratory meal.

As everyone ate and conversed, the Queen turned to Aurora. "We are so pleased to have you among us."

"Thank you, your Majesty," Aurora shifted in her chair. "What are your plans to take on King Zagan?"

The Queen pulled back stunned, "I will have no talk of war plans tonight."

"But we must start preparing for battle," Aurora admonished.

"I will decide what must be done when it is time," Eleanor declared. "We must be cautious when dealing with King Zagan."

"My Queen," urged Argus, "ya know Zagan will not be leavin' Thurnadan castle untouched. That is why yer Majesty sent us to gather the Descendants from the Academy, nay?"

"I refuse to lead our soldiers into death when we don't know what we are up against."

"But I do," interjected Aurora. "I have seen and battled the Sharnin Army."

"Enough," the Queen commanded. "Now I will hear no more talk of this tonight." She stood and the men stood up as well. "In fact, I will take my leave for tonight. Malcolm?"

"My Queen?"

"Let us retire for the night."

"Whatever my Queen desires," he agreed. Eleanor stood, and as Malcolm pushed his chair back, Aurora grabbed his arm. He looked at her and gave a slight nod, then removed her hand from him as he turned to go.

Aurora watched them leave, a look of worry on her face.

****

Malcolm closed the door of the royal bedchambers as his wife glided over to the window. He admired Eleanor in the soft moonlight. He moved to her slowly. Wrapping his arms around her waist, they both looked out the window and onto the garden below.

"I am so happy you are home," she whispered.

"I will always come back to you," he assured her. He kissed her bare shoulders gently.

"Did you get enough to eat at the banquet, you must be ravenous from your travels?"

"Ravenous I am." Malcolm shifted his hands to the back of her gown and helped it find its way to the floor. She turned to him. Her piercing eyes bore into his. She gently removed his tunic. She ran her hands over her husband's muscular bare chest. In one strong motion, he took her into his arms and carried her over to the bed. He was indeed ravenous.

****

A faint golden light played across Silvia's bruised face as she strained to open her eyes. Her whole body ached as she was barely able to rise. The camp her Sharnin captors had set up the night before was now her residence. Unsurprised, Silvia noted that her armor and weapons had been stripped from her, her clothes were filthy, and her braided hair had come undone. But, she was glad to simply be alive. A change of guard occurred around their cage as Silvia surveyed her surroundings. The wolf she was tied to rolled to its side and made a series of gurgling, snoring sounds.

"Silvia!? You're awake!" a loud whisper came from behind her. Silvia turned her head slowly, the rope around her neck causing chaffing and scabbing.

"Ryder!" she exclaimed, fighting back tears when she saw her horribly beaten companion.

"Shhh," he hushed her, looking about nervously.

"You're alive," Silvia breathed, keeping her voice low as to not attract attention from the green-clad soldiers.

"And so are you!" Ryder's face was covered with blood from the cut just below his hairline.

"How many Sharnin soldiers have you been able to count?" Silvia asked.

"Why?"

"How many?"

"About thirty or so," Ryder looked around at the others lying with them. "And only the two of us actually able to move. Everyone else is worse off."

"We need a plan." Silvia stated bluntly. "I can probably take half of them."

Ryder whistled through his teeth. "Half? That's bold. What do we do with the other half?" Ryder breathed heavily.

"That's where you come in." She looked insistently at Ryder.

"Keep your voice down!" he whispered.

The Sharnin soldier guarding them scowled threateningly before pivoting and continuing his surveillance. Silvia began rubbing at the ripped flesh around her lashed-together wrists.

"Don't," Ryder reached out to Silvia but quickly pulled back again, "it only makes it worse." Silvia stopped her fidgeting but remained silent. Ryder sighed, dropping his head into his hands. "War from within it is." Ryder forced himself to continue, "I guess I've lived long enough for today." His hazel eyes smiled with glimmer of optimism, "If the remaining few of us are going to have any chance of staying alive, we need a plan."

Silvia watched as the guards changed. Her eyes lit up and she turned to Ryder, "I think I have an idea."

"Great! Then get us out of here."

****

Aurora lay still in an unfamiliar bed in the north wing of the castle. A cold draft swept through the small room. She could feel the rush of the air, the beat of footsteps throughout the halls, the dance of flames in the torches outside. She could feel the dreams of the slumbering soldiers downstairs, the whispering of the water in the nearby stream, and she could even feel the hushed breathing of the stabled horses. However, Aurora could still also distinctly feel the ghost of an icy blade cutting through her throat. The memory of her companions' words of warning before their magic built up inside her was perfectly distinct in her mind. They had left themselves defenseless so that she might survive; they had died to save her, but how could it be? How could it be that she, alone, was to aide Thurnadan in this war? An unrelenting knot pulsed violently in her stomach.

She shivered as her memory continued to play out in her head. Every moment returning in even more vivid detail...

On the backs of the beasts were stone-eyed soldiers. Her companions, even as strong and well- trained as they were, struggled to defend themselves against the rain of arrows. The group was compiled of teachers and students, all with magic.

A man had come upon them, walking slowly, with no visible weapons. His presence had caused the soldiers and their mounts to shudder, hold their fire, and retreat a bit. Her companions tried to use the momentary pause to their advantage. A few of the younger, more rash Descendants had called on their various magics – fire, earth, air, water, forms of animals, and tricks of mind – but nothing more than aimless sparks had come from their frightened fingers, their bodies too drained of energy to continue. It was then, after turning in stunned silence to one another and to their Dan'te that they focused their attention on the man on foot. He had a slight figure despite his weighted middle, short graying hair, a long white and green cape, and olive green eyes. With one arm raised and outstretched, he smirked when they looked at him.

The man laughed, "Strange, is it not? To have no power, to simply..." he paused, "be ordinary." His small smirk spread into a smug grin. As he slowly curled the fingers of his extended hand, three of her novice companions sank to their knees, clutching their hands to their heads. The man narrowed his eyes and threatened the rest of her group. "See these weaklings? You think a little magic makes you strong? Keeps you safe? It's a lie. The only thing that keeps you safe is power! Can't you see that you are on the losing side of this battle?"

"Zagan!" the elderly Dan'te called out. "Why can't you leave us? You possess your own magic, surely you have enough to accomplish your own feats without the torture of our people!"

"Silence," Zagan ordered, his voice echoed in all their heads though his lips remained still.

"Zagan!" the Dan'te yelled again. "How dare you force yourself into my students' minds! You coward! You were a coward before, you are a coward now."

Aloud, the man spat, "You taught me well, old man, yet resist the modern way of the world and of magic. Magic not only needs to be feared, it needs to be shown respect! Kind hearted leaders are destroyed, not respected. Fools, both of them! And you as well, for believing them. It's a pity none of you will actually reach Thurnadan." He snidely chuckled.

Aurora could feel the tension in the air as the coils of magic wrapped around her friends began to choke the life from their bodies. They convulsed where they knelt. Anger welled up inside Aurora as she looked at her baffled, frightened, and wounded companions. She brought her arms up behind her then threw them forward. Blazing gold sparks flashed from her fingers in hot rage. The wind swept down and the snow billowed up. The tundra wolves tumbled together in fright, causing their riders to shout and fall. Zagan remained still, watching her.

"Kill them!" he ordered. "Every last one of them." His soldiers deserted their mounts and drew their swords.

"How can you?" the Dan'te cried out as the soldiers closed ranks. "You call yourself 'Commander'! You call yourself 'King'! You are *unworthy of those titles! You are unworthy of your magic! Release my students. Face me."*

"Face you? No. I'd rather simply destroy you." Zagan drew a sword and slashed across the Dan'te's chest leaving him to bleed to death.

Aurora knelt beside her Dan'te. His hand in hers.

The last connection Aurora had had with her companions replayed continuously in her head. It was an order from her teacher:

Save Aurora at all costs.

Six

Eleanor's magic heavily saturated every single corner of Malcolm's mind. He could not remember most of what had happened the night before. All his thoughts were consumed with love for his Queen; nothing else filled his head. Malcolm rose from his luscious bed, careful not to wake his beautiful sleeping wife. He dressed quietly but moved slowly, for his concentration was lazy, and in no hurry to rush. The air in his chamber tasted sticky and sweet, like cinnamon and honey. He neglected to call a servant for aid dressing, and instead nonchalantly exited from his bedchambers alone and in his breeches.

"My Lord," the guards at the end of the hall bowed hastily to the King as he passed. They refrained from inquiring where he might be going unattended and with no shoes on his feet or pants to cover his undergarments.

****

Aurora sat alone on the edge of her bed as the sun shone through her window. Slowly, the anguish she felt over her memories melted away. She could still feel the pulsing tremor of her companions' magic as it ran though her body. This made no sense to her. How could she possess their magic as well? She wanted to explore what happened on a deeper level, but she instead focused her mind on the events around her, as they reeked of imminent danger. Her eyes glowed a fierce blue as she tapped into her Seer's ability.

Calming her emotions, she let the whispers of earth, air, water, and fire float through her like the weaving of colored threads caught by a playful breeze. There was distress everywhere. The moods of people flooded Aurora's mind as her Seer's Sight and Elemental magic worked together. She sensed violent bloodshed and terror in the east along the Thurnadan-Sharnin border, especially in Caerwyn. Narrowing her attention to just the castle grounds, Aurora felt the apprehension of the on-duty guards. Overall, the residents were pleased that their King had returned but deeply vexed about the war. Beneath their frail veil of pleasure seethed a giant wave of panic. Deep below her, she could feel the earth trembling with the guards' alarm. There it was, the source of the panic: a prisoner had gotten free.

The bedroom spiraled around her. He was familiar to her. Memories caused her to gasp for breath and she clutched at the headboard of her bed. Why was the Queen not rushing to capture and return him? Her Seer capabilities were too clouded by emotion to look further. She stood up, composed herself quickly, and readied herself for the storm that was brewing outside her chamber door.

The King was up and moving about the halls. Aurora was suspicious he might have been sleep walking since his steps were unsteady and his words were faded and muddled.

Argus, however, was burning with exasperation in a room full of maps. Aurora moved past him, choosing to give him her attention later, in person. Cheerful good mornings came from the kitchen with talk of a maid, Bridget, being unusually tardy. Always curious, Aurora focused to see Bridget down by the garden and a young man walking towards her. Aurora was met with Donovan's green eyes staring straight back at her. Her surroundings slammed back into focus as the distance her mind traveled sliced across her like a sharp wind. Aurora swayed and collapsed, her head hitting the floor, vision blurred.

"He's found a way in," she sputtered.

****

Bridget was wandering about the garden letting her finger tips graze the petals of the flowers that surrounded her. Their scent was intoxicating. She bent down to take them in fully when a voice from behind her gave her a startle.

"How was the banquet, last night?" Donovan inquired, tucking a strand of hair behind his ear he had assumed the persona of Hugh once more.

"Oh, hello, Hugh."

"I didn't mean to give you a fright," he apologized.

"That's alright. It was lovely, actually. But those soldiers can sure put away the stout."

"Ah, yea, the Queen's drink. Haven't had the pleasure of drinkin' it myself. But I heard it's quite sweet, yet bitter."

"You should have come, everyone was invited."

"Oh, not me. No, no. I'm happy out 'ere."

"Speaking of the Queen, she will rise soon and I must greet her. I should go," Bridget scooted away from Donovan.

"Must you?" Donovan mused, reaching for a lock of Bridget's chestnut hair as she slipped out of his grasp. He stood to follow Bridget saying, "But it's been so lovely talking to you, your skin is as fair as the clouds above, and your eyes could light a candle's flame." Bridget blushed and bit her lower lip while self-consciously twirling a stray curl around her fingers, the one Donovan had aimed to grasp, to be exact.

"Well," she finally responded, "I am here in the morning when the weather is fair, may we meet again soon."

Bridget turned to go. Donovan caught her by the wrist and gently pulled her back. Face to face, Donovan let his features soften as he stroked Bridget's jaw. He leaned down slowly to ever-so tenderly kiss her.

"Hugh!" Bridget pulled away reluctantly. "I hardly know you!" she whispered willing to sacrifice almost anything to be locked in his gentle kiss.

"Then I will wait until tomorrow to get to know you better," Donovan cooed. "Tomorrow then?" He stepped back a pace, like a school boy, seeking one final reassurance.

"Tomorrow," Bridget agreed as she hurried toward the castle. Donovan watched her until she was out of sight then looked about for any witnesses to their intrigue. Satisfied that there were none, he smiled. He was certain that one more encounter with Bridget would grant him unhindered access to the castle. *No one questions the Queen's personal maid.* Donovan remarked snidely to himself.

Donovan shifted into a small frog and tucked himself into a shadowy crevice of the bridge to think. Charming Bridget had been quite effortless, but he was now faced with what to do with the King and Queen. He was torn. Imprisonment was an eternal risk. Their escape would mean his immediate demise.

Killing Malcolm would be easy but he didn't know whether to automatically count Eleanor as a force against him or hope that he could win her over. Their family relation was a well-kept secret. All Donovan was sure of was that his half-sister was bound to make things difficult. He didn't relish the thought of killing her but circumstances being what they were, they would most likely both have to die.

Donovan scratched his slick frog-head against a pebble as a light rain began to fall. He dozed and thought, plotted and yawned. He remembered feeling like someone had connected to his mind earlier, someone who seemed so familiar yet strange. As the rain began to fall, he drifted off to sleep.

****

Eleanor woke with a pleased smirk. Soldiers could fight and die, fate could be reckoned with, and men could turn the tides of war, but nothing could compare to the power of a woman's seduction. She had bought herself a fair amount of time before anyone questioned her. She had broken the laws of magic, but, she had done it in order to make the right decisions for her Queendom nearing a time of war with the Sharnins. They would see that eventually. They would forever idolize her.

The Queen rolled gracefully out of bed then stretched and flexed her toes against her wolf-fur rug. Manipulation and allure were her weapons, but she had no protection, no shield. The assailing fear of loneliness and rejection that overwhelmed the Queen with every breath she took, snared her to her love-drugged husband and finally pushed her into action. With Malcolm indisposed, Eleanor would simultaneously be able to keep him out of her way and protect him while she reclaimed her authority.

She knew if Donovan returned there was a high probability of Malcolm's sudden and violent demise. Despite their relationship being a twisted bond of affectionate love and passive-aggressive bitterness, Eleanor did not want to see Malcolm die.

Like her husband, Eleanor declined the aid of a dresser. But, unlike Malcolm, she knew precisely where she was going. Breakfast of sweet cream and berries took the Queen mildly off track, but only for a short while. Methodically, she sat before her desk with ink, quill, parchment, and the Royal Seal of Thurnadan. She wrote a brief but imperative letter, sprinkled it with powder to hurry its drying, then called for a courier. The Queen was pleased when a courier about her own age, male, with a naïve disposition, appeared at her door.

"You are to carry this letter to the leader of the Sharnins attacking Thurnadan's villages," she instructed. "I am quite certain you can follow the trails of carnage and fire to their camps." Eleanor gestured the young man forward until he was intimately close to her. She set the crisp note carefully into his hand then leaned forward until her lips nearly brushed his ear.

"Say nothing to anyone. Deliver this and return to me promptly. If you do as I have instructed, you will be greatly rewarded."

"Of course, my-my Lady," he stammered. "It will be my pleasure," he added with a blush.

"Ancients' speed to you," she gently pushed him toward the door. "I await your return." The courier bowed and hurried away. Eleanor murmured to the empty room, "Poor sap."

****

All morning Silvia and Ryder had discretely been trying to plot their way out of the Sharnin camp and it rested on one small chance of seduction.

"It's our only chance. We don't have any other options," Silvia whispered to Ryder. He closed his swollen eyes and rubbed at his left shoulder where a fall from his horse had nearly broken it. Silvia pursed her lips. "Think of how long it's been since these men have even seen a woman."

"I won't let you do this. There has to be another way."

"This is the only plan. Besides, if I can get into a tent with the leader, I'll kill him before he can touch me," Silvia muttered under her breath. She also knew that she would need do nothing more than walk in the room to excite them. Then she could make her move. There were only a small handful of survivors, and with no one to assist them it was indeed their only real option.

"Just be careful," Ryder urged as a Sharnin Sergeant came over to his fellow soldier.

"Hungry?" the Sharnin bellowed. "Take a break, mate," he ordered the man who had been guarding them all morning. He turned his back on the soldier and looked over the captives as the leader of the camp approached the cage.

"Wonder which of you I have to thank for my new scar," the Sergeant growled. When his gaze fell on Silvia his expression rapidly changed. A lewd grin pulled at his lips. She had adjusted herself to be seated in a suggestive position.

"Well, well, what's this?" he breathed licentiously, attention slithering over Silvia's exposed skin. Silvia resisted the temptation to cringe. "Thought you common folk were against a warring woman!" He chuckled. "Though I don't suppose the fightin' men would mind a little female affection after a long battle." Silvia's eyes burned heatedly but she held her tongue. "Face like yours," the soldier leered, looking elsewhere, "must have a pretty name?"

"Silvia."

"Sillllvia," he drawled, his eyes blurred with an odd mix of emotion. "Absolute pleasure to make your acquaintance," he slithered. "Wade, at your service." Silvia's skin crawled.

"Don't suppose you'd want to make a deal? How about some decent food for a tumble or two?" Silvia mused to Wade.

"Perhaps something could be arranged," he replied. "Though I don't actually think I need permission," Wade guffawed.

"And I, sir," Silvia replied curtly, "doubt you would find a broken back very comfortable to sleep on."

The soldier raised one eyebrow unnerved not by what Silvia had said but by the straight face and utter seriousness with which she had made the comment. "Am I to understand your talents for *warming* a man may be too potent for me?"

"Unless you're the type of man who finds the warmth of his own blood comforting, I suggest you find some manners before approaching me."

"Then should I say please?" Wade sneered.

"Do you want to deal?"

"I'd be delighted to. Though, my lady, I am not a man who tires easily."

"I believe I am up to the challenge, assuming it is worth my time."

"I'll have you take leave of your pitiful friends then."

"In exchange for decent food?"

"Yes," Wade inclined his head briskly. "It is a deal."

Silvia smiled disdainfully. She knew his and her idea of a 'tumble' were two very different things. After glaring down at the other captives and promising to return momentarily with food, the soldier turned and left. Silvia quickly worked out the details of her attack in her mind before his return.

Seven

Aurora moved tentatively through the castle in search of Argus. She did not want to make a sound or risk being detected. Her velvet gown fell softly down the stairs as she peeked around empty corners. She needed to ask him about the prisoner's escape. She wanted nothing more than to settle her fears, but she knew that would not soon happen. She arrived at the large, beautifully carved door to the drawing room. She could hear Argus' voice but the door was bolted shut. Aurora knocked and called out but no one answered. She stepped back a few paces into the shadows of the hall then projected her vision into the room. Her eyes lit blue as she melded her Seer power and her Handler magic in order to take hold of one of the guards within the room. She could now see through his eyes. Argus, the two other guards, and the King were seated in the room but no one was speaking. The sweetly absent-minded expression on Malcolm's face was the exact opposite of Argus' set jaw and penetrating, frenzied gaze.

"Yer Highness," Argus cautiously spoke, breaking the silence, "don't it bother ya ta' have the Sharnins destroying your lands an' stealing tha' lives of yer people? We got word they attacked Caerwyn. The attack on the Snow Lands' should tell ya' just how much danger is out there. Even yer own prisoners are gettin' free from the dungeons runnin' from here an' yet neither you nor the Queen ain't doin' nothin'! Nothin'! Pardon me, Sire, for speakin' so blunt, but how does your peoples' agony an' deaths not fill yer mind wit' the need to battle, Sire? Protect these lands."

The King hummed obliviously.

"Sire?!"

"Eleanor will deal with it," Malcolm slowly drawled.

Argus' breath hissed from between his crowded teeth and his eyes bulged with distress. The guards' attention darted back and forth between the two, not sure whether to call for additional guards.

Aurora's mind shifted focus over to the charts and maps on the table. Over three dozen villages within the borders of Thurnadan were blacked out on the map, with arrows pointing towards the castle.

Invading forces were almost to one of the main trading cities, Layton, a half day's ride from the castle. Aurora's mind recoiled in horror. Layton was where she had almost been captured by Sharnin soldiers. *The quaint little village in the valley, the merchants bustling down the streets, the artisans at work in their shops. Could it be they are the next victims to suffer under Zagan,* she thought. She cringed at what she knew Zagan would do to those villagers.

Her attention shifted back to Argus. "And what do ya plan to do about Donovan breakin out'a the dungeons? That reeks a trouble fer sure, yer Highness." Aurora stiffened at the name. She wished it was not the Donovan she knew from her days at the Academy.

"Devious woman," Lairson profaned, lips pinched and yellow-green eyes flaming. Aurora blinked heavily, jumped back and struggled to regain the balance in her body.

"Lairson?"

"You terrible, devious woman! I knew you were a mistake to rescue! Spying on the King, are you? I'll have you executed."

"You will not, you know as well as I do something is amiss."

"That is no excuse to eavesdrop on a conversation meant only for the King."

Aurora rolled her eyes, suddenly dismissing her annoyance with Lairson. "Don't forget it was your King who asked the Academy for help," Aurora snarled. "And I am the Academy now."

"I'll make sure he sees the error of that request!" Lairson threatened, "I'll have your neck in a noose soon enough. That's a promise."

"A promise I'm sure you'll have to break," she spun away from the doctor and strode off down the hall. "It takes," she said quietly, "a whole lot more than a rope to kill a Healer and you know it."

Unsure what to do with herself until the Queen requested to see her, Aurora's thoughts drifted. She knew she was strong. She was, after all, the one that had control of all the elements. And having the magic she did was unheard of and therefore extremely intimidating. Her entire life her abilities had be growing, even when she was at the Academy. She couldn't help but remember...Donovan.

When she was sixteen, Aurora had been matched in a practice battle against Donovan. She had felt no apprehension at the pairing. She had battled Donovan a thousand times or more and never lost. Donovan, then fifteen, was skilled beyond measure in Shape Shifting but that was his only talent except for a little aptitude for manipulating air. She was not arrogant, but she certainly was not intimidated. The battle started as usual with sparks of silver and green, some hits and some misses. Wind, earth, and animal tangling together and tearing apart. Suddenly, Donovan disappeared. Aurora had stood still and searched mentally for his aura, yet found nothing.

"Dan'te?" she had turned to her teacher, "Dan'te, what happened to him?" Their puzzled expressions mirrored each other. An unexpected loss of breath made her sag to her knees. Her teacher had risen to his feet as fear flashed in both their eyes. "Help," she had gasped. Sparks flicked from her fingers as she tried to coax her magic into saving her. A cold coil of seemingly solid air sucked out the threads of oxygen that attempted to sooth her screaming lungs. A satisfied laugh filled her head.

'You learn quickly, Son,' the voice said. Aurora had choked from confusion and lack of breath. Desperately grasping at her neck, attempting to free herself from the coil, she had started to lose consciousness.

'RELEASE HER!' her Dan'te had ordered. The coil had responded by shrinking then slithering from her windpipe and out of her mouth. A cloud of blue-green mist collected before her as she panted and brushed tears from her eyes. Donovan's figure formed from the mist and then solidified.

'Why did you stop?' the voice sounded again. Donovan winced.

"Father," he had replied apologetically, "she is my friend."

The voice laughed again, a laugh that was familiar to the Dan'te, but he couldn't quite place it. Aloud he had said, "You have no friends. Not here. They teach you nothing except how to dampen your talent and make it less useful. She is one of them. She is not your friend."

"Zagan!" her Dan'te had interrupted before barely managing to fight off the intruder who Donovan had called Father. That evening, Donovan had disappeared from the Academy, but not before he had whispered a threat in Aurora's ear: if she ever battled with him again he would surely kill her.

"Can you See your own death yet?" Lairson disturbed Aurora from her memories.

"I can certainly assure you of yours if that's what you seek," Aurora rebutted.

"I'm warning you! If you — "

"Lairson! Doctor! Where have ya been?" Argus roared, bursting out of the chamber doors and down the hall toward Lairson and Aurora. "Here I were lookin' for you, 'here ya are. King Malcolm has completely lost 'it, I think he caught somethin' out there, come." Argus grabbed Lairson by the shoulders, ignoring his shocked expression, and thrust him toward the door.

"Constable, of course!" Lairson yipped in trepidation. His feet came off the floor and his gangly limbs struggled to align themselves as he stumbled across the hall. Argus marched behind him, muscles tight under his form-fitting sparring clothes. Aurora knew he must be in his mid-fifties, but he moved with an ageless strength and grace.

"Ain't you comin'?" Argus called back to Aurora. With a sigh, she followed the bumbling doctor and powerhouse fighter.

The King sat slumped in a chair in the drawing room when they met him. The three guards had been dismissed. With just his finger, Malcolm attempted to sign documents.

"Your Highness?" Lairson bowed, searching for signs of ailment. The King patted the doctor on the cheek tenderly.

"I am getting ready to think about potential solutions to some issues that may've arisen in the Queendom," the King said as he slumped back against the chair. Lairson's face hardened, his thoughts coming quickly. A moment later, after masking his suspicions with a confused expression, he turned to face Argus.

"He's lost his mind!" he sniveled.

"Exactly what I told ya, ya thick-headed guttersnipe! I don't need no doctor to see that. I be needin' a doctor to get his mind un-lost!" An awkward pause filled the air. Aurora, Argus, and Lairson stood in frozen bafflement with only the faint humming of the King as he pondered filling the silence.

****

Silvia looked around Wade's tent. The bed was plusher than she expected for a Sharnin soldier. She surveyed her surroundings, taking in all the things that could be used as a weapon. The ties of the door, the splintered leg of the chair, even the small knife for carving fruit. She plotted out how she would undermine Wade to make sure she trapped him before he realized she was not just a soldiers' whore.

"I'm not to be disturbed for the rest of the afternoon. Not for any reason. Understood?" Silvia eavesdropped on the conversation occurring outside as her eyes scanned around Wade's tent. The soldier lifted the flap to the tent and warily tied it closed behind him.

"You're still dressed," he commented, mock disapproval dripping from his lips as he smiled in anticipation. "Shouldn't we change that?"

"Are you always such a knave?" Silvia raised her eyebrows in haughty annoyance. Her mind screamed and raced as she frantically tried to think her way out of the situation. "Are my companions well fed?"

"It will be taken care of," Wade assured. Silvia forced her attention not to follow the path of the belt he was dropping, for she did not want to alert him of any ill intentions. She slowly started to unlace the cords from her blouse. Four steps was all it took for her to be just within arms-length of Wade.

Silvia felt suddenly weak and small standing next to the muscular man who was over six feet tall. His eyes began to hunger as Silvia loosened the cords of her top, causing more of her chest to be exposed. Silvia suddenly had a pit in her stomach; Wade's eyes looked hauntingly familiar. He reached out for her but she danced away from him.

Silvia steadied the shaking in her hands, returned to where Wade was standing, and gently tugged at the ties holding his pants up. His loose green trousers fell to the floor. Silvia allowed her eyes to drop as well, taking a split second to locate the knife attached to his belt on the floor and notice a large dagger still strapped to his calf. Silvia sashayed away again, running her fingers along her hair then continuing down the length and curve of her figure, avoiding her few remaining healing wounds. She loosened the ties of her own trousers. Wade let out a short whistle and stepped toward her. Silvia gulped hard but kept her smile from faltering as she stepped back and he came forward. She lay back on the bed and undid the last three cords on her blouse. The soldier sighed, smiled, and came down over her. As quickly as she could, Silvia grabbed the dagger from his calf holster and brought it up toward his throat. But, just as quickly, Wade snagged a knife from under his pillow and held it tightly to Silvia's throat, just a drop of blood spilling out at where the tip of the knife was dangerously close to permanent harm.

"You didn't really think I'd be foolish enough to not recognize a fighter when I saw one?" Wade sneered. "You may have the skin tone of a peaceful Kailani but your eyes scream soldier." Silvia remained in mute, fearful shock. "I'm disappointed in you though. Would you not know that a warrior never sleeps without a knife by his side?"

"So now what?" Silvia sputtered, trying and failing to sound calm.

"Now we try to figure out who lives until one of us gets sick of the other's voice and slices their throat," Wade replied with no mercy.

"Well then, if that's the case, you talk first."

****

Argus raked a hardened hand over his short hair and sat down heavily on a chair near the King. Lairson fidgeted but said nothing. Another long silence ensued. Finally, Aurora knelt before Malcolm. She focused, looking into the King's eyes but was instantly interrupted by Lairson.

"What do you think you're doing?!" the doctor barked.

"Obviously," she replied, her voice thick with annoyance, "you don't know how to help the King. I, however, might."

"Get your witch eyes off my King!" Lairson growled, yanking Aurora by the shoulder.

"Lairson!" Argus jumped to his feet and grabbed hold of the doctor. "That ain't no way ta' treat a lady!"

Lairson spat, "She's no lady." Nonetheless, he lifted his long fingers from Aurora's shoulder. He had no want for Argus' strength to be turned against him.

"You think ya' can restore his senses?" Argus asked Aurora, his expression pleading.

"I'm honestly not sure. I am, however, very sure that if I looked into his conscious I could at least figure out what's ailing him. May I try, sir?" Aurora half-smiled.

"All right then," Argus agreed.

"NO!" Lairson could not help but screech. "Absolutely not! Argus! As the High Constable, protector of the Queen and

81

King, surely you have more wisdom than to allow this witch to have mental control over — "

"Do not forget, my goal is to aide Thurnadan," Aurora hissed, "I am aiding in return for saving my life. I want nothing more than I have already been given. If you disrespect me again Lairson, you will have my attention upon you which I assure you is not something you can handle." Aurora's eyes flashed, the colored spirals in them brightened with magic. She stood, back straight as a spear, and scowled at the doctor. Although she was small in stature, her posture was threateningly full of anger and authority.

"Your power has made you evil!" Lairson raged back. Argus stepped forward, attempted to draw his sword to break the two apart but was met with such intense looks from both Aurora and Lairson that he stepped back again and remained quiet.

"I do not understand how you, a Descendant yourself, still do not trust me." Aurora reprimanded the doctor.

Lairson, unwavering, looked her square in the eye, "You are a witch of the highest order, and evil in nature. You deserve to burn for all eternity. You know nothing about Thurnadan. You vile witch!"

"Bastard!" Aurora yelled, raising her arms. "What did I say about calling me 'witch'?" Silver sparks danced from her fingers. Lairson took a few paces back but Argus held his ground. The Constable had fought with steel against magic before and won, and he would do it again if need be. A tiny flick of Aurora's wrists caused a circle of flame to erupt around Lairson, trapping him. She glanced back over her shoulder and saw that the King sat unmoved, still humming to himself.

Taken aback by this sudden outburst, Argus shouted, "What are ya doin'?"

"Teaching this imbecile a lesson," Aurora replied, her voice boiling with fury. Aurora walked steadily toward Lairson, pausing just outside the fire ring. Jaw set, eyes bright, and red hair glowing, Aurora flicked her wrists again. A gust of wind spiraled through the fire causing the flames to lick closer to Lairson and climb higher toward the ceiling. The doctor trembled and shrank in on himself in an attempt to get away from the violent flames.

"Stop that, there is no magic allowed in the castle," he implored. Aurora's expression smoothed into a passive calm. She reached through the fire slowly, clenched the knotted ties of Lairson's cape in her fist and pulled him forward so his long nose was less than a breath away from the seething flames.

"Open your eyes, fool! The carpet is unburned, your own clothing is not singed, and I did not cry out when I passed my arm through the circle. Just because my skills can be a weapon and can be used for harm does not mean they have to!" Aurora released Lairson and took a step back. "I do not know everything, but what I do know is this: humankind was never intended to possess magic. Whether you call the Ancients creatures or gods, fortunetellers or simply myth, we have books full of counsel, prophecies, and instructions because of them. From these books, my masters thought it wise to teach me control, restraint, compassion, and kindness. I was raised to use my magic — my gift — to the benefit of all!"

"The Ancients are nothing more than old men's scary stories of fire-breathing, wicked-tempered dragons!" Lairson screeched. "If you believe your magic came from them, you truly are a fool!"

"Walk through the ring, you spiteful, pathetic man. You won't be harmed. Let's test what you know." Aurora huffed loudly when Lairson failed to move. She waited, impatiently tapping her sandal-clad foot on the floor. The doctor remained immobile. His eyes were fearfully wide but his face was pinched in abhorrence.

"I will not believe you," Lairson spitefully insisted.

Aurora flung wide her arms as vibrating sparks cascaded from her hands. Cinders scattered throughout the room and sparked, quickly blazing to life. Crystals of heavy, wet snow blurred and billowed around them and the floor rumbled and quaked beneath their feet. The very breath was sucked from the room and everything fell deathly still. Aurora's magic surged back into the room with the force of a tsunami, using her abilities, Aurora forced her way into Lairson's mind.

A wall of fear is the weakest defense there is. Trust, hope, and love are much better alternatives. Believe me, Lairson, I will not harm you. Not unless you give reason that I must. She breathed deeply and retreated from his mind.

Arms back at her sides, the floor fell still and the snow and fire vanished. Nothing in the room appeared to be disturbed. The King clapped seemingly in appreciation of the elemental show.

"Once more!" the King cheered gleefully. Argus' mouth hung open and he stared unblinking at Aurora. Lairson straightened his clothing, trying to regain his composure.

"Is all of your magic just an illusion?" he sneered condescendingly. Aurora's face tightened in hot fury. She snapped her fingers and Lairson's cape disintegrated in a quick and savagely vibrant blaze of fire. In a split second, a small pile of ash lay on the floor at his feet. Although brittle with fear, Lairson's body remained untouched by the flame.

"I will have you beheaded," Lairson gruffly stammered, "for your use of magic."

"I suggest, Lairson, that you stay out of my way from now on," Aurora stated pointedly. "Argus!" Aurora barked, snapping the High Constable back to life. "Please, may I have the doctor escorted from the room and a servant called to clean up those ashes. I would hate to stain this beautiful rug."

"Yes, lady," Argus agreed; Aurora had won his respect. She took a deep breath then turned and knelt before the King.

"Her use of magic-" Lairson quibbled. "Sir, you must have her punished! She broke Thurnadanian laws!"

"I never saw nuthin'," Argus coughed, then winked at Aurora.

Aurora cocked her head to one side and connected with Lairson's mind. *You will not challenge me again, or I promise you Lairson, it will be the last thing you do and there will be no healing from what I have in store for you.*

"Get out of my head, witch!" Lairson stormed off down the hall in a huff.

Argus and Aurora shared a smile before she turned her focus back on the King. "Alright, let's see what's ailing you, my Lord," she cogitated as she closed her eyes and entered the King's mind.

Eight

The back of Silvia's left ear itched. Her legs were going numb under Wade's weight and her arm was growing weary from holding the knife to his throat. Neither Silvia nor Wade spoke. Both their nerves started to fray as the silence painfully continued. Practically nose to nose, Silvia could not help but notice the laughter lines around Wade's eyes and an old scar that ran from the bridge of his nose, across his cheekbone, and ended at the missing tip of his left ear. His skin was tanned yet clean and Silvia was perplexed that he smelled good in an almost familiar way. His washed-out brown eyes, however, gave Silvia chills that she made futile attempts to control.

Finally, Wade broke the silence. He sniffed, adjusted his arms to redistribute his weight across Silvia's hips then gracelessly said, "I think I know you."

Silvia was taken back by his words and rather befuddled facial expression. "I don't think so," she hesitated. "Why?"

Wade replied forebodingly, "I don't much care for the idea of slitting a woman's throat. 'Specially one I know I previously exchanged pleasantries with." He elaborated, "You look awfully familiar." Silvia looked blankly at Wade, shocked that the man was so casually talking with her instead of killing her. She felt like a sinister game of cat and mouse was being played at her expense. "You said your name was Silvia?" he twitched. She narrowed her eyes. "That's rather intriguing."

"Why?" she inquired pensively.

"My name is Wade," he reminded her.

Silvia looked hard at the soldier, "Wade?" She resisted the temptation to shake her head since there was still a knife to her throat. Her instincts of self-preservation roared at her to kill the man and be done with it, but if it could save her life at this very moment, she was happy to oblige. "Why do I care what your name is?" Silvia licked her dry lips, still trying to work up the courage to dig the dagger into his flesh and make him submit to her request for freedom.

"It means nothing to you?" Wade questioned.

"How'd you get that scar?" Silvia abruptly asked. She recognized the scar and those eyes. She searched her memory for a time when she was someone she never cared to revisit.

"I've been in a lot of battles, sweetheart," his eyes stormed, though his expression was deadpan.

"Don't call me sweetheart. There's nothing sweet about me," Silvia growled.

Wade burst out laughing, causing Silvia's blade to jolt and make a shallow slice across his windpipe. He flinched and pulled away as a single drop of blood fell onto Silvia's exposed breasts. Both Silvia and Wade froze, looked at the spot of blood, then met eyes. Silvia swallowed hard, "Why do you think I look so familiar?" Wade cocked his head to the side, lifted his knife from Silvia's throat, braced himself on his knees, and raised his hands in a half shrug-half surrender.

Silvia now realized this was a game for him. That he had indeed seen her before, and was toying with her. She was still pinned down. She was getting ready to make her move when she realized he was about to tell her the truth. Piece by piece.

"You were down by the lake when I scouted Caerwyn," Wade snorted without mirth. Silvia did not reply. "I could have killed you at any time," he said grimly.

"But you didn't," Silvia baited him for more information. She was afraid of what Wade's intentions might be now that he remembered previously seeing her.

"No, I didn't kill you. Oh, but that's not all," he laughed emptily. A leering smile spread across his lips as his eyes wandered down Silvia's figure. "Why is it that no one's kept a better eye on such a pretty woman?" he purred, his cheek muscles jerking in mischievous questioning.

"If you're wondering," replied Silvia in a flat tone, "why no man is by my side, I'll willingly inform you that it's because of your kind." Silvia wrenched herself out from under the soldier, toppling him off the bed before sitting squarely across him. She held his knife hand down as she set her blade back on his throat. "It's because of your kind — that he's dead," Silvia hissed.

"Unfortunate," Wade replied unfazed. "But Silvia dear," he continued to murmur, "no need to take your anger out on me." Silvia glared down at him furiously. "Why such a change of heart? You liked me quite well last time we met," he bantered.

"At the lake? I'd hardly call that a meeting."

Wade smiled the most unnerving smile Silvia had ever witnessed, and uttered, "Oh Silvia, the Battle. Clodith and Sharnin. I was there for you when you needed consoling."

Silvia blanched. "What," she reluctantly asked, dreading the answer, "are you talking about?"

"Oh, Silvia, don't insult me so! I know you remember me! In your suffering after the Battle you were quite open to my consolation."

"Filthy pig!" Silvia screamed, suddenly recalling, with gut-wrenching horror, exactly who the beige-eyed man was. She went to dig her dagger into his throat but he was too quick for her. After a tangle of body, loose clothing, and blades, Silvia found herself trapped under Wade once again, only this time without her knife.

"Now, darling," he whispered, conflicting emotions flashing across his face, "it's not nice to stab people. Besides, imagine the guilt you'd feel later, knowing you'd murdered your old lover?"

Silvia growled, "Upon your death, I swear I will forget your very existence."

"I knew you remembered me."

****

Donovan awoke with a start when he heard some nearby children discussing whether they should kill the frog then skewer him on a stick and roast him or to simply roast him and assume that that would kill him, should they catch one.

"My papa says this is how the people in the castle eat ever'day," the leader boy bragged.

"Even the people in the dungeons!"

The little girl's eyes widened, "That's why that bad man broke out, I'll betcha."

"I heard he's real scary!"

Now more than ever, Donovan did not want to risk being seen. He knew that if he was seen changing forms it wouldn't take long for the children to let everyone know that a shape shifter was near the castle. Someone would put two and two together and figure out that he was indeed the prison-broken Descendant. Then all hell would break lose in a hunt for him. Eventually, he would get caught. Donovan brooded in frustration, determined not to have a return visit to the dungeon. After all his years of training, with all the magic he possessed, and all the forms he could take on, he refused to let a group of children be his downfall.

He also knew he needed to get to his father. He had an 'in' at the Thurnadan castle, now all he needed was to know his father Zagan's battle plans, and he would be able to conquer both thrones. They rightfully belonged to him. He would give Descendants free use of their magic, yet he would never fully let them out of his control. He knew better than that. Donovan would stop at nothing until he had had everything that was rightfully his. Everything he had been robbed of. Yes, he would take it, and the Ancients' Aide to whoever tried to get in his way.

****

Aurora backed away from the King. She took a deep breath and collected her mind, extinguishing the glowing light from her eyes.

"What is it?" Argus asked Aurora.

"We should speak outside." Without another word, she was out in the hall. Argus on her heels. "He's under the influence of magic."

Argus asked Aurora as he paced the hall. "Who by?" he growled. "What for?" Fury burned in his eyes. He longed for a sword, dagger, staff: anything he could use to burn off his aggravation. Argus pointed sharply at the room behind them, "He is da' only man who could end the slaughters an' he's gone an' lost his mind to a soppy world of myth an' dreams!"

"Calm yourself, man! Losing control benefits no one here," Aurora admonished.

Argus' old buried reservation about Descendants flared up, but dampened down again when he laid eyes on Aurora's sweet, concerned face. No one would have even known what was wrong had it not been for her magic. She was trying to help and Argus knew it.

"Argus," Aurora paused, "are you familiar with all in the castle possessing magic?" Her features wilted with unease and her eyes held obvious fear. "It would have to be a Handler, or a Spinner who knows a spell of persuasion. I don't think anything else would do that." Aurora and Argus felt their eyes drawn back to the absent-minded King through the doorway. "His mind was clear and unfettered when I reached out to him in the mountains," Aurora blinked heavily, the thick dark lashes rimming her strange eyes softened her expression. "Argus?" she cajoled after a minute or two had passed in silence. Argus took a startled breath and tried to calm his agitation so he could think clearly. "Who are the castle's Descendants?"

"'Fraid I don't know of many of 'em. People keep quiet 'bout their magic. The head cook though, he been known to possess a touch. Perhaps he'd know of a few of ta' others 'round here."

"What magic does he possess?"

"Seer."

"What?!"

"But most of the Descendants in the castle ain't very strong on account of them not gettin' to use their magic much."

"Well it's a start at least," Aurora said as she tugged at her dress sleeves. "I think it's best if we head to the kitchen immediately. Argus, I can't regain King Malcom's mind unless I know what magic caused this."

"But why would someone be doin' such a thing to the King?" Argus inquired.

"Someone doesn't want him to be part of this war."

"My bones feel somethin' awful about this."

"We should get to the cook, see what he knows. Think it's safe to leave the King alone while we pursue the cook?"

"I'll call a guard."

****

Mouth full and heart heavy, Ryder gagged violently, suddenly realizing that he and his companions had been duped. "Damnit," he seethed, dropping his bowl. "We're fools."

"Whatya' waste that for, mate?" the man beside him asked.

"Open your eyes! Force yourself to see what you have before you!"

"What the —?" Ryder's companion smashed his bowl on the ground. "There's maggots everywhere!"

Frantically, Ryder knocked the food from his companions' hands. "Don't eat another bite! It's not what you see. Our minds have been altered by a Handler! There's no mutton, no potatoes! It's rotted porridge!"

The posted Sharnin soldier laughed sadistically as he watched the captives spit, curse, and vomit. He winked when Ryder glared at him.

"We have to," Ryder stopped, the taste of bile poisoning his nose.

One of his companions calmed his retching and said, "we have to get out of here."

Ryder ground his teeth in aggravation, causing pain to shoot through his jaw. He could not help but think that if things continued the way they had been, the maggot-infested porridge might be their last meal. Irritation and fatigue wrapped vice-like around his heart. To distract himself, he eavesdropped on the jovial exchange between the soldier posted to watch them and another that had stopped by to share large mugs of the stolen Queen's Stout from the ale house in Caerwyn.

"Fools blithely ate that slop up," the first solider bragged.

"I can smell that," the other laughed. "So, the Commander says it seems Thurnadan's as good as ours. He's been having Mind Handlers scope out Layton to see what they know. It seems no one at the castle cares that we're taking over!" He slapped his fellow soldier on the arm good-naturedly, "Drink up mate! It's only a matter of days until we be lazy castle watchmen eatin' Thurnadanian pheasants and ravaging their women. To the overtaking of Layton, then Thurnadan!" The soldiers laughed heartily, clunked mugs together, and tilted their heads back finishing their pilfered stout. After a few more similar comments and boisterous guffaws the second soldier nodded farewell and returned to the tents. Ryder was quickly forgetting his pain as pure loathing overwhelmed him. Horrible images of destruction, Sharnin take-over, and of what Silvia might be enduring at this very moment tormented his mind.

****

The Queen took the afternoon to sit in her elegant garden of vanilla and white orchids. She wanted life to resume as normal as not to raise any suspicion. Her white marble bench was cool even in the strong sunlight. The vanilla orchids bloomed for a short while, once a year, so the green rows of her vanilla beans were covered with snowy billowing flowers. Eleanor knew that the timing of today's bloom was no accident. She plucked a flower and methodically twirled it in her fingers before tucking it into her hair. She looked over her husband's schedule for the week as she tossed pieces of biscuit to a flock of birds. Her mind was heavy. She noted that Malcolm was due to converse with the Head of Infantry that afternoon and that Kailani, the land to the south, was hosting a New Moon banquet the following evening. Eleanor was certain that the more people Malcolm was around, the more likely she would be exposed. She hoped that if everyone's attention was on war and prison breaks, no one would give the King much attention. She had even arranged a search party to look for Donovan as a distraction, knowing perfectly well that Donovan would not let himself be found.

"Bridget?" she summoned her maid who was standing in the grass a little way off. "Have an apology letter sent to the Head of Infantry that the King is not feeling well and will not be able to meet today."

"Yes, my Lady," Bridget curtsied. The Queen debated whether or not she should go and check on Malcolm to ensure her magic was still working as Bridget curtsied, her eyes on the floor, then turned to go.

"And have send a decline of invitation for the Kailani banquet. The King is worn from his travels," Eleanor instructed. "Then hurry back." Bridget curtsied again and left the garden.

Eleanor was beyond apprehensive; she had noted Bridget's odd behavior throughout the day and had begun to think it had been a mistake to involve the maid in freeing Donovan. She contemplatively looked out over her garden: Donovan had turned many of her citizens into traitors by recruiting them to join forces with Sharnin against Thurnadan, but it had been all at Zagan's orders. The Queen hoped that her involvement in freeing her half-brother would appease the

Sharnins and perhaps spare Thurnadan from Zagan. Personally though, freeing Donovan meant Eleanor's promise to their mother to get him out of imprisonment had been fulfilled, she was now free to do as she pleased with him.

"Donovan probably won't even credit me for his freedom," Eleanor scoffed aloud. She thought that perhaps with the Sharnins and their King pacified, and Malcolm's mind half dissolved, she could rule more forcefully. She would finally be the Queen she was meant to be. "What is the point of having a title if I do not wield the power and influence it bears?" she aimed her question toward the birds at her feet.

Letting her thoughts fade to less frustrating things, Eleanor gazed upon her garden to settle her mind. It was serenely quiet. But the Queen hated the quiet and hated being alone, which she noticed uneasily that she very much was. Even the birds had begun to wander away.

"Bridget?" she shouted, wondering why the maid had not yet returned.

"Eleanor." The Queen heard her name. She sought the owner of the voice for it was not Bridget's. She saw no one. Eleanor sat perfectly still, trying to keep her nerves from fraying any further. "Eleanor, you naïve girl," chuckled the voice as a blue mist appeared before her. The Queen gulped loudly as the mist solidified into the form of a heavy-set man with olive green eyes.

"Zagan," Eleanor gasped, and desperately attempted to steady herself.

"Hello, my dear. Don't look so shocked! Surely you do not think so poorly of me as to not expect a personal expression of gratitude for helping my son?"

"How did you find out so quickly?"

95

"I have over a thousand Descendants, you fool," Zagan clucked. "You do, after all, live surrounded by humans."

Eleanor gritted her teeth, "Must you always insult everyone around you?"

"'Tis a guilty pleasure of mine," Zagan smugly replied.

"What did you really come here for?" Eleanor huffed.

"You invited me," Zagan sat down beside the Queen. "I intercepted your messenger boy just an hour ago. I do so hope you didn't expect him back." Zagan grinned. "Sorry if you were expecting him to return alive, but I just could not let him go running back to you with the knowledge of our whereabouts and numbers." The King laid his arm around Eleanor's shoulders as she twitched her head in a slight nod of annoyance. "I do adore you so," he pouted. "I did hate to kill off one of your pets."

Of course, I did not expect the man back, Eleanor pushed into a mental connection with Zagan, something she had not done since she was a little girl at the instruction of the Queen Mother. *I am not a doll with nothing but air for brains.*

Since when?

Why did you not just bring your army and take Thurnadan now?

Where is the fun in that? I love seeing you sweat.

No more games, Zagan. Eleanor pushed out of their connection.

"What do you have to say to my offer of truce?" the Queen asked, "I will happily grant you safe passage through Thurnadan into Kailani in exchange for peace."

He shrugged, kissed Eleanor on the cheek, and said, "No sorry, my dear Eleanor, I reject your truce. I will take Kailani anytime I feel like it. I could see your head on a stake whenever I desire and believe me I will make sure it happens in good time."

****

Lairson sat with his feet propped up on the polished, wood desk in his chambers. He chewed on a piece of gum tree bark and mumbled to himself. "It's unfair. Lairson heal this! Lairson heal that!" He kicked his boots off and screamed for his assistant, "Boy! Get in here!"

"Yes, master?" the assistant scurried into the room tripping over some rather large tomes he had left on the floor.

"What in the King's name is wrong with you boy get on your feet!" Lairson admonished his clumsy assistant. "Get over here. You are old enough that if you were born with magic, it will soon develop and your blood will darken. If you do possess magic," he glared threateningly, "make sure you respect it."

"Ye-yes sir," the boy replied, perplexed.

"That woman! She reeks of magic and yet is completely unaware of the magnitude of her abilities, of the destruction she is capable of! She can raise wind or fire as though it's warm breath on a cold morning! An ignorant, childish woman, of all people! And that type of strength!" he continued to rant.

"Doctor?" the boy raised his hand, trying to figure out what his master was so distraught about.

"What irks me most though," Lairson held a finger up in the air. "What irks me most is that although I don't read nor practice the Ancients' lore, I am very familiar with what it says. This girl—this clash of bloodlines—I bet is thought to be the Scarlet Prophecy come to life."

"What is the Scarlet Prophecy, sir?" asked curiously.

"Forgive me that I—a responsible, well-trained, well-educated man of practice and knowledge—think those old tales are nothing but idiocy." Lairson stared at his wooden cabinets: every herb, concoction, and salve was neatly labeled and placed precisely. They were in alphabetical order from left to right and according to potency from top to bottom. "No one respects what I do," he continued. "They think that because I have magic that's all there is to healing. They forget that I studied medicine and know the body intimately. I have worked my entire life," the doctor pounded his fists on his desk, "to have this workplace and my title. And still I get no credit or acknowledgement." The doctor chomped down on his bark but was taken aback when the bite came down on his tongue. He stood and paced his small work room back and forth. He violently kicked at his chair and watched as it toppled to its side. Its plush cushion tumbled away.

"Sir, the prophecy, what does it say?" the assistant squeaked, his posture self-protective.

"Oh, alright." Lairson sat across from the boy and leaned in to him, "The Scarlet Prophecy tells of a young woman, hair as red as the flames of dragon's breath, who will be chosen to receive all Nine Gifts of Energy. And with all Nine Gifts she will be able to conquer and bring together the Descendants to be more powerful than even the Ancients were in the Pure Age of the Ancients."

"Wow," the boy's eyes lit up, "that's truly amazing. Do you really think she could be the one?"

"There is no 'one' you fool boy! What I do know is that woman will be the downfall of us all."

"But if she is supposed to bring the Descendants together? And you're a Descendant…"

"You don't get it, boy. She will bring war and destruction. The Prophecy says that she will conquer us." Lairson turned away from the boy. He fumed, "I will never kneel to her!" Lairson strained for breath, "This room is stuffy! I need air!" Lairson twitched as he tried to subdue his anger.

His assistant watched, mouth agape. "Master?"

Lairson froze when he saw a bottle of Seer's blood. "This never happened," the doctor said without lifting his eyes from the bottle. He let out a hissing breath through his bark-dyed teeth. He winced, closed his eyes for a moment, and then steadied himself to walk heavily but oh-so-calmly to a window. He eased open the window, a tense, fake smile on his face then briefly turned to his assistant, "Leave."

"Yes, Sir," the boy squeaked, jerking his mouth closed.

Lairson nodded curtly, smile distorting into a snarl, "And I don't want to hear a word out of you about any of this. Understood?"

The boy rushed out as Lairson returned to the cabinet and stood staring down at the bottles.

"Vile little monster, to burn my cape!" he commented to himself. The doctor could vaguely remember a story he had heard as a child. His father had been regaling what he knew to be the rumored formula to the Indigo Venom. The exact concoction that could, in small doses, allow the ones with magic to be controlled, but with a larger dose they could be stripped of all magic. The doctor rubbed his chin pensively as he was trying to remember the correct ratio of Seer's blood, snake venom, and a highly flammable powder made from the roots of the large-leafed selva tree, only found in Kailani. But now, only a few teaspoons were left of the Seer's blood he possessed. The gears in the Lairson's head started turning: teasing out a grim and spiteful plot. He wondered what would happen if he made the Venom with Aurora's blood and then used it against her. Surely, he would be able to destroy her.

****

As Zagan stood to leave, Eleanor couldn't resist one last insult. "You think you deserve all of the Lands, do you? I will let you in on something. You will never be more than a recipient of my mother's lust. You will never be loved. She loved my father, she could never have loved someone as weak as you," the Queen spat.

"How harsh, pum'kin. I think my pride's been bruised," he winked. "Speaking of your mother, you know that every time I see you, you look more and more like her? Such a beautiful woman." He traced a finger down Eleanor's ear. "Being like her would not be a bad thing."

"Zagan!" Eleanor jerked her head away from his touch.

"Same soft skin and beautiful hair. You even smell like her."

"Enough!!!" Eleanor stood up and stepped away from him abruptly. It was his power she was being drawn to, not him. It made her wonder if her mother truly wanted him or if he made her want him.

"You can never manipulate me. You, or your pathetic excuse for a son. He received none of my mother's attributes, he and all his darkness are a replica of you," Eleanor growled.

"Do not speak so harshly of your brother," Zagan teased.

"I will do as I please. You think Donovan will take the throne by blood lineage and then you can rule him? He is afraid of you, Zagan. But not that afraid," the Queen retorted. "Do not be surprised when he undermines even you."

"Dear heart," Zagan said dripping with sarcasm, "you are smart but not near smart enough. I will give him a tiny piece of land, and he will rule that. He would never be capable, ever, of ruling anything larger than a small hillside." He smiled sheepishly at the obvious shock on Eleanor's face.

Zagan shrugged his narrow shoulders. "I set Donovan up, Eleanor. How have you not figured this out? He was snooping around the castle, shifting, recruiting, killing, and generally stirring up trouble, because I told him to! I knew the Mother Queen would not be able to kill her own son. I knew she would lock him away instead. While he was in there, I had him acquire information of your castle and military plans."

"You wanted Donovan imprisoned? And the plans you heard are meaningless. My husband is no longer in charge."

"Oh, we shall see my darling," he said as he started to fade into blue mist.

"You are twisted, Zagan. You are cruel and horrifying."

"One more thing, Eleanor, you might want to keep your guard up," the voice of Zagan rang in the Queen's ear, making her shiver in disgust. "I'm getting ready to dispose of you," he sneered as he vanished entirely.

Nine

Donovan had decided the best course of action would be to Shift into a small winged insect as to not be detected by the nearby children. As he began to focus his magic, he was suddenly spotted by one of the children. They lunged at him, creating a giant splash as he shifted into a gnat.

As he flew farther away, Donovan mentally sighed and hoped the splash was large enough that the children had not been able to see him shift, however, if he had stayed just a few moments longer he would have heard the beginning of the manhunt that would ensue.

"Hey! That frog was a Shifter! I saw it! I had it in my hand as it Shifted!" cried the little boy who had moments earlier lunged for what he thought was his dinner. "We need to go! We need to tell the adults! There's a Shifter breaking laws!"

The children dropped everything they were doing and ran to alert the village.

****

"Wade, you don't want my death on your conscience, not after everything we've been through, everything I haven't even told you," Silvia begged, afraid of the dagger pressed against her throat. She knew at this point there would be only one way to save her life.

"Convince me not to," Wade whispered in a coy tone, lust filling his eyes again.

"Wade!" Silvia began to panic as she grasped for something so deep, so forgotten, that she knew by telling him the truth she would live, but he would die. With his death, the last of her memory would go with him.

Wade's left hand traced the edge of Silvia's jaw, though his dagger stayed still. Silvia squirmed. Wade locked his knees against her legs and settled himself across her hips, letting his weight lay across her body. He smiled. Silvia shuddered. He lowered his weapon to her side, blade still threateningly close to her flesh. He touched his lips to her cheek, moved down along her jaw, and dipped across her neck. Silvia shuddered again but Wade did not seem to notice.

Mouth dry and eyes closed, Silvia half whispered half sobbed, "I did once love you, even if only for a night. Then you left me. Alone. With child."

Wade's head jerked back, his eyes snapping wide open. "What are you talking about?"

"Desperate loneliness and a heart destroyed by the loss of everything I loved. I had thought maybe, just maybe, I could lose myself and their memory if only for a moment and you gave me that."

"Battle after battle, threat after threat. I watched everyone I knew and loved die and it killed me inside. And then you! And then I had this life inside!" she breathed.

Wade, shocked by her sudden honesty, and the impact of her news, slid off of her and slowly settled himself on the floor. Wade could not pick his head up out of his hands because they were the only thing that could hold the weight of this revelation.

Silvia felt a pang of sympathy toward the diminished man before her. She leaned forward again to say something but could not find the words.

"A child? I have a child?" Wade stated suddenly, a bit of hardness returning to his expression.

"*We* have a child." Silvia was torn bitterly.

Wade looked up at her in shock and disbelief. "I had a family back in Sharnin," Wade haltingly elaborated. "But when I got word that my brother had been executed by some self-righteous magic-hater, I felt so furious and vengeful that I joined the Sharnin army. What a fool I was. My family was killed while I was out raiding innocent villages. But when I returned, I had nothing. So I became a soldier once again. Zagan promised freedom and an end to all the suffering we have endured."

"And you believe him?"

"Yes, he has shown us that Descendants are powerful allies, and you are either with us to build a new world where Descendants don't have to hide or obey laws, or you are against us," Wade expounded. "Zagan gave me hope. Following him gave me purpose, but now you say I have a child? Was it a boy or girl? Do they still live?"

Silvia hushed the thoughts spinning and thrashing about in her head. She sat up, but Wade did not move. She realized that if she acted quickly, she could grab his knife and stab him before he had time to defend himself. Silvia's eyes lit up but darkened just as quickly. She knew killing him would do her no good and she would indeed feel like a monster afterward.

"It was a boy. We had a son." She looked at Wade, noticing how he had aged yet remained lean and muscular. His hair was beginning to thin yet his shoulders had not curved and his movements were still nimble. He was checkered with scars but they only served to accent his obvious strength. Wade dropped his head into his hands and rubbed his palms to his eyes.

Silvia was tired of Sharnins, tired of everything they had robbed her of, and it hurt her soul to the core to know what came next, but no matter what the cost, she had to free her comrades and end this constant war and death. She looked Wade square in the eye.

"I am a solider. I am a Descendant. I am a woman who deserves to lead in battle. Please let me go now."

****

Ryder, was wide awake despite the heaviness of the warm afternoon air. The stationed soldier had become drowsy from the stout he had drunk and he leaned heavily against a horses' water trough. The shadows of the late afternoon were long, overlapping from tent to tent forming an overwhelming, thick blanket. Ryder slipped quietly through one such shadow, until the rope tied around his ankles was pulled taut. He silently positioned himself behind the soldier.

A few of the brightest stars had become visible as the soldiers' jovial singing and drinking had settled into a more somber mood of mumbling nonsensically. It was oddly calm for a camp of soldiers a few nights before a massive battle, but Ryder supposed it was simply because they were confident of their victory. Apprehension made his eyes dilate despite the swelling of the wound on his forehead; he had not told his companions what he had planned because he did not want to unnecessarily raise their hopes. He winced, clenched his teeth, and focused on the task at hand.

The posted soldier's head bounced slowly and his fluttering eyelids exposed his sleepiness. A few moments later, he became still. His lips were parted, his eyes closed, and his chin near touched his chest. Ryder waited for thirty seconds, one minute, two minutes... The soldier remained still. With stealth, Ryder extended his bound-together hands to the

105

Sharnin's weapons' strap. Ever so slowly, he extracted a dagger from its sheath. With the blade firmly in his fingers, Ryder scuttled back toward his companions as the soldier continued to snore.

Quick as he could, Ryder sawed through his bonds then woke his companions with a finger to his lips to keep them from crying out. They had observed that there was only one row of tents between them and freedom but that there were also horses and tundra wolves stabled nearby that would make their escape much more difficult. It was every man for himself out there. If an alarm was raised among the Sharnins it would mean the end of all of them until they were a fair distance outside the camp.

"We'll meet at the far side of the woods and head toward Layton," Ryder whispered. The others bowed their heads in agreement as they finished cutting their bonds off. Now with his hands free, Ryder could reach the key of the cell and with a click it unlocked and squeaked open. The sound nearly woke the guard but within seconds his snoring returned. Ryder signaled for his companions to scatter and disappear. He breathed deeply to calm his nerves then headed toward the heart of the camp. "I have to find Silvia." Right hand clutching the stolen dagger, Ryder skirted sideways along the ring of tents. His bulky frame made invisibility within the shadows impossible but he managed to go unnoticed anyway. Ryder's heart grew heavier with each soldier-filled tent he passed; he knew it was only a matter of time before someone noticed the captives' absence.

"Silvia?" he loudly whispered into the darkness. "Silvia?"

A woman's muffled voice caught Ryder's attention. His ears perked up as he strained to hear any sound again. He doubled back the way he had come then snuck one row deeper into the tents. A small lantern weakly illuminated the dirt in front of Ryder from the seam where a tent's flaps met the ground. Ryder's fingers trembled as he untied the knots holding closed the cloth door.

"Silvia?" Ryder gasped. He entered the tent to see both Silvia and Wade sitting on the floor in similar stages of undress.

Wade, startled by the intrusion, was immediately knocked to the side by Silvia as she flew to her feet and prepared to fight him.

Ryder, knife in hand, was at her side.

Ten

The cook was chopping carrots and parsnips as he prepared for the evening meal. The kitchen was filled with scents of meat stews on the stove and freshly baked bread in the ovens. "After last night, I've been a little slow going ta'day. Too much o' the Queen's Stout, I had!" The cook rubbed his protruding belly. "Ah, so you wanted to know somthin' now didn't ya?

Aurora chimed in, urging the cook for a swift answer. "Yes, we need --"

"You want ta' know who in the castle's a Descendant, eh?" the cook paused to look at Aurora and Argus as they sat on three-legged stools in the kitchen, tensely munching on a wedge of cheese and a loaf of sourdough. "And I don't suppose you'll be tellin' me whys you're wanting to know?"

"Perhaps at a lat'r date," Argus frowned. Aurora and Argus watched as the head cook bellowed out orders to the kitchen staff then hefted himself up on a stool across from them and tore off a piece of bread for himself. Aurora was becoming agitated that this was taking so long.

"I ain't in any hurry to be thrown in the dungeon for disobeyin' the High Constable," the cook nervously gnawed on his piece of bread, "I jest fixin' to make sure I won't be named in anythin' evil comin' outta this." Argus nodded in agreement and the two men shook hands.

"Alrighty then. Well I's got the Seer's sight myself. Got the Inking and am all official, as ya' can see," he laughed as he pointed to his left eye. I also have the tiniest bit of mind handlin', but ain't never developed it much. My wife's got shifting, a number a' soldiers sculpt fire, couple whisper', an', well," the cook cleared his throat, "both the Queen's maids got spell-spinning talent. Lairson heals," he bit his lip, contemplatively. "Castle is one a' the few places in Thurnadan that it's mostly safe ta' be a Descendant."

"Because of that, are there a lot of Descendants here?" Aurora asked.

"Most certainly. But seein' as the laws prevent us from using it, we mostly just have magic but no real use for it."

"I don't understand," mused Aurora.

"Hey missy, not all of us here can afford no fancy education for magic."

"The Academy welcomes all. Or it would if..." Aurora trailed off; the words hurt too much to finish.

"Who else then?" Argus prompted.

"A lot of the servants have a touch of magic. But major strength, I can only think o' one. That be the Ivory Queen herself."

Aurora was pale. "Queen Eleanor has magic?" Argus asked, in total astonishment.

"Oh, Ancients yes! I don' believe I'm the only one seein' it," the cook huffed good-naturedly, his cheeks puffing out as he did so.

"So you know she does?" Argus pressed.

"She's a Mind Handler, I bet," the cook leaned in to them. The shocked looks on Aurora and Argus' faces made the cook uneasy. The cook gulped in nervousness and his skin paled, he may have just sealed his fate.

"But, maybe I be wrong. I'm just a lowly cook after all, what could I be knowin 'bout the Queen. I just know how she likes her eggs in tha' mornin'."

"How do you know this?" Aurora whispered.

"Well I- uh," the cook stuttered. "I don't remember," he raised his shoulders apologetically, suddenly afraid for his life. Aurora looked long and hard at the cook.

Argus shook his head, "If she has an Inking, it must be covered same as yers."

"Surely the Queen wouldn't break her own laws!" Aurora scratched at her chin. "She would have to have an Inking but also a spell set to hide it and her veins. With how pale her complexion is, the purple would noticeably show."

"Have ya lost what's left o' yer wits?" Argus half snorted, half coughed, "Even if she do have magic, she ain't gonna' cause trouble with it."

"Why wouldn't she? And if she didn't do it to the King, then who?" Aurora scowled. The cook cocked his head to the side in baffled curiosity. "What about Donovan—"

"Donovan wouldn't be foolish enough to stay here in the castle after his escape," Argus cut in, "an' would never cast a weepy spell' like this." He paused, "Nor would the Queen."

"A weepy spell? Like what?" the cook pestered, leaning forward across the table. Aurora fiddled with her hair then rubbed her eyes; she was exhausted and was still not back to her full strength. Argus drummed his fingers on the table, deep in thought. Neither of the two seemed to have heard the question. The cook pulled back, huffed, then slid off his stool.

"If I ain't of further use to ya', I thinks I be turnin' back to my stew," he grabbed a spoon and walked to the far side of the kitchen.

"Now what?" Aurora asked, her voice sharp with displeasure. "If the two I believe to be guilty are unquestionably innocent in your eyes then who is to blame?"

Argus met Aurora's harsh gaze. "Queen Eleanor ain't exactly one ta' harm the King. An' as for Donovan? Well, he's long gone by now we both know that."

"Fine then," Aurora snapped. "I agree about Donovan. The Queen however," Aurora trailed off, her lips pursed, "I am suspicious of." Aurora pinched the bridge of her nose in an attempt to fight off a growing headache. Argus slammed his fist down in exasperation.

"Fer what reason?" Argus yelled.

"I don't know!" Aurora shouted back.

"Then how can ya be suspicious?" Argus asked, calming down only slightly.

"Then tell me, how it is, that nobody knows she's a Handler?" Aurora rebutted, voice tight.

Argus finally had no answer for this. After a moment, he looked up at Aurora, defeat in his eyes.

"Argus, please," Aurora touched the soldier's arm. He pulled back, disquieted, but said nothing. "It seems implausible, I know, but hear me out. She has the skill and has kept it hidden, plus, she had the opportunity," Aurora withdrew her hand, then continued, "when I was found in the Snow Lands outside Achlese, I warned the King. I had seen this coming, and tried to tell him. I cannot see into her mind completely, which can only mean one thing - she has Handling capabilities. Perhaps that's why the King could hear me at all. If another had reached into his mind before he would be open to any who were strong enough."

"I should throw ya in the dungeons myself for spyin' on tha Queen's mind!"

"I only did it to protect the King when we first arrived. I swear. When will you believe that I am only here to help? We want the same thing."

"Fine," Argus pulled his dagger from his boot and started stabbing small holes in the wood of the table. "Ancients, them witches gonna be the reason we all die," he growled.

"Excuse me?" Aurora hissed.

"Ya know what I mean," Argus waved one hand sideways in a dismissive manner.

Suddenly very awake and very angry, Aurora curtly replied, "No. I'm afraid I don't."

****

"Ryder get back," Silvia urged.

"No, I will not let him live," Ryder seethed, his hand felt white hot against the dagger in his hand. His intense eyes not leaving Wade's. He grabbed Silvia's blouse on the ground and covered her with it. He hugged her close to him to save her modesty.

"Ryder, I need you to stay out of this," Silvia winced, "we were acquainted a long time ago, and I have unfinished business with him that requires both my undivided attention as well as my sword."

Wade snorted and muttered, "Acquainted? That's an interesting way to put it." He rose slowly, acutely aware of Ryder's wary gaze.

The three fell silent; the tent cramped with an almost palpable discomfort. Wade went to dress, which Ryder begrudgingly allowed. However, when he went to collect his weapons belt from the ground, Ryder approached him menacingly. Pain sliced from Ryder's arm into his neck. Now though, was no time to reveal his weakness.

"Wade, Ryder and I are going to walk out of here. You are going to count to one hundred before you sound the alarm. Do you want to know why? Wade?" Silvia coyly snarled.

"No," Wade snapped. "I think not."

Silvia's momentary feeling of strength quickly gave way to frustration. She set her jaw and tucked her chin in; anger seethed from her pores. In a quick motion of dismissive bad humor, she dropped her hold on her blouse. The dirty white shirt fell in a heap on the floor. Neither man could help but see Silvia's naked form out of their peripheral vision. Ryder turned his eyes away in gentile properness but Wade turned to look, there was still hunger in his eyes for her.

After a split-second distraction, Wade used Ryder's turned back against him. He latched onto Ryder's wrist, yanked his blade free and tossed it away. Wade simultaneously drove his shoulder into Ryder, knocking him off balance and sending him to the ground. He pinned Ryder down then smugly turned his head to look at Silvia. Her patience dissolved and her expression grew menacing as Wade's eyes wandered across her body. She glared as Ryder struggled. Wade drew his own dagger from his belt.

"I'm not," Wade grunted as he lowered the blade to Ryder's throat, "a fan of intruders." Silvia, in a moment of brashness, lunged at Wade and met his gaze with a full-force slap across the face. The sound of contact rang in his ears as bright red welts instantly sparked on his cheek. The shock sent him reeling. Silvia kicked Wade in the chest to get him off of Ryder.

As Wade splayed out backwards, Ryder rolled to his feet and quickly re-armed himself with Wade's fallen dagger. Cradling his stinging jaw, Wade cursed vehemently.

"Enough!" Silvia raged.

"Here is why you will give us aide. Yes, I was with child and had a son. In fact, so far as I know he is alive and well. You have a son, Wade. He has his own life, you have grandchildren. I will not tell you where he lives unless you give us the head start I've requested." Silvia pursed her lips.

Wade's eyes opened wider than seemingly possible. "You lie. You whore, you lie."

Silvia's expression was hard. Both her self-consciousness over her undress and her sentimental feelings toward Wade had burned away. "I swear on our son, who I had named after his father, that he is alive. Let us go, let us free our comrades, and I will get you the name of his village and when you arrive, you will ask simply for your next of kin and state who you are. That will be all of the proof you need. I never hid who you were from him, he believes you are a great hero. He is in the Snow Lands and knows nothing of the terror you have inflicted."

"Two minutes," Wade muttered, beige eyes lowered to the floor.

"I suspected as much," Silvia grunted. She blinked once then methodically turned around, picked up her clothes, redressed, and led Ryder out of the tent by the arm. Ryder heaved a sigh of relief although his eyes were still wide in surprise.

"Run!" Silvia hissed.

****

Eleanor remained in her garden until the chilly night air gave her goosebumps. Bridget had eventually returned after completing her task but, after seeing the frightened irritation lining the Queen's features, she had not said a word.

114

As shivers began to run through Eleanor's body, she steeled herself against the worst-case scenarios playing out in her head. She forced herself to believe that Zagan's visit changed nothing. Determination made her posture stiffen. One way or another she would have to deal with the Sharnin King. Now knowing the sheer number of Descendants he had at his beck and call caused her to rack her brain for any and all of the Descendants she knew of in Thurnadan.

"If Malcolm had given our Descendants Venom, the tables would be turned right now," Eleanor seethed to herself.

"Your Highness?" tentatively Bridget inquired. The Queen fluttered one delicate hand dismissively.

"Nothing," she chewed on the inside of her cheek before opening her eyes again. "Indoors. Come now. We will catch colds sitting out in the evening air like this." Realizing she had to finally tend to Malcolm, the Queen moved hastily down the hall. Bridget followed.

"I will not be needing your assistance," the Queen dismissed her maid.

Bridget bit her bottom lip, her brow creased, "My Lady, if I may. The evening is still young. I will stay by your side."

"Not necessary."

"Highness—"

"Bridget. What has gotten into you?"

"Nothing, nothing. My apologies. Pardon me, please."

Suspicion and irritation flashed across the Queen's face as she turned away, "Go on your way." The station guards nodded to the Queen as she marched down the hall and into the study.

"Good evening, my love," Eleanor greeted her husband. Perplexed at the sight before her, she froze.

The King was bent over a large table which had been covered in a campaign map representing the Temperate Lands. He was using the markers that normally represented troop movements as toys. He waged a fictional battle with the small green and blue figurines. "Die Sharnin scum!" the King shouted as he crashed the pieces together. "For the Queen! You scurvy rats!" The King continued to play with his new dolls for a moment before realizing Eleanor had walked into the study. He looked up at her and gave an innocent smile. "Sweetheart," he gushed, rose, and engulfed the Queen in a hug. She blinked excessively, trying to appear surprised at Malcolm's actions. The last thing she wanted were rumors that she was the reason for his condition. "Thought I would relax a while, read a bit," Malcolm hummed happily.

"Read?" the Queen looked at him incredulously as she could see no book in the vicinity. "How are you feeling?" Eleanor queried, nervously.

"Fine, fine," he cooed.

"How about some dinner? I think a meal would do us both good."

"I will accompany you if that is your wish, Eleanor."

The guards stepped forward to follow the Queen and King out of the room.

"We can tend to ourselves, men," the Queen directed. They seemed not to have heard her. "Leave," she snapped.

The guards' eyes shifted as they hesitated, knowing Argus had instructed them to stay with the King no matter where he went or who he spoke to. But, they knew they could not disobey an order from the Queen herself. That would result in immediate and certain death. They saluted and backed off.

With her hand on Malcolm's elbow, the pair exited the study and headed off down the hall.

116

****

Donovan had not wanted to meet his demise in the web of a spider, so he found cover in some foliage and shifted out of his gnat form and into that of an unassuming sparrow. He reached out with his mind hoping to connect with his father, but Zagan wouldn't allow him access. Feeling no choice but to go to him, he shifted again. Using the much more efficient wingspan of an owl, Donovan made good time flying east toward the Sharnin border. It infuriated him, however, that night had come so quickly. He needed to be back to Thurnadan to meet Bridget in the early morning, and flying was taking its physical toll. But, it was imperative he see his father. He needed to know what he was planning. Zagan had promised him Thurnadan, and he needed to know what information he required in order to ease the invasion of the castle.

Scanning the earth beneath him with his owl eyes, Donovan observed a few human forms running with vigilance through the forest. Although he thought it odd, the woodland creatures were highly alert but did not view the fleeing people as threatening. Donovan followed suit, ignoring the people and concentrating instead on the trickles of smoke making the air ahead of him hazy. It was clear the Sharnins had wiped out a fair number of villages and were steadily moving west, deeper into Thurnadanian land. Donovan flew straight into camp, shifting forms to a large beetle a mere thumb's width from the side of a tent. He dropped safely onto the coarse fabric just as a bugle sounded a brassy alarm. Soldiers sprang from their tents as quickly and steadily as they could. Donovan mentally smirked as he listened to the commanding officer ranting at his drunken men as they came to attention.

117

To the ranks, he barked, "Men, our failed little watch-dog here has let our captives get away," he growled. "Find them!!"

Donovan slid down the tent side as he shifted into his true form. "You will be demoted for having no sentries currently stationed around this encampment," he interrupted as he came around the tent corner. "Because you never know when an intruder may arrive uninvited. 'Evening, Captain." He grinned and bowed slightly, "For your information, your escaped prisoners have already gotten a considerable distance into the forest."

"Your Highness!" the Captain blubbered, shocked at Donovan's sudden appearance. He hurriedly sent six men to the camp's perimeter. The rest of the soldiers saluted, trying to hold back laughter at their Captain's flush of embarrassment.

"At ease, gentlemen," Donovan instructed. "At present, Captain, I think the captives are a waste of your time." Donovan shrugged. "Thurnadan is quite aware of our presence; the escapees can serve no harm to us, they have no knowledge of our plans nor are they in possession of any strong Descendants," he became serious. "We are a breath away from conquest and I have not had an opportunity of recent to converse with the King." Donovan smiled tightly. He dismissed the men then firmly placed his hand on the Captain's upper back, "Where is my father? Take me to him," he curtly ordered.

"He arrived just hours ago. This way," the soldier led Donovan through the camp to Zagan's tent.

****

Aurora's severe tone caused Argus' head to rise sharply and his eyes to pop open. "Witches?" she spat. "Did you really just use the term 'witch' while I'm sitting right here next to you?"

"Please forgive me," Argus said reluctantly. "I'm an ol' soldier who's had too many bad run-ins wit' yer kind. My mouth be speakin' but there be no brain attached. Forgive me." Aurora's temper did not calm in the slightest.

"Hear me now, you thickheaded bludgeon of a man!" She roared. "If I have yet to prove myself to you I know not how. I am sick of your kind looking at me with disdain as all I try to do is help you. My kind has healed your wounds and brought rain to your crops and still you isolate us. We fight and die beside you in battle and yet you continue to denigrate us. Those of my kind that have brought an ill reputation to Descendants and done evil were being manipulated by Zagan and those of his ilk. They were bound and shackled to the conviction that killing those who have no magic is the only path to having a life without fear!" Aurora paused to swallow past the lump in her throat. "I grew up surrounded by all things magic and legacy. I was taught to believe that the Ancients saw the beginning of time and foretold its ending as well. People believe the Ancients are everything from gods to demons, all-knowing creatures to complete myths. Some people say that magic was stolen from the Ancients, some believe it was a gift, others think it was a reward of conquest and Zagan uses this. Zagan has played on people's superstitions, played on their fatigue and anger, and because of that, he will win this war and kill all of you, unless his army of Descendants is able to break free of his hold. If you are told something enough you start to believe it's power over you, that is what Zagan does best. Breaking you down until you have nothing left but to trust the man feeding you the lie. You have been forced into believing that we are evil. I am not a

119

'witch.' I am not evil. I am not one of Zagan's underlings. I am to be feared only by those who follow Zagan." Aurora locked eyes with Argus. He could see her eyes start to glow a soft blue as she delved into his frustration-filled mind. Although Argus felt nothing, he knew Aurora was using her Seer's magic.

In his memories, Aurora saw the pain he had endured, the battles he had fought, the reasons behind his loathing, the loved ones he had outlived, the deeply-loved family he had lost during the Battle of Clodith and Sharnin, the burdens he bore from abandoning his homeland, and the anxiety he struggled with as he tended to Thurnadan's crumbling Queendom. As she withdrew from his mind, Aurora was struck with a premonition. Her surroundings faded into nothing as visions swarmed her mind:

She saw that war was inevitable, and that a grotesque and penetrating magic would soon scorch the gentle hills of Thurnadan. Bodies lay in smoldering piles, blood ran in streams through cobblestone streets, and the sky was heavy with screams of agony. Aurora saw that the Temperate Lands would be torn asunder and that the man before her would meet his demise. Lost in the trance of her magic, Aurora clutched at Argus' stout forearm for support. The lines faded as Aurora's premonition ended and she slowly opened her eyes. She removed her hand from Argus' arm.

"What's wrong?" Argus inquired fervently.

"I had a premonition." Aurora spoke with a new depth of understanding in her voice, "They seem to come at the most inopportune moments."

"I admit yer gifts have me a bit intimidated an' tongue-tied." Argus ran his hands over his head. "So what'd ya see?"

"I saw burning trees in a valley, not far from the castle. It can be seen at a distance. Descendants fighting Descendants."

"The only nearby valley is Layton."

"Yes. Layton," Aurora realized. "That must be where Zagan is heading next."

"But we don't have any of yer fightin' Descendants. Where they be comin' from? There's nary enough here in the castle to be makin' a battalion," Argus snorted.

Aurora and Argus mused for a moment they both came to the same answer, "Layton!"

"They must be hidin' out in Layton. But how are we to know they be on our side?" Argus questioned.

"Many Descendants have succumbed to Zagan's mantra of violence and used their abilities for harm, but we're not all evil," she sighed. Argus saw the sorrow and fear reflected in her posture as an introspective silence filled the room. For the time being, the discord between them had dissolved.

Eleven

The Queen was keenly aware of the eyes of her servants watching her as she took the King into the dining hall. They strode down the hall, passing torch after torch, the privacy of the study fading into the distance. She felt their eyes scrutinizing every step.

"The King is not well, he must eat," she explained to the servants. She was reluctant to increase the attention focused on them by even a small amount more. Most of the servants had gathered in the quarters downstairs for their late-night dinner. They finally approached the door to the private dining room. It swung open with a loud crack that echoed through the hall.

Eleanor sat across from Malcolm at the small round table. *How is it possible for me to so ardently want your love and yet just as equally wish you dead? Oh Malcolm, why could you have not just stayed out of my way. I know I can do this but not while you are here. Why do you love me?* The Queen thought, feeling slight disgust at herself.

The Queen smiled sadly as she listened to the deep, full beat of the music and the sweet, expressive voice of the singer in the corner of the dim-lit room. She remembered when her grandmother had explained to her how servants were always more loyal and harder working if they were given their own time and space within the castle. There had been many, many generations of Crowns peaceably passed from mother to daughter. An occasional son had reigned, but no matter male or female, at all times, for as long as anyone could remember, the ruler of Thurnadan had had a good and noble reputation. *It's a good thing mother cannot see me now,* she thought to herself as she mused over whether or not the ends truly justified the means.

Guilt oozed through Eleanor's mind, knowing that Zagan was murdering her subjects and that she was adding to the chaos instead of properly protecting her people. Part of her wanted to seek the council of Malcolm but the other part of her hungered for the opportunity to prove herself as a strong and steadfast Queen. The festive music grew louder and billowed into the hall and drew the interest of the few remaining attending servants. Mercifully, the Queen dismissed them for the evening. She was pleased to be left alone with the King for now. Stronger than ever, she felt the need to take back her rule and re-establish her Queendom. She longed for the freedom to do as she pleased but also the adoration and encouragement of a doting husband. She was tired of merely being pacified with attention and false influence.

"I am plenty full," Malcolm mumbled sleepily. His eyebrows scrunched together. "Dinner?" he said more loudly, cocking his head to the side. His eyes filled with confusion. He looked to Eleanor. "When did we come to dinner?" his sentence hung uneasily in the air, his eyes much more focused now. "I cannot remember. It just seems like..." his mouth slowly fell open as he gazed at Eleanor and leaned into her gentle touch at the back of his head. Eleanor dove once more into Malcolm's mind. Apparently, the effects of her magic didn't last as long as she had hoped and would need to be reapplied more frequently.

A loud bang followed by a crash came from downstairs, silencing the music and startling the Queen. Eleanor's eyes darted around the room realizing there were far too many witnesses for her liking. "You may all go," she dismissed the servants as well as the musicians. Without question or hesitation, the onlookers fled the room. She shook her head at the distraction then refocused her magic. Malcolm relaxed into the cushion of his chair and grinned with child-like innocence. A little bubble of spit dribbled from his lips. Eleanor had gone too far, she had infused too much confusion into his heart and brain. "Damn, I spoiled his mind," she cursed and bit her cheek. She called out for a servant.

"Highness?" a maid curtsied.

"Call the doctor, immediately!" the Queen demanded, fake alarm shaking her voice. "The King is not well," she pleaded. "Go!" she yelled once more. She grimaced as she helped Malcolm wobble toward the door and out into the hall.

Lairson, trotting alongside the panic-struck servant, met the couple mid-way to his chambers. He took one look at the lovesick King then glowered at the Queen. Eleanor jerked back at his harsh gaze but quickly recovered, dismissed the servant, then followed Lairson into his medical room. Once the door was shut firmly behind them, she attempted to influence the doctor to get him to care for her husband without suspicion. Unfortunately for her, Lairson was ardently focused on the slouched King.

"I find it irritating, my Lady," Lairson said crossly as he settled Malcolm on a couch, "that you are perfectly willing to overwhelm one's mind with intentions that are not their own knowing that you have no way to remove that magical imprint if you so need." The Queen choked and jolted back.

"Excuse me?" she asked.

"Oh must we play games. I think you have done enough of that now, haven't you?" Lairson spat back.

"Why, I do not know what you are talking about?"

"Come now," Lairson teased.

"Can you help him or not?" the Queen pleaded.

"I don't know what you are carrying on about. You know what you did. I assume you want me to dose him with a reversal tonic?" Lairson inquired, locking his hooded eyes on the Queen. "And truly, you were unaware of my knowledge of your magic?" Eleanor pursed her lips, eyes narrowed. "Your secret is safe with me," he smiled craftily. "Not to fret. But we must be more careful. Mind Handling is tricky, if you are untrained, as you can see." Lairson indicated Malcolm who was drooling everywhere and humming to himself.

"Where are my soldiers? Where are the little green men and the tiny kingdom?!" the King shouted as Lairson looked questioningly at the Queen. The Queen met Lairson's look with a simple shrug.

"How did you know about me?" the Queen replied tersely, trying to keep the anger out of her voice.

"Magic can't hide from me," Lairson stated without further explanation.

"Does anyone else--"

"Know about you?"

"Yes."

"My Lady, suspicions are inevitable when your husband suddenly becomes a blubbering idiot. He reeks of magic to the point that my healing magic views him as diseased!" A low growl escaped from Eleanor's clenched throat. Lairson tilted his head a bit to the side in an apology. "In general though, my Lady, no. I swear on our Ancient bestowers I have kept the information to myself."

"That's not very comforting considering you don't believe in the Ancients" the Queen replied snidely.

Lairson simply replied with a sarcastic shrug. He turned to his work table and picked up a small vial he had been tampering with earlier: it was filled with a thick, purple liquid.

"What is that?" the Queen felt the need to whisper.

"Salvation," Lairson whispered back, his smirk turning unnervingly devious. The doctor stuck his thumb and forefinger into the sides of the King's mouth, his hand wrapped around his chin. He opened Malcolm's mouth and tipped seven fat drops of the liquid down his throat.

"That will bring back the good portion of his senses," Lairson informed the Queen before releasing the King from his grasp.

"What," the Queen broke out of her trance to snarl, "pray tell, is that?"

"Why, the only thing that can undo and control magic, Your Majesty, the Indigo. When used on someone such as the King, who is without magic, it acts as an anti-venom of sorts," the doctor purred. Eleanor grabbed Lairson by the upper arm and forced him to look at her.

"I do not—" the Queen was interrupted by the revived King.

"What happened to the music?" Malcolm asked in a sweet voice. "It was so pretty!" Lairson chuckled as the Queen released her grasp.

"The Queen Mother tasked me with making Indigo to help control prisoners," Lairson replied haughtily. "Yes, your mother was privy to the ancient formula. Why do you think Zagan was so keen to bed her? He didn't want her affection, he wanted her power! As you well know, my Queen, a Handler's power is most effective as pillow talk. Your bastard half-brother was simply a byproduct of effective intelligence gathering." Lairson said in his usual nonchalant tone, "Now

126

Zagan has what he needs, courtesy of your mother, to control the Descendants. And thanks to me you now have one slightly used, slightly less vapid, King. You are welcome! What you are holding is the last of what I have. Without Seer's blood, I can make no more."

The Queen's face fell. "Seer's blood? Seer's are so rare these days. The woman Malcolm brought is a Seer but not likely to agree to parting with her blood."

"But, if we can convince Aurora to join our cause, we can make a trade. Her blood for her people." Lairson continued, diverting his eyes he became solemn for a split second as he remembered the unpleasant experience of collecting the blood.

"So what you mean to tell me is that we can make more with Aurora's blood and we can control the Descendants?" Eleanor questioned, eyes bright with curiosity. She finished scrutinizing the bottle and handed it back to the doctor.

"Yes, precisely," Lairson responded.

"And you have everything else you need to make--?"

"The Indigo Venom. Yes."

"Who else knows about this?"

"I am the only one who knows, my Queen," he said making his place known.

"Then Aurora shall assist us, whether she has the desire to or not."

"I think that is a fine idea, my Queen, a fine idea indeed."

****

Silvia and Ryder heard the war call of a Sharnin bugle as they fled deeper west through the woods. Their ears strained to hear the sound of pursuit as tremors of dread skidded through their bodies. Silvia's voice stuck in her throat like sap

127

to a tree, unable to ask Ryder what their plan was. She was unsure how she felt about her interactions with Wade and did not want, nor know how, to explain her history with Wade to Ryder. Anger and perplexity was a mire around them.

****

"Quite the gift you have for your prodigal son!" Donovan bowed deeply to Zagan, his fist on his heart. "I shall be inheriting a double throne?"

"I see your arrogance hasn't changed," Zagan replied, not looking up from the desk inside his tent.

"Father?" Donovan questioned, the jovial tone in his voice fading. "It's been over two years since I was imprisoned. Are you not pleased to see me?"

Zagan slowly raised his head to stare into his son's eyes. "Pleased? Why would I be pleased? None of the information you relayed to us was anything more than common knowledge." Donovan's posture slumped. "No. I am not pleased. I am disappointed."

"Surely you can't expect the utmost of secretive meetings to take place in the dungeon, father, I had hoped you wiser than that. I have done everything you have requested. Your anger towards me is unwarranted."

"I expected more from you, Donovan! You are not worthy of any title." Donovan's expression crumpled with shame. His heart raced and his throat tightened. "You are a waste of my time," the King growled.

Shock made Donovan stutter, "I-I spent two years locked up without seeing the sun or breathing fresh air because of a mission you sent me on! All I wanted was to succeed for you.

To have my own Kingdom, for you to honor your word. I got you the formula. Now where is my crown!"

"You failed in every aspect of your intent. Proud, I am not." Zagan's face held no kindness or remorse, "Get out of my sight, Donovan. You have squandered enough of my time."

Donovan could not believe what had just occurred. He found himself unable to move.

"Go, or I will make sure you meet your mother in the hereafter sooner than I'm sure you would like," Zagan threatened.

Donovan, dejectedly turned and left. *How could my own father reject me?* His sadness was very rapidly becoming a white-hot rage. If his father wanted to take Thurnadan, he would need assistance from the inside. Assistance Donovan already had. Donovan realized he had done all of the work. He was respected within the Sharnin camp. He would master both Thrones and lead the Descendants. Except he wasn't a fool enough to think he could control them. Granthan, the leader of the Sharnin Descendants, was civil with him. *I can earn their respect while executing my own needs.* He reassured himself. He left the tent in search of Granthan within the Sharnin camp.

"Donovan!" Granthan called out. He was a tall man, lean but muscular. Greying at the temples due to surviving into his middle years. "Just wished to know if you had further instruction for us from King Zagan. Any news?"

"No." Zagan's harsh words echoed in Donovan's mind. "Why do you follow my father?" Donovan asked boldly.

"My Lord?" the Descendent jerked back, surprised. "I- I, used to live in Clodith, in freedom. But I am a Wind Whisper and I dealt with more of people's cruelty and suspicions than I could stand. I needed guidance for my gift, not punishment and ridicule. Zagan promised us our own land to the north, we must first defeat all that stand in our way. He told us that the Indigo gives our gifts rest while we prepare for our next battle on our way to freedom. The land to the north of the Snow Lands is high above the seas and we will see no limitation to our gifts. The fields are green and fertile, with rivers of pure blue water cutting through them. We can finally make a home for ourselves."

"His words are lies. The Indigo takes away your powers so you will not revolt. Listen to me Granthan, as I swear on The Ancients and everything that I am. There is no freedom, there is no north beyond the north. And even if there was why would he give you such a prize? As soon as Zagan conquers the lands near and far, you will be destroyed."

Noticing the guards drawing near on their rounds, Donovan knew Granthan was skeptical and he had one last chance to make him believe.

"Do not eat your rations in the morning. Let your magic return. There is a woman in the castle who is a Seer. Zagan will be after her. Use your mind to find Aurora. Have faith in my words and find Aurora. She will bring you truth."

Granthan grimaced, "Surely this will be over soon. Our lives will be freed."

"Find her."

Abruptly, Donovan shifted to wolf form. He howled once with great sorrow, teeth gleaming and eyes bright, then took off toward Thurnadan's castle. Vowing revenge against his father, heavy breaths plumed from Donovan's lips; his pace quickened with the fury of betrayal. He did not wish to side with Eleanor and Thurnadan, but if that was what it would take to bring Zagan down first, he was willing to do so.

Donovan slowed his pace only as he reached where the forest met the loping, grassy hills of the castle. He growled, then ripped up the soft soil by a stream. Anger burned in his body so badly his eyes teared up and his skin itched. He wanted to sink his teeth into his father's throat and show him just how much of a mistake he had made by disowning him. Donovan paced back and forth on the bank and twitched his tail viscously. His eyes snapped open when he stumbled across a badger's nest.

The badger hissed and struck a clawed paw out. Donovan pounced, teeth barred. A moment later, the striped creature was dead, though not before it had left a slice across Donovan's snout. Pain brought him back to his senses. Irate, Donovan rinsed the wound in the stream then set off again. He had to get to Bridget. He had to get to Eleanor.

He would have his retribution.

Twelve

"Ryder," Silvia broke the silence. "Why aren't they following us?" she panted as they ran.

"I overheard a soldier," Ryder snapped, his breath coming in puffs.

"Saying what?" Silvia pressed.

"That Layton was next and then Thurnadan was guaranteed to be theirs."

"Why don't we see Queen Eleanor, King Malcolm, and a caravan of troops flooding through these woods to come to the people's rescue? Why don't we hear the war drums sounding from the grand castle? We should be knee deep in Thurnadanian soldiers by now!"

"Why are the Sharnins plowing west without hindrance? Has no one reported the destruction of Caerwyn?" Ryder replied crossly. He was tired, furious, and frightened, as was Silvia.

"You think we're doomed?" Silvia queried hoarsely. Ryder did not bother to respond. "We need to get to Layton to warn them," Silvia insisted.

****

Donovan reached the castle grounds in the wee hours of the morning. He blinked his wolf eyes in fatigue then shifted rapidly into his alternate human form, 'Hugh', and perched on the bridge of the far side of the garden he and Bridget had previously conversed on. He rubbed at the cut on his face that ran from under his eye to the tip of his nose. Although it was a shallow wound, it stung fiercely. Just when Donovan was

132

about to give up on Bridget, she swept gracefully from a castle door and came over to the bridge.

"Hello," Bridget replied sweetly, sitting down and neatly arranging her skirts.

"Morning," Donovan grinned shyly. "How are you?" he inquired.

"I don't know," Bridget replied forlornly. "Everybody is acting so strangely. Both the Queen and King, all the servants too! Last night everyone had such a peculiar mood about them. News from the surrounding land gets worse every day, and still we do nothing, so maybe people have accepted being conquered. After all, we are severely outnumbered by Sharnin." Bridget sulked, her eyes shifted over to Donovan then back to her own feet.

"I have heard some terrible things," Donovan added.

Bridget smiled faintly then looked up to meet Donovan's tender gaze. "My!" she gasped.

"What?" Donovan startled.

"You've got quite a scratch!" Bridget gushed, her eyelashes fluttering.

"That! No need to worry! I got into a bit of a wrestling match with a badger is all."

"A badger?"

"Yes, he was quite an opponent," Donovan smiled lopsidedly, pleased with himself for his acting. Bridget's expression darkened harshly for an instant before her shocked and caring smile returned.

"Fine don't tell me, but perhaps you should have it looked at? Those wild animals could make you ill!" Donovan shrugged bashfully. "Come with me this instant!" she demanded. "I'll get the castle's doctor for you."

"Oh no, I couldn't, it's so early," Donovan protested.

"Come," Bridget insisted with a giggle, tugging at Donovan's arm as she rose to her feet. "Huuugh, come on!"

"Fine," he relented, though he dragged his feet as he followed the maid. Despite his pouting, anxious expression, he was pleased internally.

The two made their way silently through the gardens and entered the castle. As Bridget led the way to the doctor's chambers, Donovan could not help but think resentfully how he could — and should — be inheriting all that he was seeing. Bridget knocked gently on the doctor's door. The voices inside quieted.

"Lairson," Bridget curtsied as the door swung open with a high-pitched creak.

"Hello, Bridget, what's the matter?" the doctor replied, distracted by the occupants of his room.

"My friend, Hugh, here had a run in with some horrible little creature." Her eyes went to Donovan then back to the doctor.

"Let's take a look at your friend. Hugh, you said?"

"Yes, sir," Donovan bowed. Donovan's formality caused a small smile to tweak at the corners of Lairson's mouth. He snorted and straightened his shoulders.

"In, in, come in." Donovan and Bridget followed the doctor, expecting to meet whomever he had been speaking to. But the room was empty. Donovan sat gingerly on the examination table. Flakes of dried blood dotted the back of his hand after touching his nose.

"Leave it alone now, boy," Lairson instructed, examining the wound. "Nothing but a scratch. It simply needs a cleaning," the doctor informed them as he wetted a cloth with a pale orange liquid and rubbed at Donovan's nose. "Guaranteed to sting for a while but it should heal just fine."

Bridget let out a loud sigh. "No need to be anxious, dear," Lairson smiled at the maid.

"How come you don't just heal it?" Bridget asked.

Lairson glared fiercely and replied, "I am a doctor, not a jester in an attraction. There's no need for magic here."

"Th-thank you, sir," Donovan gulped. Suspicion flamed blatantly from Lairson's expression.

"Have we met before?" the doctor asked, his mood shifted and his eyes sparkled. Donovan shook his head mutely. Bridget sensed the tension in the room, chuckled with discomfort, swished her skirts over to Donovan's side, and took his hand to get him to his feet. Without warning Lairson's door burst open. Revealing Eleanor standing in the doorway with a dumbfounded Malcolm.

"Lairson I do not know what I have done we need more Venom now!" The Queen bellowed.

"Your Majesties!" Bridget exhaled, dropping into a deep curtsy. Donovan 'Hugh' followed suit with a bow as Lairson slapped a hand over his face in exasperation.

The Queen paused, not having realized Bridget and Donovan were in the room. Lairson groaned. Eleanor's face froze into a deeply puzzled frown as her gaze fell on Donovan. When their eyes met, her blood ran cold.

****

Aurora sat bolt upright in bed. The hushed voices of the wind had risen to blood-curdling shrieks and the earth shook violently. Every sense she had told her to run: that the castle was becoming a home to evil. Aurora shivered despite being beneath a pile of blankets and having the morning sun pouring through the blue and white stained-glass windows and across the floor of her room. She knew she had to get a hold of whatever evil was now in the castle, and unwillingly crawled out of bed. She crept from her chambers to the throne room at the heart of the Thurnadanian castle.

The throne room was devoid of people. She stood in the center of a large orchid engraved in silver into the black marble floor. She turned to face the throne. The seat to the right had a large and ornately carved back: gilded in gold and silver and featuring the Queen's signature vanilla orchid. The seat to the left was slightly smaller. Carved from a single timber and featuring a lion's head at its top.

Aurora arched her neck and back. Mouth open and arms extended over her head in an elongated oval, Aurora called on her power and pleaded with the Ancients to tell her why the earth wept and shuddered. The voices and auras of her companions sang in her mind with the hum of her magic as she let her arms drop slowly apart. A thick bubble of flames, wind, water, and dust swirled around her.

She knelt, slowly bending and straightening her fingers. Reaching toward the elements that surrounded her, she pushed away her fatigue. "Show me the path to freedom so that I may fulfill your command. I am ready!" She cried as she reached for the answers she sought.

She bent her elbows so the back of her hands lay flat against her cheeks then forcefully threw her arms to the side. Sparks danced across the floor as her eyes began to glow a bright blue. Aurora wandered the castle with her mind. Fear, anger, and danger lurked everywhere. She sent her thoughts out beyond the castle walls to every mind she could reach. She whispered encouragement into Thurnadanian citizens minds. She sent pleas of mercy to Sharnin soldiers, and a sorrowful sense of morality and love to all Descendants. *Fear not my family, I am coming for you, I have built the trust I need, the time will soon come for you to understand. Peace will soon be upon us.* Was the final message she implanted in the minds of the Descendants outside the castle. She swayed with the rhythm of time, the melody of the elements, the beat of consciousness, and the harmonies of something she had not ever heard before, the harmonies of war. As she continued to sway, her Inkings began to come alive. The power coursing through her violet veins made them glow and dance. The vortex of elements swarming about her began to thunder and move with her. As the lights and sounds grew to a crescendo, Aurora became certain of the task ahead of her. At the very moment she accepted her fate, her Inkings stopped their incandescent glow and the elements fled her presence. The room became still once more as Aurora collapsed exhausted onto the giant silver orchid at the center of the throne room, her red hair draping across the black stone.

****

"Out," the Queen snapped. "Bridget, get out."

"But," the maid huffed, appearing rather flabbergasted. The Queen glowered viciously until Bridget curtsied and left the room. Hugh moved as if to join Bridget in her escape.

"Not you, boy," Lairson admonished.

"Well, well, well," Eleanor seethed, her eyes boring holes in Donovan. "Welcome back." Donovan clenched his fist and mentally kicked himself. Bridget hovered by the door with her ear to the wall.

"Did I miss something?" Lairson inquired.

"Silence, Lairson, or I will set my magic on you and turn your mind to porridge," the Queen flamed. Donovan twitched his eyebrows, then nonchalantly yawned. "Change to your real form *now*, Donovan," the Queen spat in disgust. "You are a fool for thinking I would not recognize you," she informed him. "If you are ever going to thoroughly disguise yourself, you will have to put aside your vanity to change those emerald eyes of yours. Shift," she insisted, infuriated.

Donovan sighed loudly, "Only to indulge you, my sweet sister."

Lairson's eyebrows shot up. Donovan stretched then shifted to the form of a large, foul, white wolf. Lairson stumbled backward in astonishment and fear.

"Delightful," she snorted. "A tundra wolf. Is that a new trick?" she asked in a mocking tone. Donovan shifted again to his true form, smiling gleefully.

"I was practicing the form just before I was disposed of in that nasty cell of yours. I had not the opportunity to fully undertake the transformation prior to today. Forgive me for giving it a try," Donovan winked with mirth and mischievousness.

"Like father, like son," Eleanor smiled, knowing this was a sore point.

"Would that it were so simple," Donovan spat, "don't you ever compare me to my father again." In an instant Donovan shifted into a green mist and flew into Eleanor's throat. She began choking violently.

"Stop that," Eleanor choked. As quickly he entered her throat he flew out. She fell over coughing as he shifted back into his usual smug self.

"Your Highness?" Lairson moved to help her. But she stood up with vigor and stared Donovan down.

"How dare you!" Eleanor quickly enabled her Mind Handling skills and invaded Donovan's mind. *So, you went running to your father and he was most displeased with you. Why does that not surprise me? And now you want to join me. That will never happen!*

She broke the mind connection and stumbled back.

"I'm sorry," Donovan confessed.

"Zagan is coming and he has the Indigo Venom?" Eleanor confirmed.

"How dare you dig through my mind!" Donovan whimpered. "Besides, that is a secret I would have told you willingly. But that is not all, sweet sister."

****

Silvia sat on a large moss-covered rock with her head bowed between her knees, utterly exhausted. They had caught up with their fellow captives. The small group took rest amongst the tall pines taking care to hide as much evidence of their presence as possible.

"We need horses," Ryder's voice dissolved the silence as all eyes focused on him. "If we can make it to Layton, they should have a Handler that can relay warning to Thurnadan."

"We have to get there and warn them of the attacks, they'll be here soon," Silvia agreed.

"Why?" grumbled one of the surviving villagers whose left eye was swollen shut below a gash on his temple. "We'll be dead before we get there," he stated flatly.

"They need a chance to protect themselves, and fighting will stall the Sharnin troops hopefully long enough to get Thurnadanian reinforcements," Ryder's stress burst from his voice, "and save Layton."

"Unfortunately, that gives the Sharnin's time to wait for their reinforcements too," Silvia added.

The most-badly injured of the villagers whispered vaguely, "I ain't goin' nowhere," he said, his far-away gaze sharpening determinedly, "'cept to find my wife and litl'n." Both Ryder and Silvia lowered their eyes.

"I second that," stated the first man who had spoken. "Besides, none of us are in any shape to travel."

"We fought and look what happened to us!"

"We were crushed!"

"Those Descendants will kill every last one of us!"

"Exactly! All I want's my wife!"

"I'm alive. Like to stay that way, too."

"Right. Why go risking our necks again? And in a valley no less. We'll be an easy target."

"Oh no," Silvia realized, "You're right. The Sharnins are not marching into Thurnadan's castle. They are drawing them into the valley of Layton to attack them there. That's why they are waiting. They are holding for their army."

The men around them began to talk of heading south, wanting no part of the war. Ryder and Silvia looked at each other as they listened to the men talk over one another, their voices becoming more and more distraught.

"You," Ryder started then waited for the men to settle down.

"You are alive now," Silvia interjected. A flicker of questioning crossed Ryder's face but he let her speak. "You are alive and, Ancients-willing, your families are safe," she paused. "Perhaps we all should have run away," she turned to Ryder for a split second then continued, "but we didn't. We stayed and fought. And because of that, many Sharnin soldiers fell."

"And what did that get us?! Pain, sufferin' an' more pain!" shouted the younger man. Silvia held up one hand to silence him.

"Yes. I know that. I know that better than any of you. I have no husband, no father, and no brothers because of Sharnin." The men diverted their eyes to look at the ground, knowing Silvia had been through an unmentionable amount of loss due to the casualties of war. "So, tell me something," Silvia forced the words from her clenched throat, "tell me why your families are safe rather than dead? Why are they not lying face-down in the damned dirt, soaked in their own blood, with Sharnin arrows in their backs?" Silvia's voice strained as she fought back tears, "Imagine if we were warned?"

The men sat in discomfort for a long moment.

"And that," Silvia closed her eyes and set her jaw, Ryder recognized her expression of resolve and reacted by standing a bit straighter, "that, gentlemen, is why we will indeed go to Layton." The men remained silent. They knew Silvia was right. Ryder's hardened heart softened; he could not judge Silvia when he did not know her whole story.

"I'm glad you're on our side. I would hate to cross swords with someone so damned determined. Also, I've seen you fight." Ryder sighed in resignation.

"Then why are we wasting time sitting here?" cheered the big man as he heaved himself to his feet, his expression intent.

"Come on, Layton can't be more than a few more miles from here," Ryder said hopefully.

The survivors stood, one by one. Pain tore through their bodies and their hearts. Despite tears running down a few cheeks, the men's backs were straight and their shoulders squared. Thurnadan had won itself soldiers: soldiers of anger, soldiers of heart, soldiers of defiant strength that fought not for land and honor but for redemption, preservation, and revenge.

Thirteen

Bridget had heard all that she needed. She was already quite aware of the Queen's involvement in Donovan's escape, so she felt no need to stay and eavesdrop any longer. She crept away from the door, letting the bickering voices of Donovan and Eleanor fade behind her. Bridget became solemn as she tucked her curls into a messy bun.

In her head, she replayed all that she had overheard. Only slightly out of breath when she reached the top of the three flights of stairs, Bridget double checked that the infrequently used tower was indeed empty. Satisfied that she was alone, she walked to the oblong window facing east and gazed out over the landscape. A shimmer of red and yellow light wafted across the hills.

"Mediara firmar," Bridget whispered as she cupped her hands together, breathed deeply, and watched as a green sphere of light grew in her palm. A man with sharp olive green eyes and a short graying beard looked out from the light at her. She nodded twice. He nodded once. Bridget knew that as much as she sorely hated flight spells, they were very frequently necessary. Shoots of golden daylight sprang one by one from the horizon. A breeze lifted languidly from the east and rolled gently toward the castle, but its sweet aroma was sourly tainted with the murky, gritty odor of smoke. Bridget gulped loudly and fought back her feelings of guilt. She took a deep breath to steady her nerves then stepped up onto the window ledge.

"Chegar apareece," she chanted. She closed her eyes and dropped forward into the open air. A gust of wind rushed up to meet her. It rolled across her body, thick and soft, but cold.

"Zagan," the words skidded from Bridget's tense throat, and off she went.

Her stomach lurched whenever she opened her eyes so she clenched them shut as she spun eastward; only the air and her thoughts kept her company. Bridget knew she had already gotten herself into trouble, but when she told Zagan the news of what she had overheard, things would only get worse. She had hoped that he would be kind to his last remaining spy in the castle. Eastward, the green rolling hills quickly gave way, through the forest, to charred earth and the smoldering remains of a village.

****

Back in her room Aurora jerked awake, her eyes flashing blue as her Seer's ability took over once more. She was certain that someone had used a substantial amount of magic nearby, she just wasn't positive due to her state. A few pale sparks were still pulsing on the windowsill and a faint smell of cinnamon hung in the air. A spasm of magic yanked at Aurora's conscious. But, as quickly as it had come, it was gone. She shook her head. Having as much awareness as she had often made her want to cry in exhaustion. She sighed, frustrated that she had missed whoever had harnessed the wind.

Without warning, Aurora stiffened as she felt someone attempting to connect to her mind. She was certain it was another Descendant but one from...Sharnin?

Aurora?

Yes, it is I, Aurora. Using her gift of sight, she was able to see a man in his middle years, soldier like, clearly in some sort of camp. He was indeed a Sharnin. She immediately raised her guard and prepared to engage in mind manipulation of the highest variety with a Sharnin Descendant.

My name is Granthan, and I am a member of the Sharnin army. These are my people, as you use your Sight, please look around our surroundings. Donovan, son of Zagan, was rejected by his father and offered to aide in our release. He is to be trusted as far as I know at the moment, he was the one who opened my eyes to the effects of the Indigo Venom in our rations. As well as Zagan's true intentions. That is how I was able to connect with you. He informed me of your involvement in the Thurnadanian castle, with regards to our escape.

Granthan, how do I know you are not lying to me?

Use your Sight, Aurora, no one has any fear of me. Not even the slightest. We are always wary of anyone who is not our kind. Even a Sharnin soldier that is full Descendant is not our kind. Aurora, you are within the Thurnadan castle, I can mind connect the current battle plans to you, and you can warn the King and Queen. They don't give us more detail than necessary, but at least it can give an advantage to Thurnadan.

I'm not sure what kind of advantage it would be, or that Thurnadan would even stand a chance against common Sharnin soldiers. The King has had his mind muddled by, I believe, the Queen. There is so much chaos and discord here in the castle, I will need time to sort this out.

Time is something you do not have, Aurora. I am sending the plans I know of. You must act quickly.

****

Lairson slithered warily down the hall, confident that both the Queen and her overindulged half-brother were supportive of his endeavor against Aurora. However, inside his chambers, Eleanor and Donovan continued to quarrel with one another while Malcolm slept soundly on the examination table.

It had taken almost an hour of arguing for the siblings to agree on a plan. They would use Aurora to distract Zagan while they attacked him, allowing Donovan to take over Sharnin, and leaving Thurnadan squarely under Eleanor's rule. Lairson suspected that Donovan would change his mind whenever it suited him though, no matter what compromises they had made.

Lairson's very own plan was to corner Aurora and lock her up, then bargain her freedom for her blood. Once they had the blood, he would let Eleanor and Donovan use his concoction to end the Sharnin King's reign, and Lairson could use it for pure paltriness. He would get great satisfaction from rendering Aurora's magic useless. Lairson stiffened when he heard Aurora's voice. He quickly tucked himself into a closet to hide, and held his breath to be perfectly quiet. Aurora paused as she walked by, but soon continued on her way. Lairson waited until he could no longer hear Aurora's footsteps and then followed her.

****

Bridget tumbled from the air into an undignified heap at the outer edge of a sleeping Sharnin encampment.

"Identify yourself!" barked a startled soldier.

"Sharnin recruit. Bridget. Devoted messenger and spy for King Zagan."

"Proceed forward," he instructed. Bridget let out a long, exasperated sigh and walked slowly forward. "Prove your loyalty," the soldier said with a squint, suspicious of Bridget's seemingly innocent appearance.

Snapping her fingers, Bridget grinned mischievously and said, "Moira sicao." She blew on the pale green orb that appeared above her palm. The soldier took a step back and tightened his grip on his halberd; the spike and blade shone menacingly but Bridget took no notice. A scene from her fighting in past battles replayed within the orb of Bridget ordering the Sculptors where to throw fire. The soldier gulped apprehensively when the tiny hologram let out an eerie howl, as the screams of the dying penetrated the silence. Bridget extinguished her magic and inclined her head in a slight bow. With his right fist over his heart, the soldier saluted in response.

"The Commander resides in his tent," he informed Bridget. "Are you in need of an escort?"

"I can find my way, thank you," Bridget smiled faintly and started toward Zagan's tent. As she walked away, she noted that the soldier warded himself against her. He kissed his fingers, placed them to his forehead, then set them on the tundra wolf crest that decorated the chest of his uniform. Over her shoulder, Bridget snidely commented, "Scared of magic, soldier? In the midst of the Sharnin army, a little light show scares you?" Neither man replied. "Fools. Fear will get you killed."

Two soldiers stationed in front of the King's oversized tent crossed their weapons to block Bridget's approach.

"Identify yourself," growled the soldier on the right.

"Sharnin recruit. Devoted messenger and spy for the King. Bridget," Bridget huffed.

"Prove your loyalty," ordered the one on the left.

"For the Ancients' sakes!" she stomped her foot in irritation.

147

"Let her in," said an authoritative voice from inside the tent. The soldiers stiffened to attention then slowly uncrossed their halberds. Bridget smirked.

"My King," she curtsied when the tent door had slid closed behind her.

"Hello, Bridget," smiled Zagan, removing a thick Clodithian cigar from between his lips. "You have news for me?" The King sat with his feet propped up on the desk in front of him, his shirt's top buttons were undone and his beard had not been trimmed yet that morning.

"I do, Sire," replied Bridget warily.

"Why," he picked at a fingernail, "do I get the feeling it is not good news?"

"Because I think it is not."

"Don't waste your energy on thinking, Bridget," Zagan's eyes flicked over to Bridget then back to his cigar.

"Yes, Sire," Bridget curtsied quickly.

"I do not keep you for your thoughts. I keep you for your observations." The King slowly lowered his feet to the floor, sniffed, and locked eyes on Bridget. "Out with it then," he instructed. "Do tell."

"Donovan is in the castle," she began.

"Impudent boy," Zagan's brow creased and his fists tightened. "I should have just killed him."

"Her Highness," the King's eyes grew dark. "Eleanor," Bridget corrected herself, "Eleanor recognized him..."

"So?" he snapped. "Why would she not recognize her own brother, no matter what form he took?"

"Well, she, Donovan, and the doctor, Lairson, seem to be conspiring together. At least temporarily. I'm sure their animosity will return soon enough but for now they appear to have brokered a truce."

148

"So Donovan's found a new puppeteer. How predictable for such a pathetic child," he hissed. "Continue."

"The doctor knows the recipe for the Indigo Venom. He is most excited about it too. He told Eleanor and Donovan about it — "

"Bridget! Curse the Ancients and let me die before I listen to another rambling word of yours!" Zagan swore. "I have a war to win! Speak straight!" Bridget winced as Zagan slammed his feet on the ground. He leaned down and pulled the collar of Bridget's dress away from her neck. "Perhaps Thurnadan's folly has rubbed off on you. Has your Inking somehow bled into your soul?" he stared at the coiled lizard Inking on Bridget's chest, her petrified breathing making it rise and fall.

"No-no, Sire," Bridget stiffened, trying not to flinch.

"You are my spy. Do your duty. Tell me the news," he lowered his voice to a controlled growl, "or I will string you up by your tongue and leave you for the crows to devour."

"It's the Descendant. There's a Seer in the castle who is most powerful."

"Now I see. You suspect they will use the Seer's blood then?" The King slowly tilted back his head and returned his cigar to his mouth, "You think with this Seer fellow, a fraction of the Descendants that we have, and a rudimentary Indigo Venom that they will defeat us? Am I understanding your worries correctly?" Zagan gave a mirthless chuckle.

"She, my Lord."

"What?

"She, Sire. The Seer is a young woman. Her hair the color of fire and blood. But Sire. She's not just a Seer, Your Highness, she has almost all abilities..." Her voice had dropped to a barely audible whisper.

"She?" Zagan grew pale. He launched out of his seat to grip Bridget by the shoulders "Her name?" he breathed, face full of rage. "What is her name?" he demanded, shaking Bridget fiercely.

"A-a-Aurora," Bridget stuttered. "My King, what is it?"

"Enough," the King sagged and his grasp relaxed. He spun around to his desk, kicked his chair viscously, swore at the pain it caused him, then spun back to face Bridget.

"Sire?" she squeaked, eyes twice their usual size.

The King whispered, "She is supposed to be dead."

****

Lairson followed Aurora as she wandered about the castle then as she went into her bed chambers, he waited frozen outside her door. Although there had been a mere drop of Venom left, he had hoped it was enough to keep her from resisting capture. He gathered two guards from the nearby hall and had them follow him. At his command, they seized Aurora and jerked her unceremoniously from her chamber. First wide-eyed and then furious, Aurora wrenched herself from the guards' grasps and scrambled across the room.

"What in the Ancients' names do think you're doing?"

"By order of Her Highness, Eleanor, the Lady Queen of Thurnadan you are to be escorted to the prison until further questioning can be arranged."

"For what?" Aurora protested.

Lairson replied smugly and laughed, "you are to be imprisoned for suspicion of magical involvement in the ailment of His Highness, Malcolm, King of Thurnadan."

150

"And if I don't comply?" Aurora countered, a few gold sparks jumping ominously from her fingers. Nervously, the guards backed off.

"You will hereby be considered a traitor. A threat to the crown. Which, I might add, is a grievance punishable by death," conceit glinted in Lairson's eyes.

"And what if the culprit cannot die?" Aurora replied stone-faced.

"There are ways of getting around such details," Lairson responded shrewdly. "I would recommend, witch, that you allow these gentlemen," Lairson gestured to the guards who came forward and tentatively took hold of Aurora's wrists, "to escort you downstairs."

"I wish to speak to Argus. I will go for now, but be advised I am going of my own free will," Aurora hissed, fear starting to itch at her heart.

"I am afraid Argus is otherwise engaged at the moment," the doctor grinned. "Take her away," he ordered the guards.

****

"Get back to the castle. Immediately. Bring me her head," Zagan bellowed.

"My Lord?!" Bridget objected.

"Her head. Or yours."

"Sire, please!" Bridget begged, dropping to her knees at Zagan's feet. "Please do not make me do this!" Her body shook and her eyes filled with tears of terror.

"Do as commanded, Bridget! Be the Sharnin solider you took an oath to be or I will have your head."

"How can a Healer be killed?" Bridget implored, eyes on the ground as she resigned herself to her fate.

151

"Bridget! You fool! The Venom! The Queen must have some of it to threaten me so," Zagan seethed. "Use it," he looked down at Bridget, his expression distorted with rage. "Drown her in it! Make her powers useless! Then she will die just like any other pitiful magicless sod." Bridget shuddered, trying not to retreat in fear. Zagan's voice was stone, "You are mine. All of you Descendants are mine! Do not ever forget that." Bridget nodded. "You are dismissed," he spat.

"At your service," Bridget rose, saluted, then turned and left the tent. Zagan turned to open a box filled with empty vials where there used to be Indigo Venom. "Guards!"

A guard came rushing in, "Yes, King Zagan."

"Bring me another Seer. Now!"

"But Sire, there are no more."

"Then find me one!" the King seethed.

"Yes, my King." The guard left without another word.

Bridget ran a few paces until she was out of the encampment. She looked down at her shaking hands. "I have become a monster. They are right to be afraid of our kind," she wept to herself.

Fourteen

Wearily, Silvia, Ryder, and their few remaining companions stumbled west. The closer they got to Layton, the more the rough forest floor smoothed into grassy plains and the craggy cliffs softened into rolling hills. Still, dragging themselves forward took an excruciating amount of effort.

"What happens if we come across another Sharnin?" worried the young man walking behind Ryder.

"Then our throats will be slit and we'll be out of our misery," the man next to him replied, his mood fouled from pain and exhaustion.

"Ancients save us," the young man swore.

A wind rushed past the group, causing the trees to sway and buckle.

"Get down," Ryder warned.

The sharp crack of snapping wood filled the air. The survivors looked at each other uneasily as the wind urged them forward before fading away.

"What as that?" the man asked with a shudder.

"Let's not swear by the Ancients, shall we?" the big man of the group replied, remembering superstitious tales from his childhood.

Silvia resolved her facial expression to mask her fears despite the raised hairs on the back of her neck. "I'm sure it was nothing," she tried to console them. "Besides, if I've judged our position correctly then we will be approaching Layton momentarily."

"Layton cannot be much further!" Ryder replied as an enthusiastic grin pulled at his lips. They climbed over rocks as the trees got thicker and thicker. The group crested a hill and laid eyes on a valley below filled with the shining town of Layton. The valley city was truly something to behold. Lush green grass, water running through the town that sparkled like the night stars, made Layton a beauty. The sunlight reflected off of the town making it almost appear to glow.

"There are five main trading cities in Thurnadan, they call em' the five jewels," an older man stated, his mood brightened by the view. "This is Layton, and boy she is a jewel!" Silvia nodded and smiled, witnessing the rejuvenation of her companions' energy. The older man clapped the younger on the shoulder.

"The Thurnadan castle lies due west. At the center of the Queendom, bordered by the trading route," Silvia added. "There, you can see it just over those mountains."

"Well," Ryder interrupted. He soberly gestured down at the hill. The survivors' moods fell once again as they reluctantly agreed.

"It is a pity our tidings be so disheartening," bleated one of the men.

"But better they know then be struck unaware," Ryder reminded him. A concurrent sigh came up from the group as they began their descent. "Follow me," Ryder encouraged.

Just before they were half way down, an arrow flew from their previous position at the tree line catching Silvia's ear. She screamed out in agony. Another white birch wood arrow flew toward her and pierced her side.

"Get down!" Ryder shouted. The men dropped to the ground, scattering and trying to find cover. The grassy slopes around them held no reprieve or protection. Only a moment passed before shouts, clanking armor, and the whinny of horses rose up from Layton.

"No!" Silvia shrieked aloud. She broke off the shaft of the arrow, leaving its head embedded in her side. She staggered to her feet, rushed Ryder and took his stolen dagger, then fled uphill.

"Silvia!" Ryder yelled. "Silvia! Silvia, dammit!" He swore and went after her.

There were a half dozen Sharnin men approaching the city but only one set as an archer on the surrounding hill. Silvia knew that if the townspeople tried to fight they would foolishly ride directly to their deaths. The Sharnin's archer would strike them down before they had crossed even fifty strides beyond their own grounds. Once again, the rage inside of Silvia gave her the strength to continue forward.

"I've got the archer!" belted a Caerwyn villager as he ran towards the direction of the arrow's origin.

The first Sharnin Silvia caught up to as he came down the hill never saw her coming. She jumped on his back and slit his throat without remorse and moved on before his lifeless body had even sunk into the grass. She looked down at Wade's blood-soaked dagger in her hand. She shook off all thoughts creeping into her mind. The next man Silvia took after spotted her a moment before she reached him. His sword vastly overpowered her dagger but, in his surprise, he acted unwisely. He lunged at Silvia, leaving his body fully exposed. Silvia spun away from his attack then countered by gouging a hole deep into his stomach. Her dagger tore through his skin and into his muscles. Blood welled around her fist as she gave her blade a fierce twist. The man cursed, sputtered, and attempted to swing at her again. Silvia dodged, caught his wrist to swing behind him, and forced him forward to his knees. Silvia dug her dagger into his throat, then grimaced as he toppled over dead. The Sharnin to Silvia's left had seen his companions die and had readied himself for attack.

Silvia charged as the man grinned. A pace away from the tip of his sword, Silvia dropped forward into a somersault. After tumbling head over heels, she came up on her feet again, body against body with the Sharnin. She burrowed her blade into his abdomen, angling her thrust up and out to savagely tear into his lung. The man gasped and gurgled then died with an expression of shock and anguish clear on his face. Silvia removed her bloody weapon and ran toward Layton. Her feet moved faster than they had since her training with her father and brothers in her youth.

"Stop!" she screamed as a brave, brash, townsman rode from the city's gates. "Stop!" she shouted again when his head swiveled toward her. Another white arrow lodging into her, the sharp point tearing a tendon in her shoulder. Silvia stumbled to her knees but fought her way up again. Nausea from the pain caused her to sway. Her vision blurred but she kept on; she wanted no more innocent deaths on her conscience. "Go back into the city," her voice cracked as she yelled. "Go back. The archer," she pointed to the hills, "it isn't safe! They'll..." she couldn't find the words to finish her sentence. She looked up to the hillside to see the archer fall to his death, the villagers had succeeded in overtaking him. A searing pain of wicked cold ripped through her muscles from the wound in her shoulder. "They're poison arrows!" Silvia realized. The knowledge made her gag. "Poison," she cried. Silvia blindly staggered the last few paces into the city. A woman's soft arms caught her as she collapsed.

"You're safe now," said a soothing voice. "You're safe."

Silvia's eyes blinked, her mind straining to stay focused. In the distance, she could see Ryder fighting the last of the few

Sharnin soldiers, but before she could see his victory her eyes gave in and closed into darkness.

****

As soon as the guards had locked the cell door behind her, Aurora projected her mind into the castle. At first, she thought she sensed that Argus was still asleep but soon realized he had been sedated. It must be Lairson who sedated him too, knowing that Lairson's handiwork was to blame for her weakness. Aurora knelt on the ground to stabilize herself before searching farther out. She felt the Venom Lairson had dosed her with taking hold over her Seer powers. She found the King and Queen approaching the doctor where he waited in the dining hall, then pushed her reach even further out. She saw that Sharnin troops were closer than she thought. "Layton," she whispered. Unrest and fear boiled within her. Aurora sighed, wishing that the Sharnin Descendants would find their morality and turn on Zagan before he devastated another village.

I have seen death and destruction. My Seer's sight weeps at what the future holds, Aurora wretched every last bit of power she could from her body in order to enter each mind she reached out to within the Sharnin ranks. *No peace will come from Thurnadan's ruin. Zagan is not your savior. He is your downfall.* The Descendants' emotional responses to her messages were so strong that even when Aurora returned her mind to her physical self, her heart fluttered with sorrow and confusion. Thoughts, plots, and frustration: nothing was certain except that all of Thurnadan was still in great danger. It was clear the Descendants were still being forced to swallow their daily dose of Venom. And with that, her head began to spin. She

157

laid on her back in the middle of her cell, trying to conserve any last bit of energy she had to fight the Venom in her veins.

Aurora felt the Energies of her companions dance inside her. But, this time, they seemed frightened. Their nervousness infected Aurora and caused a small whimper to escape her lips. She clenched her jaw closed and focused on her search. Her mind continued to travel through the castle. It quickly landed upon the doctor's chambers.

Donovan was clearly an uninvited guest in the doctor's chambers. Lairson, out of loyalty to Eleanor, had not reported Donovan's presence to anyone, but nonetheless, did not want to engage with him on any level. Donovan was tinkering with some of the doctor's herbs. Aurora was about to examine the herbs more closely when she felt a tug at her thoughts. Her eyes snapped open but she kept her mind in the doctor's chambers.

Hello again, Aurora.

Aurora cursed at herself. She knew Donovan had felt her presence and connected to her. *Donovan,* she reluctantly answered.

You do not feel happy to see me.

This surprises you? she replied. Donovan's laugh filled her mind.

How are you enjoying my former residence down there?

I truly loath the fact that you and I have a mental connection.

Does that mean you haven't missed me? Donovan retorted.

What are you doing here? Aurora snapped.

Helping Thurnadan, same as you, Donovan brayed.

I have a hard time believing that. After all, you were locked in the dungeons for offenses against the Crown, why would you now help? Why are you here and not stuck to King Zagan's side?

If you ever say my father's name again I will end you. I am helping Thurnadan, I have not yet decided, however, if once you and your people are free, if I will re-capture you for myself. Eleanor is graciously giving me the crown of Sharnin, after we defeat my father. Did you know you can destroy a Descendant by strangling their conscious while in a mind-connection? Donovan asked.

I dread to know how you learned such a forbidden technique. However, if you think you are up to the task I invite you to try. That is if you think your mind is stronger than mine.

You and I are bonded, I know I could snap your mind like a dried twig. I could render your senses utterly useless right now.

You could try. Aurora's aggravation and fear was returning her to their younger days of teenage fighting. *Don't forget, I'm a Healer.*

Yes, of course I remember that. And a cocky bunch of people you healers seem to be. You are not indestructible, Aurora. And neither is my father. Donovan snapped, *Everyone reaches their limit eventually.*

Let go of my mind, Donovan.

You are scared of me, aren't you? With good reason. Donovan's tie on her loosened. *My threat still holds true and it always will.*

Aurora's body melted into the floor when their connection broke. After a moment, her healing powers returned her strength. She doubted that Donovan was truly aiding Thurnadan, but if he had indeed turned against Zagan it gave her hope that others would follow in his footsteps and abandon the army. Some pieces of Thurnadan's predicament had fallen into place in Aurora's understanding: She knew Eleanor, Lairson, and Donovan were plotting something. She also figured King Malcolm's affliction, as well as hers and Argus', was a result of their plotting. There was much

159

uncertainty, but perhaps there was also a chance for the Queendom's survival.

Aurora's magic pulsed under her skin. She brought herself to her knees as her mind and mouth filled with the words of elemental magic. Aurora touched one finger to the lock on her cell and the cool metal softened into putty. With a wave of her hand the door swung slowly open.

"Freeze!" bellowed a guard, his sword drawn and pointed at her.

"Sorry," Aurora unapologetically snapped her fingers as she got to her feet. Sparks fizzed from her hand and the packed-dirt wall of the underground prison bulged forward and engulfed the guard. Aurora was stunned at her ability to move the earth.

"What the—?" the guard startled as his weapon clattered to the floor and his body became locked tight in a blanket of soil.

"It will wear off in a little while, I promise," Aurora guiltily reassured him. "You won't be harmed." She touched an icy finger to his lips and a seal of air kept him from calling out to the other guards. She went to a torch on the wall and put her left hand into the flame. When she withdrew it, she was holding a ball of fire in her palm. She carried the flame in front of her as she moved her way down the passage to get out of the dungeon. As she came across more guards, she dealt with them in the same manner she had with the first. A series of mummified guards filled her wake. When she sensed she was directly under Argus' chambers she extinguished the flame and called on her Grounder magic. The mountain Inking on her right wrist began to glow an emerald green. She steadied her breathing and looked at the ceiling above her. She then reached up as the stone ceiling parted and a platform

160

made of hard packed earth rose up beneath her bringing her directly into Argus' chamber. She came upon a slumbering Argus, the ground closed beneath her feet and she took a step forward. No sign of her escape was visible. Not one speck of dirt out of place.

She took a deep breath and walked over to settle herself at the foot of Argus' bed. She laid her hand on his forehead and the other on his chest.

"Come back to us, Argus," she urged with her healing magic. Spirals looped from her fingers into his body and picked apart the sedation that had him near death. But he didn't move. Aurora sat back and looked at her hands. "Why isn't it working? Why can't I heal him?" Aurora panicked. She drew as much energy as she could manage. She pressed her hands onto Argus and poured everything she had into him.

"Come on," she prayed. She waited. *Open your eyes,* she urged.

" — don't go!" Argus violently shuddered awake.

"What?" Aurora asked as Argus opened his eyes. "It's alright. It's me."

"I hada' dream. My wife was still here! It- it seemed so real," Argus looked around confused and saddened. Aurora jumped to throw her arms around him then quickly stammered back.

"I'm so glad you're alright," Aurora's mood shifted, "Where's Lairson?"

"Why do ya' ask?" Argus' eyebrows twitched. "An' why are ya' here?"

"I just freed you from the near-death sedation your sweet and docile doctor issued you," Aurora snorted.

"Lairson?"

"Yes, Lairson," Aurora huffed in annoyance. "Are all men this thick-skulled after waking?"

"Hey!" he protested, but his drowsiness had dissipated. His eyes rolled upward as if he was examining his own brain. "Thank you," he said reluctantly.

"Get up. We have work to do."

Argus tumbled out of bed after Aurora turned her back. She paced around the room as she spoke, "Lairson's gone off! He knocked you out and locked me in prison."

"Prison?!"

"Yes, prison, don't interrupt! Our time is sorely limited. The Queen, I am completely certain, is the one who poisoned the King's mind. In addition, Sharnin troops have fully invaded and are currently circling your eastern trading city, Layton. I have done what I can to reach out to the Sharnin soldiers mentally, beseeching them to lay down arms. But," Aurora rubbed anxiously at her eyes, "our situation looks more than a little dire."

"How do ya know all this?" Argus inquired. Aurora ignored him.

"You ready yet?" she snorted, hands on her hips.

"What ya be plannin'?" Argus asked while strapping on his weapons' belt and sheathing his sword.

"You're the High Constable, aren't you? You tell me," Aurora replied, vexed.

"Here," he frowned, handing her a slim, jeweled dagger.

"I hardly think someone with my abilities needs a piece of metal to protect them," Aurora half-smiled.

"You will if we go to war. Just slip her in yer boot. Ya' never know when a blade'll be needed."

"Yes, sir," Aurora replied, touched by Argus' concern.

"The obvious start is ta' find the Queen."

"Argus?"

"What?"

"One problem."

"What?"

"It's the Queen who issued my arrest."

Fifteen

In the center of Layton was the Main Hall, where Silvia and any other who had been injured in the first attack were taken. It was a wide-open room with beautiful arching mahogany beams spreading across the ceiling. Their intricate carvings of waves and jumping fishes told the story of this riverside trading city. The afternoon sun was bursting through the high windows of the room. Their amber glass warmed the room as a cool breeze ran through it. The Descendants of Layton were busy helping those who fought for them just moments ago.

"Have you not heard?" Ryder struggled to get his warning out between gasps of breath. The pain in his knee was excruciating. "Please, don't fight. Gather your people. We need to evacuate," Ryder begged.

"We will not run away! We are no cowards!" bellowed the townsman.

"It is not cowardly to avoid running into the arms of your own murderer!" Ryder objected, clutching at the arrow in his knee. The loss of blood from the wound in his neck caused Ryder to sag to the ground, unable to keep himself up any longer.

"Layton," seethed the man, "is a city full of strong men and women. How dare you think some fool group of ruffians could overpower us?"

"Sharnin," Ryder stated. "They are Sharnin."

"The army of Sharnin? How many?" the man asked apprehensively. He fell silent, his shoulders slumped.

"All of them," Ryder rasped, holding up a Sharnin arrow for the man to see. Its white birch wood shaft gleamed with blood and its tail of green feathers flickered in the breeze.

"Sharnin colors," the man whispered, his expression bleak.

"Most of the eastern villages have been destroyed. The Sharnin have Descendants fighting with them. They have slaughtered everything and everyone in sight. Within those woods aren't ruffians; it's the combined forces of trained military and powerful magic."

"How can it be as you say?" The man closed his eyes for a moment in an attempt to calm his emotions, "Why has the Queen not issued a warning? Why has she not sent troops?"

"We have been trying to find out the same thing," Ryder looked away dejectedly. "I do not mean insult to your strength or skill," he frowned sourly, "when I tell you it's certain death if you step foot outside these walls. Who knows how many Descendants Zagan has amassed by now. You cannot win this battle alone." His words were soaked with remorse, "We need the Queen's Army if we are to survive."

"Then we will prepare for war," the man replied briskly. "The Healers will tend to you as soon possible. When you are well, I will show you that the true might of Thurnadan does not lie at its center but rather within its trading routes." Ryder sagged as the man turned and strode purposefully away.

The man walked out the open door and stood silently for a moment, almost like he was in a trance.

"What is he doing," Ryder asked a nearby villager.

"He is reaching out with his mind to the other villages nearby. Perhaps they will aid us, or at the very least be able to protect themselves from these attacks.

The man came back into the Hall. Ryder watched as the crowd fell impossibly still.

"The other trade cities have been warned," the man bellowed back toward Ryder as the light on his face diminished. "Word will spread quickly." A grumbling went up from the crowd: part war cry, part stubborn excitement, and part fear.

"I can tend to you now," said a murmuring voice. Ryder turned to his left and met the eyes of an approaching woman with a sweet face. "My name is Gwendolyn. I'm a Healer. I can help you." She was a sweet woman, her gracefully aged face aligned with her tall posture and beauty.

"Silvia, is she—?"

"She has a unique gift, your friend," the Healer cleared her throat. Ryder's brow furrowed. "She'll be just fine," she smiled, ignoring Ryder's questioning look.

"This is going to hurt, a lot." Gwendolyn reached out and swiftly snapped the arrow in two and pulled each side cleanly out of his knee. Gwendolyn then quickly placed her hands on either side of Ryder's knee and rubbed vigorously. A silver glow engulfed both her hands and Ryder's knee. He screamed out in distress as pain shot through his body. When she lifted her hands, Ryder's wound had vanished. "Sorry, my healings are sometimes rather harsh," she chuckled mirthlessly. "Lean forward," she instructed. Gwendolyn pressed her long fingers into his neck. Her touch was scorching but his wound mended swiftly. The light traveled down into his shoulder and Ryder cried out once more as the last of his wounds mended.

"The woman I healed—your friend, Silvia—will probably be awake by now. Would you like me to take you to her?" Gwendolyn asked.

"Please," Ryder nodded gingerly. He nearly fell when he tried to get up, nausea sabotaging his balance.

"Let me help," Gwendolyn said before carefully leading Ryder by the elbow toward a nearby house. "Your other companions are resting in my home just next door. I've healed them. All but one," the woman cringed. "He was too badly injured. A poisoned arrow took his life before I had the chance to save him. I'm sorry."

"Thank you," Ryder breathed. "It's only by your hand that we're not all dead." A twinge of knowledge and emotion that Ryder did not comprehend momentarily crossed Gwendolyn's face. "Silvia is in there," she said, blinking slowly as she pushed open the door. Ryder followed her into a small, tidy chamber. Silvia struggled to sit up when they entered.

"Silvia, for Ancients' sake, lay still!" Ryder chastised her with a laugh. Silvia smiled weakly in reply. Gwendolyn bobbed a polite curtsy, her eyes meeting Silvia's for a brief moment. Ryder caught the wordless conversation but did not pry. Gwendolyn turned and left, securely shutting the door behind her.

"Did you warn the townspeople?" Silvia asked hoarsely.

"I did," Ryder reassured her. "It'll buy them a little time at least. The other cities have been warned of Sharnin's move on Layton. Layton's Handler sent word." Ryder and Silvia fell into a musing silence. Ryder speculated on what Gwendolyn had meant when she said Silvia had an 'unique' gift. He could not help but wonder how a someone could take that much of a beating and still be so enduringly tough. "Silvia, how are you still alive?" he broke the silence by inquiring tentatively. She did not respond. "Silvia?" he prodded.

"Have you really not noticed that my blood is the color of wine, Ryder? I have unique Healer magic."

"What?" Ryder's head jerked back in shock.

167

"It's just that the type of healing I have isn't what you're accustomed to," Silvia reluctantly explained.

"You mean, our men, y-you could have helped?!" Ryder sputtered agitatedly. "Me? Our companions? You could have helped us all!"

"No, Ryder, it doesn't work that way. Not for me it doesn't. My magic is extraordinarily strong but it's internal. And internal only," Silvia struggled to make Ryder understand.

"I did notice the color of your veins, but I didn't ask. I didn't pry! And now I find out you sacrificed the others to save your own skin?" Ryder's body convulsed as though he had taken a blow to his gut.

"No, Ryder, listen to me!" Silvia gasped.

"How could you?" Ryder cried, backing away from Silvia.

"I cannot heal others," she harshly admitted. "Only myself and only when I have enough energy." Ryder locked his eyes onto Silvia. Outrage, pain, and suspicion flooded his expression.

"Then where is your Inking?" Ryder questioned.

"I found a woman in Kailani that helped me to permanently hide it. It comes out when my wounds are severe enough. It was too much of burden to bear, to be scolded for not helping those around me. My body heals itself seemingly without limit. As for healing others, even if I extend my magic to its maximum, it heals only my own body. Ryder, I am no help to others," Silvia's chin dropped to her chest despondently.

"But you didn't even try," Ryder spat.

"I have tried. I have," Silvia agitatedly ran her hands through her hair, her eyes still lowered.

"I cannot accept that," Ryder ground his teeth stubbornly.

"How would you like to witness the deaths of everyone you love?" A hot huff of air shot out of Silvia's mouth. "How would you like to watch everyone you ever cared about suffer and die knowing the whole time that you can heal yourself but you cannot heal them? That's like asking a Whisperer to start a fire or a Shifter to read your mind! Being a Descendant doesn't make anything and everything possible! It doesn't work like that." Her voice was awash with rage and anger, her blue-gray eyes flashed, "I watched my neighbors, my brothers, my husband, my father, and now my own mother die while I remained strong." Silvia's energy went out of her in one long breath, "When you have endured that much soul-destroying, heart-lashing pain then maybe, just maybe, you'll understand."

Gwendolyn re-entered the room with stout and bread in hand. She set the tray on a table next to Ryder, studied his face, then sat at the foot of Silvia's bed.

"I see you chose to tell him?" She aimed a tender look at Silvia. Ryder glared. "And he does not understand."

"I can hear you," Ryder growled, irritated that Gwendolyn spoke as though he was not in the room. Silvia pursed her lips.

"Perhaps I can help?" she suggested.

"I'm not interested in excuses," Ryder remained stubborn.

"Not excuses. Facts," she hummed sweetly as she poured stout for the three of them. They sat in silence for a long time, sipping in stubborn contemplation.

Gwendolyn paused, deciding how best to phrase what she had to say, "There are three variants of Healers." She began in a quiet tone, "The first and most common is what I have. It's the type of Healer who can tend to others but is still vulnerable. You stab me and I will bleed until the wound has been stitched by a doctor, you bring a person with a stab

169

wound to me and I can heal them in a minute." She sipped her stout again, then continued, "The second variation is the most valued. It is the Healer who can heal others and themselves. In battle, or in the midst of a plague, it is they who are the most valuable." Silvia winced, preparing to hear what Gwendolyn had to say about the last type. "And the third is what Silvia has." Ryder stared down at the floor. "It is where the Healer can cure themselves but not others..."

"Why have I never heard of that type of healing?" Ryder asked defensively.

"It is very uncommon. Or at least, no one truly knows how many have that form of healing magic."

"Why not?" Ryder snapped.

"Self-healing is a heavy burden to bear and is most often bore alone. Those who claim it rarely let their abilities be known to others, and unbelievably, a large faction with the ability never know they have it. They believe they possess nothing more than extraordinary luck. Makes for a great soldier though," Gwendolyn smiled at Silvia.

"Why would they not tell people they possessed it?"

"How did you react when Silvia told you?"

Ryder's cheeks reddened at the embarrassment of accusing Silvia only moments earlier.

"People become jealous or resentful," Silvia whispered, "which often leads to violence."

"Sometimes though, it is a whole family that shares the secret," Gwendolyn prompted. Both Gwendolyn and Ryder waited for Silvia to speak.

"Almost everyone in my family carried the magic though none as deeply as I," Silvia confessed. "We all have the Healer's Inking. However," Silvia bit her lip when she saw Ryder's eyebrows shoot up, "we all wear high collars, scarves, or keep our hair down to hide it. We keep our magic as secret as we can, but we still feel a duty to use our abilities righteously. We have always tried to help protect others." Silvia smiled half-heartedly, "Thus the reason I come from a long military line. We make the perfect soldier. My family was full of skilled fighters who rarely grew weary or sick, and we heal quickly from battle."

"You said your family members were all dead," Ryder remained suspicious. Silvia did not reply. Dark memories of her deceased family flooded her mind. Her stomach churned as she remembered burying them. Their wounds too severe to look upon their bodies.

"It's a sad fact of life that eventually even the strongest of us must fall," Gwendolyn said softly.

"There are some wounds that you simply cannot heal from," Silvia whispered.

****

The mood in the castle shifted as Eleanor began to plan her attack on Zagan and the Sharnin Army. She paced the length of Lairson's chambers and he worked fervently at his massive desk covered in papers and medical tomes. "The declaration must be made," Eleanor nodded curtly as her small silver crown gleamed in the candlelight.

"Is it really necessary? I mean, once we have Aurora's blood, you can depose Zagan. And I doubt his people will fight without his orders. There may be no need of a war," the doctor admonished.

"Lairson —"

"Besides, if we simply dispose of him —"

"Lairson!" Eleanor shouted in annoyance. "It is not your place to question the instructions of the Queen," she growled. "Donovan and I know Zagan far better than anyone else. I also know that if I wait any longer to order the troops into battle there will be no country left to support me," the Queen finished as Lairson sulked.

"Troops? I had troops once," Malcolm purred sweetly, his head cocked to one side.

"I hate to admit it; you were right all along. My dear husband, I should have trusted you. The Sharnins have been using Descendants to slaughter all of our subjects," the Queen grimaced at her husband.

"My!" The King's eyes grew wide and his magic-drugged mind fought to regain control of itself. He could feel the importance of what his wife had just said but could not figure out why it mattered to him. He coughed and gave up his struggle.

"Get me the High Constable!" Eleanor called out to the guard stationed in the hall.

"My Lady?" Lairson raised a finger hesitantly and ground his teeth together.

"What, Lairson?" the Queen huffed impatiently.

"I- I took the liberty of... sedating Argus."

"You did what?" she snarled, spinning around to look at the doctor.

"He seemed to have befriended Aurora. And well, he was getting suspicious about, you know," Lairson gestured toward the King with his eyes.

"Fine." The Queen called after the guard. "I will find him myself, thank you." She smiled tightly then turned back to Lairson.

"My Lady, I did not mean—" Lairson blubbered, but Eleanor cut him off.

"How dare you?" she hissed icily. Her eyes narrowed viscously, "When the Venom is made, bring it to me. Until then I do not want to hear your sniveling voice nor see your spiteful face nor even spot the back of your greasy-haired head out of the corner of my eye."

"My Lady!" Lairson objected.

"Keep working," the Queen said flatly. The doctor froze. She leaned forward and hissed threateningly, "We're running out of time, doctor. Work with haste."

"Yes, My Lady," the doctor blinked rapidly as the Queen turned with a whip of her cape and slammed the door behind her.

****

"The Queen issued yer arrest!?" Argus repeated back to Aurora in disbelief.

"The one and only," Aurora crossed her arms. In agitation, Argus ran both his hands through his hair. A knock sounded on the chamber door.

"Argus?" called a sweet, feminine voice.

"The Queen!" Argus breathed. "Hide," he instructed Aurora. Loudly he responded, "I ain't decent. One moment." Aurora rushed across the room and climbed into a nearby wardrobe. Argus shrugged apologetically and eased the doors closed leaving them open slightly so Aurora could survey the room.

"Are you clothed?" Eleanor called out. Argus strode back across the room and opened his door.

"My Lady," Argus dropped into a deep bow.

173

"Argus," the Queen's voice softened. Aurora strained to hear their hushed conversation. "I hardly think I would mind seeing you indecent," she murmured, raising her hand to rest on the back of his neck. Argus chuckled, closed the door behind them, and raised one eyebrow mischievously. Aurora peeked out through the slightly ajar door to the wardrobe and muffled a gasp of astonishment.

****

Bridget landed unsteadily on a tower's window ledge. She was back in the Thurnadan castle once more. The evening air was thick and heavy with the warm day still lingering. She let out a long breath and tried to settle her terribly frazzled nerves. She wondered which was stronger, her fear of Zagan or her repulsion toward killing a woman who had done her no harm. She understood that if she did not do as ordered, Zagan would destroy her. But, if she did murder the woman, her guilt would consume her. Bridget rubbed her eyes wearily as she mentally reached out to a soldier of the Sharnin army that she had known in years prior.

I can't do this anymore Xenos, she shuddered.

Playing both sides is not an easy task, he replied.

Zagan wants me to murder someone! How do you endure this? Bridget's eyes watered. *How do you watch your men ravage and kill? How can you stand behind Zagan's brutality? I won't do it anymore,* Bridget mentally whispered.

Bridget! Zagan will have you killed!

Not if I'm not the only one, Bridget implied. *If enough of us desert-*

I've heard rumors amongst soldiers of a voice — a mental connection — pleading for them to lay down arms. Is that you?

174

No, it is not. There's a woman, Aurora. Zagan is threatened by her. She's powerful and a Seer. That's who he wants to see dead!

I just cannot – the mental connection between Bridget and Xenos faltered.

I know you're afraid. Bridget sighed bitterly, *I am too. I'm terrified. But I refuse to become a monster like Zagan.*

I have to go.

Be careful. Bridget let the connection fade as she descended from the tower. She began to move about the castle, sneaking around corners as to not run into Aurora, or the Queen, or Donovan for that matter. She did not want to run into anyone. She paused only when she came near the study; the hall was heavily lined with soldiers. Bridget put on her cutest face as she approached a younger looking soldier at the end of the rank.

"Why all the somber looks?" she asked, tucking a loose curl behind her ear.

The soldier's eyes darted sideways then back at Bridget. "Sharnin invasion is in full force," he whispered.

"Oh no!" Bridget blinked innocently.

He nodded vehemently, "The Queen called a meeting with the High Constable. Only one reason she'd do that!" The soldier looked about, "Issuing a Declaration of War, I reckon!"

"Soldier! Stand at attention!" bellowed a man from farther down the hall.

"Sorry," Bridget giggled, batted her eyelashes, and turned away. She rushed down the hall, asking herself how she had become so ensnared in this turmoil.

****

"My dear Constable," the Queen sighed. Her hand still firmly resting on the back of Argus' neck. "I am in desperate need of your help."

"As you be wishin' my Queen. How may 'dis humble man serve?" Argus drawled, his mind swimming with the Queen's magical influence.

"It seems the Sharnin army feels bold enough to invade Thurnadan through Layton," the Queen explained as she strolled away from Argus'. "You know the law. An order of war must be issued by the Queen, blessed by the King, and declared by the High Constable."

"Time ta' deal wit' them Sharnins, aye?"

"I am afraid it is unavoidable."

"There be many a death ahead of us," Argus' grimaced as the Queen lowered her eyes to the floor, genuinely saddened. The Queen responded, but in too low a tone for even Aurora's straining ears to hear.

"Then my Queen, we shall declare war," Argus stood tall, ready for battle.

"Yes. We will," Eleanor smiled.

Argus and the Queen then composed themselves and left the room. Aurora's thoughts reeled. She gently placed a hand to the wooden door of the wardrobe and let herself out.

"Ridiculous. Absolutely ridiculous," Aurora huffed, overwhelmed by both the absurdity and the direness of her situation. Aurora worried about the Queen's use of power on Argus. If he went into battle as absentminded as the King, he would not return with his head. Aurora waited until she heard the soldiers march away down the hall. The door was now clear. She crept from Argus' chambers, mindful of the servants' presence throughout the castle.

Aurora? Donovan's thought knocked at her consciousness then waited for her reply to form a connection. She ignored him. *You are supposed to be in prison,* he laughed.

So are you, she could not resist shooting back. Unfortunately, it was enough for him to latch on to her mind.

Come down to the doctor's chambers. You and I ought to have a discussion.

I'm not interested, Aurora replied dismissively.

Oh, but you should be, Donovan tempted her. Aurora rolled her eyes and relented.

Why? she frowned.

Because if you come willingly it will save me from having to kill you.

Oh, how considerate of you, Aurora said sarcastically.

I thought so too, Donovan chuckled. *Aurora, we could join forces against my father!*

Aurora recoiled, *Now why would I do that when I do not trust you?* The magic of her companions trembled inside her.

What was that? A touch of fear flickered into Donovan's connection.

What was what? Aurora asked with equal surprise.

So will you come? Donovan's thoughts steadied again.

You didn't say please, Aurora sneered and wrenched her mind away from him. Aurora risked damaging her mind by breaking the connection so abruptly but she felt the awful pain worth it.

****

Fear and anger had spread through Layton; it weakened the people's good intentions and soured the air with agitation. Men and women, armored from boot to helmet, stood ready

177

for instruction. Silvia, Ryder, and the rest of their companions shuffled tentatively to join the townspeople in the town square.

"Any news?" Ryder hoped.

"War's been declared. Troops at the castle are assembling," a man stepped forward to address Silvia and Ryder. "I'm sorry I couldn't greet you earlier. I'm the High Councilman of Layton."

"'Bout time," grumbled one of the surviving villagers. The others shook their heads bitterly.

"But what does that mean for us?" Silvia inquired. The councilman looked grim and said nothing.

"'Means we beg the Ancients to let us live until reinforcements get here," the young survivor mumbled.

"How long?" Ryder swallowed hard.

"Foot soldiers at a marching pace? It will take them hours to get here. If, of course they are not delayed even the slightest. If the Sharnin troops are as close as you say, the Queen won't make it here in time to assist us."

"What?!" the young man squeaked. Ryder patted him on the shoulder in consolation.

"I'm uncertain that even mounted troops could make it by nightfall," Ryder reluctantly admitted.

"Even at a full charge?" Silvia questioned with a grimace.

"Yes," the councilman replied, "but it's hard to be optimistic when it has taken this long for the Queen to get involved, and Malcolm is nowhere to be seen apparently."

"Well, let us pray that the Sharnin's will not attack until the morning. Until they arrive we must not waste a moment. We must busy ourselves preparing," Silvia declared.

Silvia's companions' hearts sank, doubting they would live through a second Sharnin battle. The councilman turned back to the townspeople, squared his broad shoulders, and pumped his fist in the air.

"War has been declared," he shouted. The people responded by shaking their own fists in the air. His voice boomed through the crowd, hushing arguments and drawing all eyes, "Though it may not be in time to save us. We will not fall without a fight. We will do whatever is necessary to protect what is ours!" His voice quieted and the people instinctively leaned forward to hear him better. "Fear not. You have been trained well. If war is what the Sharnin bring to Layton then its people will show them what a foolish endeavor it is," he flung out his arm, pointed a finger toward the hills, then grinned menacingly and shouted, "let us meet them on the field of battle and send them to their deaths!" A roar went up from the people and they raised their fists and cheered. "I want a guard set up 'round the perimeter of the city at —" The councilman wheezed in pain and sagged to his knees, a long birch shaft ending in a wickedly serrated arrow head protruded from his throat.

A cry of shock escaped Silvia's lips. The townspeople froze, not knowing whether to surge forward to aid him or rush back away from the reach of the arrow. Silvia lunged forward, catching him as his head slumped to the side and his last bloodied breath left him. Silvia's knees gave out under his weight and the people gasped in horror. Gwendolyn rushed through the paralyzed crowd, dropped to her knees beside Silvia, but saw there was nothing she could do.

The eyes of the townspeople widened and their faces grew pale. Armor glinted harshly in the silence; the frantic reflections causing the horses to paw at the ground and huff the air. Ryder watched for further attacks but the brilliant blue sky remained clear. Gwendolyn's hands trembled like autumn leaves in a storm as she anxiously checked for a pulse, a breath, anything that could allow her to give the man back his life. She drew her red-stained hands away from his figure and stood again, her face blank. Her dress caught at her ankles as she spun around to look out over the city.

She sought out the eyes of the people. When she spoke, her voice was wrought with sorrow, "Draw your swords, mount your horses, and archers go to your posts. The war has begun." The people hesitated, unsure whether or not to follow the orders of the small woman who spoke to them. "And if," she yelled with sudden passion, "if any of you claim an ability," a murmur of unrest threaded through the people, "for the sake of the man next to you, hide it no longer. We will need every added strength we can get." Silvia hefted the man from her lap and gently laid him on the ground, then stood beside Gwendolyn in consolation. "All our lives we have been taught that our magic is a curse and a burden. But today, it will be our salvation!" Gwendolyn called out.

The people of Layton stood dazed by what had just transpired.

"Go!" Silvia shouted, forcing the townspeople into action. "Today your magic can be the difference between life or death!"

"Get down!" screamed a woman to Silvia's right as another arrow flew through the air toward Ryder. Everyone dropped to the ground. The arrow, however, never hit its mark. Brightly colored sparks trailed through the air from the outstretched hand of a man to the hovering arrow. His skin was ghostly white and terror blazed from his eyes. Silvia cautiously stood back on her feet. She smiled at the man and reached up to curl her fingers around the shaft of the frozen arrow. The sparks faded.

"You're a Wind Whisperer," her smile broadened. The man nodded grimly. The people collectively stood and shuffled under cover of the surrounding buildings, their moods mixed with apprehension and curiosity. As another arrow fell toward the city a short stocky young man strode forward confidently. He touched his fingers to his lips then flung out his hand. A streak of fire arched into the air intercepting the approaching arrow. The Inking on his wrist shone fiercely. Others jerked back in surprise, but Silvia watched intently as the arrow turned to ash.

"A Fire Sculptor!" Silvia said. "Thank you." Soon, another and then another braved the revealing of their magic. There were sixty-two in all.

"We must stop the archers!" Ryder charged.

"No, wait. Listen. Why aren't they raining arrows down upon us now?"

"There is only one archer," a villager exclaimed.

"That's right. He's only one. A scout perhaps to see our numbers. That means we have time," Silvia assured the group.

"Look! There he is," a villager said and without missing a beat he sent a spear of ice flying through the air and into the heart of the Sharnin soldier. Everyone watched as he tumbled forward, hitting every rock on the way down the cliff.

"That takes care of that," Ryder stood stunned.

"Now we must prepare for war. They could strike at any moment and, Queen's army or not, we will be ready!" Silvia pumped her fist in the air as everyone cheered. "Let's get to work." The group dispersed. Ryder approached Silvia.

"I'm sorry about earlier. It's just you hear so many stories about Descendants and I--" Ryder rubbed the back of his neck and looked at the ground.

"It's okay," Silvia reached forward and grabbed his shoulder. "We will fight, together."

Ryder nodded. And for a brief moment he let his body relax.

Sixteen

Aurora crept warily down the hall, avoiding the soldiers that seemed to have doubled in number over the course of the day. Reluctantly, for she was afraid she had made the wrong decision to confront Donovan, she knocked on the door of Lairson's chambers. No one answered.

Donovan, you bastard, where are you? She sent out her thoughts to find Donovan.

"Right behind you, dear," replied a purring laugh. Aurora jumped and her skin crawled. "I was going to go look for you but I guess I should have simply waited," Donovan smirked. "Thank you for coming."

Aurora ground her teeth. "What is going on?" she seethed, trying in vain to cool her flaring temper.

"How about we go inside to discuss this?" Donovan ushered her into the doctor's chambers. "We would not want some overeager soldier to see you and escort you back to prison, now would we?" He smiled sweetly as Aurora threw a menacing glare at him.

"I could say the same to you."

"Who would ever put a silly little boy in prison," Donovan shifted into a small school boy, no more than nine years old.

"Will you stop it with your tricks?"

"Oh, why? It's part of the fun of magic. Don't get mad at me because you're not a Shifter."

"You know nothing about me!" Aurora was fuming now.

"My, my. Temper, dear," Donovan spat as he turned back into his true form.

"Donovan, you're toying with an entire population of people! Your egotistical nonsense has gotten completely out of control!" Aurora paced around the room, stopping only long enough to ferociously clench the back of the doctor's couch to keep herself from attacking Donovan. "Sharnin wouldn't last a month under your rule."

Aurora.

Granthan, this is the wrong time to connect.

Aurora, you must listen. I was able to convince some of my companions and we have avoided this morning's rations. Our magic is beginning to return. You were right, thank you. I was not able to convince all of my fellow Descendants, but a fair number of us no longer wish to fight for Zagan. Those of us who flee will fight for Thurnadan. However, I fear Zagan will notice our magic returning far earlier than the scheduled battle and those who remain will fight to their last breath. We must move now.

Granthan, the Queen will be on her way soon, war has been declared, I will make it as soon as I can.

Our gratitude Aurora, without you we cannot defeat Zagan.

"Whatever do you mean, Aurora?" Donovan batted his long blond eyelashes then shifted to his mundane peasant form, Hugh. Aurora twitched in questioning but the door swung open before she had a chance to say anything.

"Well done," Lairson grinned a sharp-toothed smile after observing Aurora. He turned to Donovan and laughed.

"Well done?" Aurora asked, watching as Donovan pouted and shifted back to his true form.

"Has he not asked you?" The doctor's face scrunched. He took slow strides closer to Aurora. "We want your blood to-"

"Quiet!" Donovan barked. Lairson turned back to Donovan, his eyebrows raised. "It's my turn now. Don't rob me of the pleasure. You see, Aurora, the most overlooked Descendant to ever live is right here in this room. But the end of the story has been re-written you see. King Malcolm is out of commission," Donovan sneered before Lairson had time to speak. "The Queen will be killed in battle. And your knight in shining armor, Argus, has been compromised. The people have followed Zagan because they seek a life free of rules and restraints on magic. They want to use their abilities with the encouragement of a reliable leader. All that is in the way between me and controlling two thrones, is my father." Donovan's lips tightened with smug satisfaction, his eyes glinted with the reflection of the room's candles. "I see no reason why I can't be quite the King. I can hear it now. 'Great King Donovan united the Temperate Lands!'"

"Wait! You said would help Queen Eleanor!" Lairson's mouth gaped. He shuddered and tried to get his thoughts around all that Donovan had said.

"Yes, I will. And then I won't," Donovan shrugged conceitedly then continued. "I'm embarrassed I did not think of it sooner. So simple. So satisfying," Donovan patted the stunned doctor on the cheek as he walked by him. Smugness oozed from his pores as he relished in the prospect of humiliating his father. He paused in his stride directly before Aurora then cocked his head to the side. "This war will end the way I want," he laughed wickedly. "No glory for my father and no redemption for my sister."

"Guards!" Lairson shouted as he bolted toward his chamber door. Donovan reacted savagely. He shifted to a bear's form, locked his oversized paws around the doctor's waist, and flung him to the couch in the middle of the room.

Make another sound and I will rip the flesh from your face, Donovan drilled into the doctor's mind. His gleaming teeth sliced together threatening. Saliva dripped from his gums and onto Lairson's cowering head. After a long, intimidating moment he let his bulky body shrink and his thick brown fur melt away. Once he was in his own form again he looked at Aurora contemplatively.

"I need your blood," he stated flatly. "But it's for a good cause."

"Sorry, I have not a drop to spare and," Aurora replied sarcastically, "I'm not frightened by your big bad bear act."

"But I am familiar with something you are afraid of," Donovan whispered as his bear body slowly vanished. A blue-green mist filled the air where he had previously been standing.

Killing you has been a plan of mine since we were young. You think I couldn't see how everyone thought you were so special, so unique? Donovan's voice looped languidly through Aurora's brain. *Now I have good reason to. Want to test your strength?* Donovan snickered. The mist funneled into a hazy thread and shot toward Aurora. She ducked and dashed to the left as the fears of her suffocating sixteen-year-old-self screamed in her mind. The mist of Donovan followed her, thinning as it traveled until she could no longer see it. Lairson had risen to his feet again but Aurora knocked him out of the way. Both hands clamped over her nose and mouth, Aurora struggled to hold her breath for as long as she could. She called on her Wind Whispering magic and sent a gust of air through the room in an attempt to blow the invisible Donovan away.

Get away from me! she yelled.

You could never be rid of me that easily, Donovan's chuckle bounced and echoed in Aurora's thoughts. She balled her fists until sparks appeared in her palms.

Don't come any closer. Aurora backed up toward the door.

Lairson, partly to keep her from leaving and partly wanting to leave himself, lunged across the couch and grabbed ahold of Aurora's upper arm. She gasped. Aurora's intake of breath was thick and clammy and tinted blue. She coughed and sputtered as she yanked herself out of Lairson's grasp. Her hands quivered in front of her throat as panic set in. The mist coiled in her throat, slithered down her windpipe, and itched up into her nose. Aurora's mouth hung open as her lips trembled and her tan skin paled.

Let me go, Donovan! she begged. Her thought weakly connected to Donovan, though she was at the edge of a black-out and too far gone to hear if he replied. Aurora sagged to her knees. Her vision smeared with gray splotches and her arms dropped exhaustedly to her sides. She wilted to the floor. A firework of magic suddenly exploded inside her. The Energies of her companions blazed up from her soul and fought against Donovan. Their care kept her safe from his control; their resistance made him jerk in surprise.

Aurora felt nothing. However, the power surge frightened Donovan to his core. He fled out of Aurora's body through her nose. The force of his bitter-cold exit caused Aurora to shudder and frantically breathe in. Her nose burned viciously. Aurora glared at Donovan as he shifted into himself. Aurora inhaled deeply, settling her racing heart. Her eyes watered from the pain in her lungs. Donovan took a step toward her, a wickedly self-satisfied grin pulled his lips wide.

"What?" Aurora coughed, rubbing at her nose. Aurora wobbled to her feet. "What?" Her word faded when she noted the crimson stain splashed across the back of her hand. She cautiously pressed her other hand against her nostrils, they came away coated in blood.

Donovan plucked a small glass vial from the table beside him. He lunged toward Aurora as she staggered back. A white-painted wall blocked her way, its gritty surface chaffing roughly against her skin. Donovan nearly danced with glee.

He wrapped his hand around the back of Aurora's head. She struggled against him. He shoved the vial under her nose. The small glass container filled quickly with Aurora's blood.

Somehow I think, Donovan exhaled, *the most violet veins produce the most disturbingly ruby-red blood.*

Stop! Aurora thought as she sent a sparking blaze up Donovan's body. The flames torched his hairs and scalded his skin. Donovan writhed in surprise and anguish, released his grasp on Aurora, and dropped to his knees. The flames lessened. *Give me the vial and I will free you from the fire.* Aurora pinched her bleeding nose and stepped sideways away from Donovan. *Give me the vial!* she mentally shrieked.

Using your magic just as my father does his! Donovan hissed. Aurora struggled to hear him, his words mutilated by the fractures of pain slicing through their mind connection. Aurora spread her fingers sharply and the blaze instantly died.

"I do not use my magic for evil," Aurora insisted. "And neither should you if you truly do not want to follow in your father's footsteps."

Donovan staggered to his feet and tried to shift the smoldering burns from his true form. Red-white burns marred his ivory skin and threads of smoke traveled up from his singed curls but refused to heal or shift. The vial, however, he triumphantly held up for Aurora to see.

"I will kill my father," he winced. "He will regret the harm he has done to me." Donovan shifted to a hawk's form and clutched the vial in his scalded talons. Aurora let him go, as there was a slight chance Donovan would have success, and at last Zagan would perish.

Donovan flew out the window and around through the castle. He flew in through an open walkway. He shifted into his true form and strode directly to an out-of-the-way closet on the ground floor of the castle. He collected the ground selva root and venom from where he had stashed it earlier under a pile of cleaning rags. Sweat moistened Donovan's hairline. His feelings of excitement and nervousness, and the pain caused by his charred skin, had finally managed to break his cool exterior. Gingerly, as to not cause an explosion, Donovan poured the root powder into the vial of Aurora's blood. He was disappointed he had not gotten a surplus of blood so that he could make more than one of the concoction, but his eyes glowed with exhilaration when he realized he at least collected enough blood for one strong dose. Donovan delicately rewrapped his long fingers around the glass and swirled the thick mixture slowly until, drop by drop, the red of Aurora's blood became evenly shadowed with the blue-gray powder. Next, one drop at a time, he added the venom. One minute then two passed as Donovan stood breathing heavily and watching the concoction with silent captivation. The liquid suddenly became an ocean of indigo waves, churning violently within the vial as he corked it. It vibrated faintly. An exuberated noise whooshed from Donovan's mouth. He stretched his neck, adjusted his grip on the vial, and recomposed himself.

"One step closer," he reassured himself. Voices resonated outside the closet. To his relief, the people went by without stopping. Their presence, however, was enough to sober Donovan's mood. He swallowed his glee and got back to work. He took a cord from his trousers' lacing and looped it in a knot around the neck of the vial. He smiled as he shifted forms. His soft-woven tunic faded from green to light blue. His black trousers stiffened to proper Thurnadanian castle standards. His fair curls drooped and darkened, his nimble figure thickened, and his altered facial features sharpened. Donovan stood still for a moment to laboriously disguise the wounds inflicted by Aurora's flames and accustom himself to his shifted figure. He let his now sharp-toothed smile settle into a scowl, straightened his collar, then gently hung the vial from his neck so it rested against his chest. As he cautiously tugged open the closet door he focused his shape-shifting on his face. The emerald color of his eyes shimmered like oil on water before they paled to a dusty yellow-green. Donovan blinked slowly, smirked, and left the closet.

Donovan, now in the form of Lairson, scuttled to the armory where he figured his sister would be dressing for battle. He took a liking to the new-found freedom this form afforded him.

His assumption proved correct for when he entered the chambers, a dozen full-armored soldiers came to attention as the Queen stood to greet him. Eleanor's small figure was adorned with the finest of chainmail, her hair was woven atop her head to fit under her helmet, and her grim expression was amplified by the war makeup that lined her eyes and cheekbones.

"My Lady," Donovan groveled.

"I assume you have accomplished what I commanded or else your slit throat may be my satisfaction," the Queen spoke in a monotone. She dismissed her dressing servants and strode authoritatively down the few steps from her platform. The soldiers relaxed their salute when the Queen gestured for Donovan to rise from his bow. He lifted the vial from around his neck and held it out for the Queen. The Indigo Venom swung hypnotically from its cord. Eleanor locked eyes with Donovan who, in turn, reacted how he supposed Lairson would. He fidgeted uneasily and sniveled a bit.

190

Suspicion slithered across Eleanor's expression. "This had better be right, Donovan," she threatened, assuming her brother stood before her and not the doctor. She plucked the vial from Donovan's fingers and set it around her own neck. "You are dismissed," she commanded.

****

The breath of the soldiers was pouring out into the chilly night air. Malcolm stood atop the grand staircase looking out over the courtyard addressing the troops. "Bless your strength and valor. May your arrows soar true and-" Malcolm paused, his magic clouded brain made saying the Troops' Blessing extremely difficult.

"And your sword," the Queen prompted from beside him. She winced as she looked at the soldiers that had assembled before them on the lawns of the castle.

"And your sword valiantly strike its mark," the King continued with an insecure gulp. "Forget not that your honor grows from the resilience of your spirit, the solidity of your bravery, and the purity of your de-devotion," the King faltered but continued, "to your country and to your fellow soldier. May the Ancients bless you with triumph or a noble death." The ranks saluted. Eleanor donned her helmet with a shudder and returned the salute.

"For Thurnadan!" the Queen shouted, pumping her well-manicured, petite fist in the air.

"For Thurnadan!" the soldiers shouted back, their own fists slamming across their breastplates. The Queen tried to control her irregular breaths, kissed her befuddled husband on the cheek, and stepped forward. Although Eleanor had previously hated it more than anything, she now was greatly pleased that she would ride into battle at the head of the troops while the King remained at the castle.

"Raise your spirits! Raise your swords! Today we fight back!" Eleanor's voice caught in her throat, emotions of anger and determination mixed with the memories of years of being overlooked and pushed around. "Today we take revenge for the pain and the torment that Zagan and his forces have brought to our land!" The troop shouted and rattled their shields in response. "Today we take back our country and our power!" The Queen's steed whinnied with elation as she mounted. Eleanor knew her delicate features appeared weak in contrast to her bulky armor and thick trousers, but her heart was swollen with a confidence she had never felt before. Her mounted soldiers came abreast her horse as a slightly disheveled Lairson joined them on his own ebony mare. Eleanor grasped the reins of her ivory stallion tightly as she whispered to herself, "Today I win a war and take two thrones."

At Eleanor's signal, the young man who rode beside her raised the Thurnadanian flag. The crossed swords and flames of silver shone from the white cloth as the flag snapped smartly in the wind. The Queen dug her heels into her horse's flanks, back straight and gaze fierce. Nearly a thousand of her highest appointed soldiers followed her east across the hills toward a Layton. Under Argus' leadership, more soldiers would follow quickly behind them. A bit of her anxiety returned as she raised one hand to her chest plate to feel for the vial of Indigo Venom. Thurnadan's fate rested between her breasts.

****

192

Bridget shivered as she watched the troops swiftly march out the castle grounds and into the night. A green haze covered the palms of her hands, letting her know that Zagan was trying to use her binding spell to talk with her. All Bridget needed to do was create a sphere in her hand so she and the King might see each other. She rubbed her hands together and licked her lips anxiously. She tried to resist Zagan's beckoning. She could not kill Aurora. She refused to become a murderer.

The Queen had entrusted many secrets to Bridget, all the while assuming her ditzy lady's maid was simply a harmless girl she could relieve her burdens to. And Bridget had played along. She had listened with a sympathetic, attentive ear, knowing the whole time that she would betray the Queen the moment she was dismissed. Bridget sighed deeply and turned her eyes away from the departing soldiers. She looked down at her green-glowing hands and almost cried with frustration.

"'Ello, Bridget," chuckled a sweet-soft voice from the shadow of the archway nearest her. Bridget startled and searched for the figure that produced the voice.

"Hugh?" Bridget called, suspecting she recognized the voice. "Or should I ask for Donovan?" she hissed, vividly remembering all that had occurred the night before. Donovan laughed and came out of the shadows. "What happened to you? You look terrible, especially since, if I'm not mistaken, that is your true form," Bridget snorted, referring to the crispy appearance of Donovan's hair and the charred burns on his flesh. Donovan glowered.

"That green glow on your palms? Is that my father trying to speak to you?" Donovan called after her. Bridget paused but did not turn back. "Have you become his new favorite toy?" He laughed before stepping back into the shadows. Bridget spun around, her face flushing with shame.

193

"Boldly spoken for the man who committed crimes, murdered villagers, and rallied Descendants into turning traitor against Thurnadan simply because his father told him to," Bridget countered. Donovan's mood darkened. His violet veins filled with rage.

"I am no longer his puppet," Donovan spat vehemently.

"Oh!" Bridget replied, a mischievously smug grin on her face. "You admit you were though? At the whim of his grand schemes?" Bridget mocked.

Donovan shot back, "Just like you, from the looks of things." Bridget sobered and defiantly met Donovan's fierce gaze. "The green glow makes me think you spun a rather strong binding spell between the two of you," he sneered. "What's he having you do?"

"I was his spy. But no longer," Bridget growled, suddenly sure in her own mind that she could no longer side with King Zagan.

"Good luck with that," Donovan guffawed. "My father is not one to treat a deserter kindly."

"I am aware of that," Bridget confessed. Her posture twisted with unease but she quickly steeled herself against her apprehension. "Neither of us have any wish to further aide Zagan. But I will not stand by and let Descendants continue to suffer."

"Eleanor seems fully committed to killing my father. I haven't decided yet if that is a good thing or if I should have done it myself." Donovan quickly changed the subject.

"You think you can kill your own father?"

"Is it weak if I can't? Or does it make me as evil as him if I can? Not that I care." Donovan mumbled thoughtfully, his emotions warring. "I do not feel it necessary for me to disclose anything else to you," he defensively replied. "However, I will tell you that I have every intention of freeing Descendants from their torments, I am going to be their hero. I am going to be the one they trust with their lives and abilities. Let's make a deal. You swear fealty to me, become my spy, and tell me everything you know. Then I will break the spell between you and my father." Donovan shook his head briskly, his expression returning to neutral. "Do we have a deal or not?"

"You tell me how to get rid of him," Bridget demanded, holding up her green-glowing hands. "And I will swear to you."

"That," Donovan laced his fingers together behind his back, a crooked grin pulling on his lips, "could be a problem. I would then have no leverage to ensure you tell me truths rather than spewing nonsense in your exuberance to be free." Bridget huffed.

"Fine," she retorted. "Queen Eleanor originally proposed a truce. If Zagan would abandon invasion, she would give him safe passage to Kailani which he would eagerly take over," Bridget swallowed hard. "She wanted to make peace with your father."

"Then she doesn't know him near well enough," Donovan snorted. "I'm surprised at Eleanor's wiliness to negotiate and her willingness to go to war! She is usually more the type to hide and cry and hope everything gets better on its own." Bridget remained mute, her lips stubbornly sealed shut.

"I will tell you no more until you have broken my bond with Zagan," Bridget crossed her arms in irritation.

"Impatient, are we?" Donovan laughed. "Well, you will need an immense number of tea leaves and," he paused for effect, "an extremely powerful Seer."

"A powerful Seer?" Bridget squeaked. "How unhelpful can you get?!"

"Well, your information did not exactly help me either."

"Zagan refused the Queen's proposal," Bridget ground her teeth, barely managing to control her temper.

"Of course he did. That was to be expected. He thinks he can rule the entirety of the Temperate Lands unaided!"

"Indigo Venom," Bridget closed her eyes, exasperated. "Well, as you know, the Queen plans to use it against Zagan, his most devoted followers, and you! To imprison you once again. She has no intention of letting you take the Sharnin throne after your father's death."

"Crafty. Very crafty of her," Donovan sneered. "Wonder who she expects to take the Crown then?" Bridget strode off without another word. "Wait! Bridget, wait!" Donovan called out in a voice as sweet as sugar cane. "Why does my father summon you now?" Bridget kept walking. Donovan's nose itched and his jaw muscles twitched. In a rush, he yelled, "The tea is used to cleanse the body and spirit. And the Seer is needed to extract the threads of the past. If the shared thoughts remain in your conscious, even after a connection has been broken, have been removed, you will be free." Bridget slowed to a stop. Donovan huffed irately and continued, "That way Zagan's magic will not recognize yours. He will not be able to call on you." A hint of a smile crossed Bridget's face as she glanced back over her shoulder. Donovan took a pace toward her, "Unless of course you are unwise enough to form a new connection with him."

"Who would be strong enough to conduct this procedure?" she spoke with grim curtness.

"I happen to know of someone, actually," Donovan wheedled.

"Really?" Bridget replied disbelievingly.

"Really," Donovan smirked. "Her name is Aurora." Bridget's skin grew pale. "Sound familiar?" Donovan rubbed his chin with his thumb and tried not to mock Bridget's shocked expression.

"Quite," Bridget replied in a coarse whisper.

"And my father?" Donovan prompted.

"Wants me to kill her."

"Now isn't that interesting."

****

Wade scratched at the ragged edge of his ear. He and the rest of his small group of Sharnin troops had closed in around Layton. The darkness of night was enough to cover their quiet entrance to the hills surrounding Layton. To distract himself from the stiffness in his fingers, Wade straightened his tunic, wiped the smudges of dirt from his boots, and repositioned his weapon's belt. Annoyed, he again noted the empty slot meant to hold his favorite dagger that had been stolen in Silvia and Ryder's escape. Curled on his side behind a rotting log, Wade eyed his fellow soldier. The archer's freckles and deep-set green eyes made him appear younger and more innocent than Wade had ever looked.

"Shall we prepare a round of arrows?" the young archer recommended.

"No, we will wait for the rest of the army," Wade implored. "They aren't far behind us. We attack at dawn."

****

Argus shook his head vigorously, perplexed by how fuzzy his thoughts felt. He paced tensely, watching the ranks of men gathering, stretching, and mock-fighting on the grounds of the castle. The men were noticeably nervous but Argus' strong and reassuring presence charged their moods with energy and excitement. He knew the Queen was unstable, yet the full force of the Thurnadanian army was following her into battle against the Sharnin. Argus gulped as an itching fever burned in his mind. He was frustrated that he could not remember the last few hours. To re-center himself, he drew his sword and practiced a few fencing forms.

"Sir?" asked a gentle voice from behind him. He paused mid-jab to turn toward the speaker. A messenger boy trembled before him.

"Out wit' it," Argus prompted him, annoyed at being interrupted.

"A lady of the castle, sir," the boy rushed to get his words out as quickly as possible, "wishes to speak to you. Says it's urgent. She's in your private study in the barracks." The boy gestured to Argus' left, toward the building that framed the courtyard.

"Thank you," Argus frowned and sheathed his sword. The boy bowed and scuttled away.

By the time Argus had reached the barracks he had recalled a bit more of the day's events, though still not much. However, he lost his train of thought when he entered his study to discover Aurora sitting uncomfortably on one of his coarse wooden chairs. He could not remember whether she was friend or foe.

"Argus," Aurora coughed, got up, and warily closed the door behind him. "What do you remember of today?" She spoke anxiously.

"Why do ya' want ta' know?" Argus replied warily.

"For my own safety," Aurora cringed. "Would you let me," Aurora paused, "enter your mind?" Argus' eyes narrowed as he grunted. "Please, Argus, the fate of every non-Descendant in the world is a snap away from being doomed. Remember how I entered King Malcolm's mind to find that he was under the influence of magic? I did no harm to him. I did my best to help," Argus could easily see Aurora's agitation; his cautiousness relaxed a bit. "Please trust me," Aurora implored.

"Fine," Argus relented, remembering with stark clarity how adamant Aurora had been in her pursuit to help the King. "But you owe an explanation afta'ward."

"Agreed," Aurora replied heartily. She placed her fingers on his temples for added concentration then entered his thoughts. Only a few seconds had passed before Aurora knew without a doubt that the Queen had meddled in Argus' mind just as she had done to her husband. Aurora grit her teeth, took a deep breath, and worked her own skills to gingerly build up Argus' mental resistance to magic. She could not erase the magic that had been cast but she might keep others from affecting him so easily in the future. With a sigh, Aurora exited Argus' mind.

"Done?" Argus asked with curiosity.

"The Queen used her Mind Handling on you just like she did on King Malcolm. You will not remember what's occurred and therefore are not likely to believe what I have to tell you. Nonetheless, I must urge you not to trust the Queen any longer." One of Argus' eyebrows twitched. He held a rough-worn hand out to Aurora to lead her to another room. Aurora hesitated, then slipped her small tan hand into his and wearily followed him.

"My lady," Argus spoke gently, "I hav' not lived to be an old soldier by walkin' with me eyes closed. I had a woman once, beautiful, strong, braver than a hundred men combined," Argus laughed to disguise the tears forming in his eyes. "She used ta' tell me that seein' people was no different than seein' battle strategies, an' strikes of a fight."

"I don't understa—" Aurora interrupted.

"She was right," Argus swallowed. "I can see you ta be sincere. I can see your intentions are honest. Whereas my Queen..." Argus strode over to the wardrobe against the far wall. He took out various articles of armor and set them on his desk. "Put 'em on," he instructed.

"I think the knife you gave me is quite enough really, Argus," Aurora protested.

"It ain't necessarily fer protection," Argus explained. "I want ya' to join the ranks. Nobody will knows you're not jest another soldier." Aurora frowned, picked up the chainmail coif then locked her confused, naïve eyes on Argus. "I'll help ya' with that," he chuckled lightly. "And no worries 'bout none of the other soldiers. I'll be keepin' my eye on you."

"Why though? Why should I come with you to battle?" Aurora questioned, still not dressing. Argus hesitated before replying.

"I 'ave a suspicion," he admitted, "that my Queen is set on doin' sumtin' foolish that may cost me the lives of my finest men."

"So you want me to fight with them?" Aurora growled.

"They're skilled fighters!" Argus blazed. He took a deep breath and elaborated, "In a battle blade to blade they'd not be stopped. But against magic?" Argus humbled himself to admit, "They have no chance 'gainst the Sharnin's ruthless Descendants." He shrugged mournfully.

"Argus, listen to me. Have no fear, many of the Sharnin Descendants have reclaimed their magic. Granthan, their leader, is going to break free those who wish to desert today. We will win the battle. We just need to make sure Zagan dies." Aurora seethed. Argus looked up in astonishment.

Seventeen

Zagan stretched, rolling his head from shoulder to shoulder, and appraised the packed-up camp before him. Animal hide tents neatly folded on the backs of horses, the fires doused and smoking, Zagan's troops fell into ranks behind him. "It's not every day," he chuckled to himself, "that I get to overthrow a Queendom and eradicate a whole population."

"Ready to set Layton ablaze when you are, Commander," the captain saluted when he came before the King.

"Glad to hear it," Zagan replied smugly.

"However, I received word that Eleanor has set out with mounted soldiers to Layton," the captain informed. Zagan stroked his short beard.

"It's time we greet the Queen," he ground his teeth together. "Move out!" he bellowed across the camp. With a curt nod, Zagan said to the captain, "The final sword of this war will be drawn soon."

****

"Why haven't they attacked yet?" Gwendolyn whispered to Silvia from their hideout behind the Town Hall.

"I suspect they're waiting for us," Silvia replied simply. Gwendolyn looked at her questioningly. "For us to make the first move," Silvia clarified. Gwendolyn fidgeted, straightened her flimsy skirt, and re-braided the end of her hair. "Have you never seen a battle before?" Silvia asked, trying not to become aggravated. Gwendolyn shrugged bashfully.

"What's the story of that dagger of yours?" She gestured at the large knife tucked into Silvia's belt, "Living in a trading city I figure I've seen a bit of everything but I haven't seen a blade like that before." Gwendolyn looked at Silvia expectantly.

"It's Sharnin," she replied bluntly. Gwendolyn shut her mouth firmly, feeling uncomfortable. "Sorry," Silvia sighed and apologized. "I started training as a very young child. Where I grew up in Clodith, everyone was taught to fight. My grandmother, a peaceful Kailani, hated that I enlisted. However, that's just the way that I was raised. Those days, everyone became a soldier. I promised myself years and years ago that I'd get out of this life."

"Clodith was fearful of a Sharnin invasion?"

Silvia nodded, "Just like Thurnadan has been."

Gwendolyn frowned, "I really do wish I could fight."

"Why did no one teach you?" Silvia replied.

"They did. Or well, they tried. I think my healing powers took offense to me trying to inflict pain," she winced.

"Well," Silvia exhaled, "you may not be able to fight but that doesn't mean you aren't a help. In a few hours, I suspect we'll need your magic far more than we'll need my sword. Do you—?" Silvia started to ask another question but was interrupted by the appearance of a dusty, exhausted scout.

"They're coming!" he exclaimed.

"Who?"

"The Queen's cavalry! They're riding this way! They're less than three hours out from here."

"Who has been told?" Silvia demanded to know.

"Not many," he shook his head. "Your friend, Ryder, sent me."

"Do not tell another person. Not one. Keep your news to yourself," Silvia harshly ordered. The scout and the Healer looked at her, baffled.

"Why ever would he keep that to himself? It's great news!" Gwendolyn exclaimed.

"And it means that Sharnins will strike all the sooner if they know assistance is on the way," Silvia grunted. Gwendolyn gulped loudly. "If we've heard news that the Queen is on her way with troops in tow, then the Sharnins have too. If Zagan's smart, he will want to attack before our reinforcements get here."

"But, my lady," the scout pleaded, "can't I give our people hope that they'll have help?"

"Hope doesn't do a dead man any good," Silvia replied sourly.

Gwendolyn's skin paled to the color of ash.

"Your message has given us a moment of warning. At least we won't be caught off guard," Silvia nodded to the scout reassuringly. "That is a very good thing. Will you tell Ryder not to pass this on either, please? Have him ready the people?" The scout saluted, though his shoulders were still drooped as he strode off.

"Can you hear it? The sounds of war are drawing close." Gwendolyn looked about pensively.

Silvia grimaced, "So it would seem." As Silvia climbed up a ladder propped against a house and settled herself against the chimney, Gwendolyn turned and followed after the scout. Silvia steeled her thoughts for battle.

****

Wade yawned.

204

"Getting too old for this job, eh?" the archer to his right chuckled.

"Aye," Wade responded glumly. "The sitting around makes my joints ridged and the fighting makes my muscles ache." The archer laughed at Wade's sulking.

Silvia came into the archers' view as she climbed atop a building. However, the two Sharnins who were tucked into the shade of a group of willow trees were hidden from her sight.

"Gonna' knock that one off?" The other archer grinned. "Or have your fingers gone too stiff?"

****

Bridget stood in the kitchen anxiously rubbing her hands together. "Do you know — ?" she cut herself off, unsure how to state her question without drawing undue attention to herself.

"What's the trouble, sweetheart? I got ya yer tea leaves din' I?" the cook asked, taking pity on Bridget. He extended a piece of bread and butter to her but she shook her head no and immediately locked her fingers behind her back. "You got quite a' stench of magic 'round ya' and a face like that makes me think yer mischief's comin' back to bite ya'," the cook chewed on a mouthful of the bread and shrugged. Bridget tucked her green-glowing hands further into the folds of her skirt and tried not to squirm.

"Well, do you — ?" Bridget stuttered.

"No, I don't know nothin' 'bout what you been up to lately," the cook frowned when Bridget relaxed a bit at his comment. "But even a blind man could sense your tension." Bridget dropped her eyes to the floor.

"Might'n you know where Aurora is?" she croaked, raising her eyes back to the cook's.

"Sorry, missy, I don't," he replied. Bridget's shoulders slumped. "I wouldn't be none surprised though if ya' found Argus, an' she were with him." Bridget brightened, stood on her tiptoes to give the cook a peck on the cheek, then turned and rushed out of the kitchen. "You're welcome!" the cooked called after her with a chuckle.

"Thank you!" Bridget hollered back without slowing her pace. She did not want Argus and his troops to leave with Aurora before she could reach them. A green-eyed house cat bolted by Bridget going at almost as swift a pace in the opposite direction as her. Recognition jolted through her. She skidded to a stop and flung herself around to look at the cat. But it had vanished. A deep shiver crossed her skin and her breath became heavy and loud in the peculiar silence of the empty castle hall. She strained to hear the receding footsteps of the cat but heard nothing. Bridget rolled her eyes at her jumpiness, shrugged, and took a step to continue on her way. But the cat's green eyes lingered in her mind.

"Donovan!" Bridget swayed, torn between evils. The troops would be leaving at any moment, Aurora and Bridget's chance to be free of Zagan quite possibly with them. As for Donovan, who knew what havoc he might be plotting, especially in the absence of the Queen and Argus. Bridget looked morosely at her glowing hands then gritted her teeth and turned back the way the cat had gone. She would just have to be strong enough to resist Zagan's summons a little longer. Somebody had to be a buffer between the mischievous Donovan and the recently deserted castle. Bridget choked from the sudden fear that grabbed her heart and made her weak at the knees.

"No!" Bridget started running. She suddenly knew who he'd been after all along. "Malcom!"

****

"Fall in!" Argus commanded as he swung himself up onto the back of his steed. The soldiers in the castle's courtyard, as well as the disguised Aurora, fell into formation and respectively saluted the High Constable. "Ready ta' send dem' Sharnins back ta' the slop filled holes from whence they came?" He laughed to ease his tension and raise the troops' spirits. "This battle ain't 'bout land," Argus' voiced deepened with seriousness. "It be 'bout protectin' our people an' doin' what's right for our futures!" The soldiers shouted and pumped their fists in the air as Argus rode his horse back and forth in front of the ranks.

"Vento viaxeira." Discreetly, Aurora fanned her fingers out. Little sparks of magic scattered from her palms and floated away. A wind curled around the men's back. The soldiers calmed, though the grips on their weapons tightened.

"About face," Argus barked. "By the right, quick march!" His expression was stony as he urged his mount forward to lead his soldiers east toward Layton. Argus glanced at the ground as it rolled beneath his horse's feet more easily than he thought it ought. An amused smile turned up the corners of his mouth. He glanced to the ranks where Aurora marched but could not distinguish her from the soldiers despite the pride that shone from her eyes. The troop, aided by her gentle wind, effortlessly swept across the earth. Aurora's magic was subtle enough that no one seemed to notice it, yet strong enough that she was sure they would reach Layton mere steps behind the Queen.

"Allow them in," Zagan ordered.

"My King?" the captain questioned.

"Eleanor and her pathetic little band of soldiers will be trapped within Layton just like the rest of the townspeople," Zagan explained with a sneer. "A thousand soldiers are all she thinks she needs? She's an absolute fool to underestimate my power so severely, and I want her last suffering breath to be filled with the knowledge that she led her men to their deaths."

"Yes, my Lord," the captain grudgingly saluted and pivoted away.

"I plan to dispose of the Queen myself though, Captain."

"Understood," he inclined his head in consent and strode off.

It had not taken Zagan's men long to traverse the short distance between their camp and the rest of the troops stationed around Layton. Assembling themselves for a siege was simple enough. Now though, the captain ordered the soldiers to clear the blockade across the westward valley road that led up to the castle. He had archers blend themselves into the grassy brush at the ridges of the hills so if the King saw fit to take down Eleanor's forces before they reached Layton, all arrows were nocked and ready to fly.

Zagan paced, and pondered, oblivious to the faltering loyalty of his Descendants, who were denouncing him one by one. He planned to have his strongest Handler rip Eleanor's conscious to shreds. Then he himself would kill her. He rubbed at the back of his neck, wishing he knew if Aurora was dead yet. He held his breath as he brought his hands out and cupped them in front of his face. A light expanded from his palms into a green sphere that shifted like moonlight.

"Mediara firmar" he growled, attempting to activate the binding spell Bridget had set. The sphere remained hollow. Zagan focused all his attention toward Thurnadan to make a mental connection with her. *Speak to me,* he demanded. *I want to see that your task has been completed.* For an instant, a tremor of Bridget's fear wisped through his conscious, but she made no reply. Angry that he was being ignored, Zagan clapped his palms together and squashed out the green light. His glassy eyes filled with fury. He stomped heavily on the muddied bank where his tent had been inconspicuously set up. He wanted to shift to mist right then, track down the wench, and wring her pretty little neck for disobeying him.

"Boy," he snapped at a stationed servant. The boy scampered forward and bowed deeply. "Bring me Xenos." The servant bowed. "This instant," Zagan roared. He had no choice but to assume that if Bridget was avoiding him, Aurora was still alive. He slugged his fist into the trunk of a willow tree. His knuckles cracked and the tree swayed from the impact. He swung again, again, again. Beads of sweat formed along his hairline as the white-gray wood of the tree became stained with smeared blood. "All my work! All my planning! It was perfect! I refuse to let one stupid prophecy about one stupid red-haired girl bring everything to pieces," Zagan kicked the base of the tree.

"Commander?" the returned servant boy squeaked.

"What?" the King jerked around.

"The Shape Shifter you requested."

"Yes," Zagan huffed. The Shifter was a hefty, indigo-eyed man with frosty white skin and not a tremor of a facial expression. The King took a deep breath and blinked slowly as he tried to subdue his temper. The shifter stepped forward and bowed. "Xenos, good to see you," Zagan snarled half-heartedly.

"My Lord," he saluted.

"How strong is your magic?" the King questioned.

"I am well trained. I am of the Snow Lands and of Sharnin. My loyalty resides with you, Sire, though my magic comes from the lands to the north."

"The Snow Lands? They are indeed a people with an overabundance of magical talents. It is a pity more of your kind have not joined my ranks. Your skills as a Shifter are said to be unmatched," the King retorted, raised one eyebrow, then looked the Shifter over. The large man dipped his head in modest agreement. "You truly are loyal to me to be able to watch as your own kind died at Achlese."

"I am a soldier," Xenos replied simply.

"Yes, I see that," the King said after he had finished sizing up the shifter. "However, it seems that you failed at Achlese," Zagan locked his eyes icily on the shifter.

"My King?" he stared back unwaveringly.

"There is a woman. A Descendant," Zagan spoke with hate so thick it stuck to his words like phlegm and sap. Xenos kept calm, steady in the King's presence despite the servant boy trembling beside him. "She threatens everything we have fought for," Zagan paused to clear his throat and recompose himself though his voice continued to come out gritty. "She must be disposed of. Killed. Destroyed beyond recognition. Finish the job that I tasked you with at the Academy. Do not make that mistake again." His features hardened to a blank slate of merciless resolve. "Can you do that?" he hissed.

"For the needs of his King, the soldier obeys," Xenos responded. The King relaxed a bit, nodded, and took a step back.

"Bring me a bone—the first joint of her spine—as proof of her death and you will never have to take orders again. I will have you retired in wealth beyond measure and peace without pause," Zagan smiled through the anger that flashed in his eyes. "However, if you fail me again in this task, the consequences will be beyond your imagination. Am I understood?"

"Yes, my King."

"Good," the King snapped. "Her name is Aurora. She currently resides within the Thurnadan castle…"

****

The nearer that Argus' troops got to Layton the more unstable Aurora felt. She was keeping the soldiers moving along at a quick pace easily enough, but her concentration kept being blurred with the influences of another Descendant. Snippets of memories that were not her own flickered across her vision randomly:

A beautiful gold-lit ballroom alive with music and finely dressed nobility, the flags of Sharnin and Thurnadan hanging together, whispered words that slipped into the ear of an ivory- skinned young Queen with sad eyes.

Suddenly, the memories were viciously shredded. A burning hatred tore through Aurora with staggering strength. She gasped and her next step faltered.

"You alright, mate?" the man beside her asked.

"Yes, fine," Aurora replied in as a deep a voice as she could muster. The man chuckled. In an attempt to block out the mental intrusion, Aurora bit her lip and focused her attention on the itchiness of her helmet against her forehead. It was not enough.

Passionate kisses then furious shouts, darkness flooded by eerie torchlight. Aurora scrambled to set up a mental block. *The young Queen shamefully covering herself with a man's dark green cloak.* In realization, Aurora yanked back the mental resistance she had just built. She reached toward the memories, searching for information, to catch something that would tell her for certain whose past she was seeing. A drifting memory caught her attention when she recognized the figure of Eleanor. She was a toddler in the memory but still very much herself. A new memory appeared before her. *Eleanor, still a young child, her blue-violet eyes wide with naive fear, her blonde hair curled sweetly around her soft-skinned cheeks. She stood in the archway of a large white room as her mother's labor-induced screams from the bed before her reverberated off the walls.* The image dissolved with the echo of a shrill baby's wail. Aurora's curiosity grew too great to ignore. She mentally probed more forcefully, searching for the identity of the Descendant but was abruptly blasted with another vivid, emotionally-charged memory. *A library, an old scroll, and her own master teacher!* Tears sprung to Aurora's eyes as the Energies of her companions trembled inside her. After a moment, the Descendant's connection to her was wrenched away. The words 'Scarlet Prophecy' rang in her ears in Zagan's voice until the memories she had witnessed dropped into darkness.

Aurora sensed the words' importance. She sighed, swallowed, and withdrew her magic from the troops so that their pace would slow to a standard march. The Queen and her battalion had just come into sight.

Soldiers guarding the Thurnadanian castle were scarce, and those who did roam the halls were preoccupied by their feelings of missed glory in not being able to go into battle. Hence, Donovan's passage into Malcolm's bed chambers was rather effortless. Donovan, still a cat, meowed loudly as he approached the King.

"And who might you be?" Malcolm leaned down toward the cat in an almost clear-minded manner. The focus of his eyes was still vague and his thought process was stubbornly slow, but Donovan knew there had to be only a little time before Malcolm's full senses returned. The cat purred and rubbed at the King's ankles. "Where'd you come from?" the King asked, a small taint of suspicion tugging sluggishly at his mind. Donovan sprang forward, shifting rapidly. He pulled the knife from Malcolm's left boot then moved to drive the blade into his throat.

"Stop!" Bridget cried out.

"Halt!" came the snarling voices of the guards behind her. Donovan made a quick decision. He shoved the King back so they both tumbled over the bed and onto the floor. The knife he had held skidded across the floor but Donovan paid it no mind. Instead, Donovan shifted forms rapidly. When Bridget and the guards rushed to the far side of the bed, Malcolm lay unharmed. Or rather, both King Malcolms lay unharmed.

****

Eleanor's mouth was dry from the journey. She had slowed her troop's pace to a moderate trot as they filed into the valley leading into Layton. Dread filled her mind as she eyed the hills above them. She was certain a Sharnin scout would have spotted them and reported back to Zagan by now.

"Be on guard," she urged her troops. "Eyes to the hills."

It was a miracle they had not yet been attacked. Her troop, soldiers and horses alike, were skittish. As the trade totem of Layton came into the Queen's view, her horse started to snort and sidestep with unease. There were no fires, no shouting, no clanging weaponry, and no blood marring the ominously serene city. The Queen was uncertain whether to be relieved or even more fearful.

"Think we beat the Sharnin's army here?" the captain wondered loud enough for the Queen riding a few paces to his left to hear.

"Perhaps," Eleanor dared to hope aloud. Without seeing or hearing a single resident, the Queen and her troop entered the city.

Or perhaps not, Zagan's amused chuckle trailed though the Queen's mind then faded away. She gulped as her stomach lurched into her throat.

"Highness!" A young man dashed from the shadow of a house and dropped into a hasty bow. The Queen gestured for her troop to halt. "For Ancients' sakes, are we glad to see you!" The man smiled openly. "News is bad, my Lady," a moment of clumsy mumblings passed before the man's demeanor darkened. He rushed on before the Queen could reply, "I suggest you and your soldiers find cover as quick as ya' can or one of them Sharnins will try to pick you off with an arrow."

"Where is the city's High Councilman? I wish to speak to him," the Queen requested. The man's face crumpled into sadness.

"'Fraid that won't be possible," he replied glumly. "He was hit with an arrow earlier." The Queen's frown deepened. "A fellow from Caerwyn has been elected to take charge. His name's Ryder." Eleanor nodded her head in understanding. "I'll take you to him if you'll follow me. He's in the Town Hall."

"Thank you," the Queen dismounted and went with the young man, leaving her captain to divide and station the troops in strategic positions around the city.

****

"My King! We've got company," a Sharnin scout knelt in a deep bow as he reported to Zagan. "To the west, a second battalion carrying the Thurnadan white and silver flag. They'll be entering the valley road shortly, Sire."

He rubbed his hand across his close-cropped hair, cleared his mind of his lingering emotions, and focused on the implications of additional Thurnadanian forces. "Let the captains know," the King ordered. "The archers can stay along the hill tops. Longbows poised over Layton. Have the soldiers move to the hills as well." Zagan pulled a cigar from his jacket pocket, tore the end off with his teeth, then grinned impishly, "Let us sound the horns of battle."

"Yes, Sire," the scout saluted.

"I want those Thurnadanians torn limb from limb and heart from body before they reach the center of Layton," Zagan laughed as he lit his cigar. "You are dismissed." The scout pivoted and jogged away.

In just a few moments, Sharnin's soldiers had assembled along the hillside. Wade and the other archers were stationed in intervals around the perimeter of Layton and the rest of the

215

troops had drawn their swords, mounted their horses, and gotten into battle formation. Zagan stood hidden at the first curve of the hills, smoking his cigar and menacingly staring down at Thurnadan's troops.

He watched tensely as Thurnadanian foot soldiers paused at the edge of the valley. He raised his left arm high into the air causing his long sleeve to slide to his shoulder.

As the soldiers filed deeper into the valley below him, Zagan's eyes gleamed with the promise of battle and his lips twitched into a roguish smile.

"Damn, that woman! She hid their ranks! She split them up, clever girl" Zagan spat.

When Argus, at the front of the second battalion, reached the bend in the road where the hills smoothed into a meadow and met with the city, Zagan abruptly dropped his arm and sent a mental whistle through the minds of his men. A swarm of arrows tore through the sky. Thurnadanian soldiers dropped to the ground in formation and raised their shields against the oncoming volley. Argus shouted orders to his ranks. His soldiers fell into formation as quickly as they could and drew their swords.

Bring them down! Zagan savagely ordered. Simultaneously, the Sharnins archer launched another volley. A war cry shrieked and echoed from the city. The battle had begun.

Eighteen

Aurora grabbed up the loose reins of a runaway horse and swung herself up onto its back. She could feel fear gripping the Thurnadanian soldiers and knew that without the aid of magic, the battle would soon be lost to the Sharnins.

Granthan and his cadre of deserters waited in reserve trying to gain enough distance from the main army to go unnoticed and join the Thurnadanians.

Aurora clenched her legs to the sides of her mount so she could cup her hands together. Nearly translucent gold light pooled and crackled from her palms. With her lips pursed, she funneled a breath across the sparks and watched as fire flared into life. Her demon flame created a wall advancing toward the Sharnin troops front line. *I'm sorry,* Aurora winced as she mentally reached out to the Sharnin Descendants who stayed to fight. Soldiers screamed and ran. But even as the Sharnins scattered, arrows from the hills continued to rain down on the Thurnadanian troops.

"Stand your ground!" Argus roared, his horse rearing and squealing beneath him. A massive gust of wind knocked Aurora back, causing her fire to change directions and roll back against the Thurnadanian troops. Aurora dispersed her wall of fire only to reveal Sharnin soldiers advancing on the city. Dust billowed up, stinging the soldiers' eyes. Argus yanked his horse around so he could look at Aurora who rode behind him.

"What's this, aye?" He gestured at the flames chasing his own men.

"It's not me!" Aurora shouted above the hissing of the searing flesh. "It's the Sharnins. Their Sculptors are attacking!"

She closed her eyes and felt the charred earth beneath her horse's hooves, felt the air grow dry with the fire's heat, and knew her magic would be pushed to its limit. Her horse bucked. She snatched at its mane and barely managed to keep in the saddle.

"Can't you do nuthin' 'bout it?" Argus yelled.

"I'm working on it!" Aurora snapped back, worry for her fellow soldiers scratching ferociously at her composure. "There's just so many of them! I can't counter them all!" Sharnin swords clashed against Thurnadanian shields, the smell of metal penetrated the air as soldiers from both sides fought and fled from the fire and the poison laced arrows that continued to slice through the air. Aurora flung one arm out to make the earth buckle and bulge until the soil nearly turned over on itself. Soldiers stumbled and shouted in surprise as the Sharnin flames suffocated into puffs of smoke.

So the pretty little Ancient's-wonder child decided to join the party, did she? a voice slid snake-like through Aurora's mind.

Zagan? Aurora swallowed the bitter taste in her mouth.

You cannot save them. Although it will be entertaining to watch you fail. Zagan's voice caressed Aurora's mind.

You will not live to see me pull it off. Aurora knew she had ignited a fire.

I tremble at your might, Zagan laughed sarcastically. *It will be a pleasure to watch you die.* He finished and let their mind connection fade.

"We're gettin' slaughtered out here!" Argus called to Aurora, ramming his sword though a staggering Sharnin. A dozen huge, white, tundra wolves bound through Aurora's ring of fire. Saliva sprayed from their sharp teeth as they pounced upon the first soldiers they came to, then tore them to bits. "And there ain't no place to fall back!" Argus' face gleamed with sweat and blood. His eyes were frantic with the fear of defeat.

"This is not nearly the end!" Aurora screamed, blocking an arrow with magic to keep it from stabbing him. Argus' eyes snapped with sudden rage. "I know you were there when Sharnin took Clodith! I felt it. I saw the moment of defeat through your own eyes," she cried, tapping the side of her helmet. "We just need time. That's all we need is to buy ourselves just minutes even, for our comrades. Get into the city and regroup with the Queen's forces."

Argus paused for a brief second, then bellowed, "Yaw!" He raced his horse away from Aurora. "Regroup!" he ordered over and over as he rode passed his soldiers.

The Thurnadanian soldiers who were still on their mounts followed Argus; the others pulled together in groups of three, backs together, to fight off the Sharnins. Several bold Thurnadanians revealed their magic by sending out waves of angry wind and storms of gravel to disorient their enemy, but still the Sharnin kept the upper hand. Aurora's eyes blazed with sparks of furious magic. She flung her arms forward and the air grew thick as wet clay. Sharnins sagged to their knees to try and dredge deep enough breaths of air to satisfy their lungs' demands. Aurora's concentration broke as she dodged a Sharnin arrow and the soldiers resumed their fight.

A torrent of water crashed through Thurnadan's troops, knocking and rolling them apart and squelching out flames as it went. Several clusters of Thurnadanian troops retreated as tundra wolves ran rampant between them. Frustration furrowed Aurora's brow. Screams from inside Layton, where Eleanor's troops and the townspeople fought, spread up the hills and filled the smoky air with fear.

219

Aurora yanked at her horse's reins to urge it into the woods. At the hilltop, she dismounted hastily and let the horse gallop away. She shed her heavy chainmail, grabbed a low tree branch, and swung herself into the foliage. Up she went, then as far out as she dared. Still, leaves blocked her view. With a snort, she lifted the knife Argus had given her from her boot, sliced off the branches in her way, and then focused every ounce of her magic on the war-torn land before her. The earth screamed in distress at the boots that beat down on it, the air wept with the chaos of gasping breaths, and the water of the nearby stream wept with the injury of spilt blood pooling in its shallows. Aurora clutched her chest in empathetic pain.

****

Much to his companion's disappointment, Wade had not shot Silvia. Though now he wished he had. The fire that Aurora had sent around Layton and into the woods had forced the archers to abandon their posts and instead draw their swords and join the fight in combat. Few arrows flew from either side of the battle as Wade, his fellow archers, Silvia, Ryder, Sharnin soldiers, Thurnadanian soldiers, and Layton's citizens alike fought with ruthless abandon within the city streets.

Silvia was fewer than six strides from where Wade crossed swords with a badly bruised man. Although sweat poured from her brow, Wade could not help but notice her perfect form and elegant technique. He also noticed how eerily attractive she looked while cutting down one of his soldiers. He watched, impressed, as she yanked her blade from the stomach of her opponent, shoved the dead man to the ground, and struck a blow to the soldier behind her all in one fluid motion.

Curse the Ancients where are the rest of our Descendants? Wade wondered as he finished off his own opponent at the same time Silvia brought hers to the ground. For an instant, their eyes locked. The scratches along Silvia's brow from the beastly attack of an enemy Shifter disappeared into new skin as Wade stared, debating whether to fight or run away.

Silvia's emotions died from her face. She strode toward Wade with grim resolve. A Sharnin soldier reached out to strike her but she deflected his blade without so much as a flinch. Spinning and neatly removing his head from his shoulders, she kept marching. Wade gulped, hesitated, then turned on his heel and fled. Silvia was distracted by another soldier swinging at her and by the time she had put him down, Wade was gone.

****

"Donovan!" Bridget cursed, "You deceitful, destructive scumbag!" Her face flushed with relief that the King had been saved from assassination. Neither of the figures on the floor responded to her ravings.

"Which one is he?" the guard to Bridget's left asked bewildered. Both Kings rose to their feet uncertainly. Bridget's eyes snapped back and forth between the identical men.

"Should we take them both to prison?" another confounded guard inquired.

"One's the King, you fool! Can't be putting our own King in prison!" the first guard growled.

"Then how do we tell which is which?" The guards squabbled in confusion as Bridget's mind raced.

"Whatever are you talking about?" one Malcolm shook his head. As the first King turned to the second, palpable shock flooded both their faces. Bridget narrowed her eyes.

"Well you're a handsome fellow aren't ya?" the King to the left admitted. "Like looking into a mirror."

"Highness," Bridget interjected, "the man you are looking at is a pathetic, self-absorbed, father-pleasing scumbag who happens to also be the Temperate Land's most infamous Shifter."

"Oooh, so he shifted into me! That's smart!" The left-hand King questioned Bridget before a gooey smile pulled at his mouth, "Am I really that handsome? Eleanor and I will surely make beautiful children." He giggled then sobered, "Why is he here?"

"How disturbing," the right-hand King commented, causing the guards to hush themselves. "First he tries to kill me and now he takes on my form?" The guards stared intently at the Kings.

"I see why you call him deceitful. His form is quite believable. Though, I think my nose is a bit smaller," the left-hand King reached out to touch the other's face, who responded by harshly grasping the second's wrist to hold him away.

"Where's Eleanor?" the right-hand King inquired.

"Yes, where is she? Bring her in. I am sure she can clear this mess up," the left-hand King chimed in.

"My Lord… Lords," a guard responded apprehensively, "the Queen has marched to Layton for war. You said the Troops' Blessing yourself."

"When?" both King's replied, turning to glare at the guard who had spoken. The first King let go of the other's wrist as both their eyes grew wide. Bridget could have sworn she saw

222

a tiny flash of a smile cross the right-hand's mouth but it was gone before anyone else could notice.

****

Zagan ground out his cigar, spat, and then shifted into mist and traveled along the edge of the woods. He was frustrated that it had only been after he sent Xenos to Thurnadan, that he had found out Aurora was within the ranks of soldiers. The King knew the Shifter's skills would have been better utilized fighting in Layton than on a futile errand. It was too late, however, to have him rush back.

It was not long before he spotted Aurora's ruby-red hair fluttering in the wind. Although her body was perfectly still, dancing lights swirled around her in a sphere that dripped heavily to the ground. The tree she sat in glowed bright olive green and pulsed with magic, the forest floor swelled like an ocean's current, and the air around her snapped with static. Awe caused Zagan to pause mid-flight; he had never seen any use of magic so pliable or strong. Jealousy filled him with a vileness so intense his mouth tasted of vomit.

"This war is mine to win," he hissed, squelching his wonderstruck feelings by turning his thoughts back to imminent violence. Wrath consumed his existence. "Thurnadan is mine to rule! She will not stop me! I am stronger than any prophecy," he assured himself. He glided forward until he was just outside the edge of her magic sphere then fully compressed into his human form in order to sit behind her on the tree branch. Aurora startled and turned around to meet his gaze. Her sunset colored eyes radiated magic and anger.

"Zagan. I've been expecting you," she swallowed hard.

223

Granthan, it's Aurora, Zagan has located me as expected. I need you to go now. Head into the city. Attack the rear Sharnin forces. Go, now is the time. You may leave Zagan to me.

Granthan sent back a message of affirmation as she looked over to see his forces descend into the mayhem.

Be safe, Granthan.

"And I, you, my beautiful darling," the King sneered. Aurora's expressions grew dark with sinister loathing.

"You murdered my mentors," she accused. "And now you have the audacity to make small talk with me?"

"You are the one making small talk. I just want to kill you and be done with all this Scarlet Prophecy nonsense," Zagan snarled.

"Prophecy?" Aurora raised her eyebrows in questioning.

The King's face went slate smooth with controlled, vehement, anger, "The Ancients had a prophecy, where a Descendant bearing all Nine Energies, hair as red as flame would come to rule the Temperate Lands. All lands familiar with the prophecy have been awaiting your arrival. But they will have to continue waiting. For you are not the one to defeat me."

His right arm lashed out; his fist smashed against Aurora's jaw and sent her tumbling. "Not on this day child!" Branches slashed across Aurora's torso and face as she fell. Zagan met her on the ground in mist form, solidified, and slammed into her again before she had the chance to stagger to her feet. He kicked his steel-toed riding boots into her stomach over and over again as she frantically rolled away from him.

"I don't want to have to kill you!" Aurora snarled, pushing herself up onto her knees. "That's not what magic is for."

"Then cry as you die, little girl. I will take no pity on you."
Zagan ignored the battle below. He pulled his fist back and let
it fly directly into Aurora's cheekbone. The skin below
Aurora's eye split and her cheekbone cracked from the impact
of Zagan's blow. Aurora wailed in primal anger as she set her
jaw in determination. She threw a scorch of fire across the
King's throat but he did not even flinch.

"You know what no one seems to understand about being
a Healer?" Zagan grunted, grabbing Aurora by her hair and
dragging her to her feet. He slammed his fist into her stomach
and dropped her to the ground again. "You still feel pain.
Luckily for me, I have learned to endure it." He shifted to mist
to douse Aurora's flame then quickly shifted back to himself.
He landed a weighty kick in Aurora's side. "I cannot believe
my soldiers did not manage to kill you. Especially after all the
trouble my Handlers went through to block your insufferable
Seer's sight from foretelling the attack on Achlese. You are a
weakling, Aurora. You're just a child who treats her magic like
a paddle ball toy instead of the weapon it is." Zagan drew his
dagger. "I wonder how long it would take to heal from being
in tiny pieces? Shall we find out?" He grinned sadistically, "I
doubt you will heal from that." The King lunged at Aurora,
but she pulled Argus' blade from her boot and thrust it into
the seam of his chainmail between his thigh and pelvis. Zagan
stumbled back with a shriek of surprise and pain. Aurora took
a quick stride away, flung out her arms, and watched as her
sparks of magic streaked up the King's legs into blue tendrils,
freezing as they climbed. Zagan struggled and coughed as the
ice around his feet and legs immobilized him. He tried to shift
but his body was made so cold by Aurora's magic that his mist
became ice itself. The King gnashed his teeth as he tore his
dagger through the sides of his own legs. Blood gushed from

beneath his chainmail as he wrenched himself free of the frozen armor.

"It does not matter if you fight me, witch," Zagan crowed, "you will lose eventually." Aurora shot him in the face with a blast of sizzling hot air. His skin instantly began to peel and the veins beneath his eyes throbbed ferociously. The King countered by throwing his dagger. "I will kill you," he screeched. The blade gouged into Aurora's stomach; she gagged and reeled back. Zagan's attention wavered as hooves sounded heavily from behind them.

Eleanor was coming from behind Zagan with her horse in full gallop. Zagan's mood was swelling with devilish pride so forcefully that Eleanor followed his magic like muddied footsteps to a swampy puddle. Pain seared through her body from the wounds on her hip and ivory cheek. Eleanor ignored the flames that singed her steed's hair and her own clothes and smashed out the emotions pounding in her heart. Her bloodied sword hung heavily at her side, sweat trickled down the rim of her helmet, and her breath came in short, raspy huffs.

"You son of a bitch!" she shrieked at Zagan from the back of her charging horse.

****

Across the field, Argus was fighting with everything he had. He was about to plunge his sword into the heart of the soldier in front of him when the soldier pleaded, "Please, just kill me." The Sharnin soldier lowered his blade to the ground in front of Argus. "I'd rather die at the hand of an honest man than win this war for an evil King."

"Run then, run north!" Argus yelled, shocked at the man's words. "There is no shame in abandoning a fight you no longer believe in!" The soldier nodded in gratitude, his eyes cloudy with dishonor and sorrow.

Argus returned to the battle, attempting to put the disheartening interaction out of his mind. Three cobble-stone blocks into the city, he was stalled by the horde of warring people. His eyes dashed across the green clad Sharnins, over the dead lying on the ground, and desperately hunted for the bright locks of Aurora's hair. Instead, what his eyes landed upon with shock and uncertainty, was the figure of a woman he had not seen in many years. Though he could not hear what she said, her lips moved in a most familiar manner and her features shifted through emotions just the way he remembered them doing. She was chasing a soldier down through the middle of the battle.

Not far from where Argus stared with his mouth agape, Silvia roared at Wade, "You cowardly fool! Running from me as if your skirts were on fire!" She charged unwaveringly after Wade. "Get out of my way," she snarled at another soldier as she wrenched her blade from his gut.

"I have reason to be afraid, have I not?" Wade responded, gesturing at the lifeless body on the ground in front of Silvia.

"You deserve the same fate," Silvia said coldly.

"I don't want to hurt you!" Wade cried out, deflecting a villager's strike at him, countering with a thrust into the man's abdomen, and rendering the man dead.

"Yet you slaughter my friends, innocent villagers, for the sake of a callous King!" Silvia screeched. She flung herself forward to cross blades with Wade.

"Silvia, for pity's sake!" Wade yelped, deflecting her blows but not making any himself.

"Fight me, you coward!"

"No!"

"Then I will kill you."

"Why do you despise me so? I could have killed you a half-dozen times and yet I've let you live!"

Silvia spat, "So that means I should pardon your betrayals? Because you didn't slit my throat?" With a scream, she managed to put a gash into Wade's shoulder. Wade jerked back and lowered his sword to the ground. Silvia paused in her pursuit in order to run her sword viciously through the low back of a Sharnin fighting with a Thurnadanian soldier beside her.

"Why are you so bent on killing me? Why not leave it to one of your Thurnadanian friends?" Wade's posture drooped. Silvia locked unwavering eyes on him.

"You would rather it be a stranger that takes your life?" she retorted. Silvia slugged her shield across the face of a Sharnin, knocking him out. "You Sharnins fight and kill with no conscience, no remorse!" Silvia took a step toward Wade but still he did not raise his sword. Opposing soldiers attacked them, though it took only a minute for Silvia and Wade to dispose of their assailants. Their swords dripped with fresh blood. "You claim innocence yet here you are fighting for evil once more," she paused to catch her breath. "And now that you are again given an opportunity to redeem yourself," she spread her hands in an inclusive gesture to the mayhem around them, "you come to take the lives of my people."

"You are doing to the same to me! Even as you speak, you are killing my people!" Wade replied accusingly. He kicked a Thurnadanian townsperson out of his way so that he could clearly glare back at Silvia.

"These aren't innocent people! They are the soldiers who chose to terrify, torture, rape, burn, drown, and slaughter innocent villagers. They fight for a King who has no soul, and for what reason? To be in control? Because, in the end, Descendants are a hundred times more powerful than a person with no magic, so why not just kill them all and take over?" Wade winced at Silvia's words. "If here in these ranks is where your love and loyalty lie, if these are truly your people," Silvia continued, rage engulfing her words, "then here is where you must meet your end." Silvia readjusted her sword grip, "Fight me. Or I will run you through just like any other Sharnin bastard."

Wordlessly, Wade raised his sword.

****

Xenos finished his journey in a far shorter time in the form of a large, astoundingly fast falcon than any man on horseback would even have dreamt possible. At the imposing battlements of the castle, he perched on the cross bar of a Thurnadanian flag to survey the landscape. The general appearance of the grounds was tranquil in the long hours of the night.

Xenos fluffed his feathers in a dismissive bird shrug then glided into the inner courtyard. He shifted to a dragonfly mid-flight up a wall before zigzagging sharply to maneuver through a window into the Royal Chambers. He found the conversation between a shifter disguised as the King, guards, maid, and King rather amusing but, Xenos knew he would get no information waiting around. Instead, he made his way to the ground floor of the castle.

"You there," the head cook called out to the Shifter as he flew by the kitchen doorway. "The lil' bug that ain't no bug," the cook narrowed his eyes. "Who be you?" Xenos hovered in hesitation. "Come on," he waved a spatula in the air as he walked toward the dragonfly. "Show yourself, 'else I be forced to smoosh ya." Xenos slowly changed his form to a young boy dressed in Thurnadanian colors. He smiled innocently.

"Try again, boy," the cook frowned. Xenos rolled his eyes as he debated whether he should make an escape or show himself. "Well?" the cook encouraged, tapping his foot impatiently. Xenos shifted to his true form but kept his clothes common instead reverting them to the Sharnin uniform he was actually wearing. The cook growled, "Guess that's close enough."

Xenos inclined his head slowly. "Might you be able to tell me where to find Aurora?" he asked politely. The cook looked up at the shifter suspiciously.

"Perhaps you should first tell me why everyone's be so damn interested in findin' her?" The cook scrutinized the intimidatingly tall, broad, pale man before him. "Or maybe jest where you're from," he locked eyes on the shifter. "I ain't never seen someone so white before... them eyes of yours, indigo an' yellow like that, I knows som'one wit' eyes like those though." Xenos gave no reply. "You tell me where you're from an' I'll tell ya' where Aurora is."

"I'm from the lands to the north."

"Interestin'," the cook stroked his chin. "Guess the tales 'bout the Snow Land's people's skin weren't jes' tall tales after all. But," the cook sucked in a deep breath, "thought you people were opposed ta' leaving the tundra."

"We are," Xenos stated simply.

"Everyone up there got eyes like yers?" he continued to question.

"I feel it is unnecessary for me to answer that."

"I feel like you're up ta' mischief an' I should call the guards on ya," the cook replied, deadpan. Xenos blinked slowly. "I've got the Seer's sight," the cook said frostily, pointing to the Inking on his face. "And it be telling me you gots secrets hid still. That ya' ain't totally in yer true form."

"Where is Aurora?" Xenos inquired again.

"Not 'round here," the cook smirked. "She left wit' the rest o' da troops. They were travelin' to Layton." Xenos' face turned from white to ashen gray.

****

Ryder led a charge of Layton soldiers and Descendants to meet the Sharnin in the gulley. The sound of swords clanging and women and men grunting was filling the singed grass. The Descendants who were fighting were spinning their spells and using their magic to fight off the Sharnin. Ryder looked over to see a Weaver fight a Grounder and a Sculptor fight a Whisperer. It looked like a storm from the deepest depths of the earth. Fire and wind, whirling around water and ice. He stood in awe at this beautiful and destructive sight.

Ryder turned back to his group just as a sword came down inches from his head. He blocked it with his own and a huge clang rang out. He dropped to his knees under the strike of the Sharnin's sword. With a nimble move, he spun on his knees. Releasing his sword he stabbed the Sharnin in the chest with his dagger. Blood ran down his arm as he rolled out from underneath the falling soldier. Retrieving his sword, Ryder scrambled to his feet to meet the next soldier head on.

Argus yanked on his mount's reins. The horse sidestepped and bared its teeth as a tundra wolf bore down on them. Argus slashed at the huge beast as it pounced, but its claws caught his chest and tore through his chainmail. Blood welled through his shirt, but he stubbornly ignored the pain. He struck the beast again and again. Argus took a final stroke at the wounded wolf's neck, then touched his palm to his chest, wincing as it came away dripping crimson with blood. Light-headed, deeply confused, and shaken to his core, he searched for the familiar face he had seen just moments before. It took him only a second to spot her again.

She was older, her hair with a streak of gray and skin touched by sun and rain, but she was still the most beautiful thing he had ever laid eyes on. Argus gulped, certain she was just a hallucination. He urged his horse closer, perplexed that she could possibly still be alive. With sudden clarity, Argus knew that she was indeed who he thought she was for no other swordsman was quite like her. She fought magnificently, with not a single wasted stroke or missed guard, just the same as she had since their training days together. A small smile touched Argus' lips despite the weakening he felt in his body. He trembled as memories of a feisty young soldier girl stealing his heart flooded his mind. However, his smile faded when he noticed who she was fighting.

Argus recognized the quick-striking Sharnin as Wade, a man he had had the unfortunate experience of crossing blades with many years before. He kicked his horse forward but could not move fast enough. Mere lengths away from the fight, Argus watched as Wade launched himself forward and brought the woman staggering to her knees. Argus bayed with wrenching dismay, dismounted, and bolted toward them.

Wade turned around just as Argus approached him. His beige eyes widened in shock for the split second before he felt Argus' sword thrust under his chainmail and into his stomach.

Argus howled, "She was my life!" The Sharnin gasped as blood pooled in his gaping mouth. He took one wheezing breath and choked, stumbled, and fell as his expression smoothed into the vacancy of death. Argus withdrew his sword and abruptly turned away. "She was my everything." He sank exhaustedly to his hands and knees beside the still woman lying in the grass. Tears streamed down his dirty, beaten face as he gathered his love's limp body into his arms. Heartbroken that the man who had stolen his wife from him in life had stolen her in death as well, Argus cradled her to his chest and ran his fingers tenderly through her hair. He ignored the tempest raging around him and gingerly kissed the woman's forehead. Blood from the gouges in Argus' chest seeped into her chainmail and tunic as his vision blurred. His mind faded into a fog.

"Silvia!" Argus wept. "No Silvia, my love. Please. Not again."

Nineteen

Lairson started to inch away from the battle as soon as the first arrows fell. He had not wanted to come to Layton at all, but he knew if he did not obey the Queen he would be removed from his castle position. Lairson had every intention of waiting out the war. He was not the type to wield a sword and shield. If pressed, he figured he could dispose of anyone who got in his way but, he did not care to risk himself that way. Tentatively, he clutched his medical bag to his chest and crept out of his hiding spot. He strained to hear how severely the battle continued.

"You a doctor?" an authoritative voice rang out toward Lairson from a broad, brown-haired man plowing his way through the battle-packed street. "The name's Ryder," the young man grunted, blocking the attack of a Sharnin who had spotted them. "Stand behind him," Ryder gestured a townsman forward. "He's a Whisperer and can keep you safe until we get inside!" Ryder gestured for the doctor to follow him, "We could use your help." Lairson nodded reluctantly as he watched the townsman form a dome of forceful wind around them. Ryder fought a path toward the Main Hall, the doctor and Descendant following after him.

"Spread the word that we've got another doctor," Ryder told villagers as they went by.

"Another?" Lairson questioned once they reached the Main Hall.

"Yes, Layton has a very skilled Healer, Gwendolyn."

"Are we safe here?" Lairson asked with apprehension, eyeing the wood-beam ceiling of the building.

"There's a Weaver keeping the Sharnins from torching the place. Rest easy," Ryder sheathed his sword and slapped Lairson on the back reassuringly.

"Are you the doctor the soldiers say will help me?" came the gentle, weary voice of a petite woman with a heart-shaped face.

"I'll gladly help such a beautiful woman," Lairson raised one eyebrow and inclined his head in a subtle bow. The Healer, Gwendolyn, blushed.

"I'm afraid the majority of the people you'll be aiding aren't nearly as pleasant to the eye," Gwendolyn replied. Ryder chuckled and turned to leave.

"Not to worry," Lairson reassured her.

"You are holding up out there?" Gwendolyn called after Ryder.

"Best we can, Gwendolyn. Just the best we can," Ryder answered over his shoulder. He unsheathed his sword and left.

"Follow me," the Healer gestured as she entered the Main Hall. Lairson choked at the stench of that swelled up from the tangle of wounded people lying on the floor. "I've been doing the best I can but I'm beyond exhausted. And they just keep coming," Gwendolyn rubbed at her neck and sore shoulder.

"You're the doctor?" Lairson's voice dripped with disbelief. Gwendolyn jerked around to face Lairson, her posture stiff with irritation.

"Healer," she said bluntly. "One of the only people here trying to save lives instead of take them." Lairson coughed in discomfort. Gwendolyn glared and bit her lip to keep from giving the doctor more of a lashing. "Washing table is on the far side," she pointed, getting back to business. "The wounded nearest us have been here the longest. I have a couple men bringing people in the double doors over there," she pointed again. Lairson started rolling up his tunic sleeves. "It's the strangest thing, but many Sharnin soldiers are becoming turncoats. So, do not be prejudice toward healing those in green uniforms. If they're in this building, they've earned our help." Gwendolyn wrung her hands together, "All the supplies we have are by the table, but we're running low. Do what you can with medicine, Heal the rest. Try to conserve your energy as much as possible, I fear we are going to need it."

"I'll do whatever you need," Lairson swallowed his pride.

"Healer," wheezed a woman to their left, "I'm so cold." Gwendolyn squared her shoulders then walked toward the woman who had spoken.

Lairson murmured in bewilderment, "There are women fighting?"

Gwendolyn stared at Lairson for a brief moment, "And dying. Same as the men."

****

Aurora yanked at the forest floor to unsettle Zagan and make him fall to his knees. Eleanor slid down the side of her galloping horse and tumbled forward a few paces before regaining her balance. Her horse trampled across Zagan, nearly crushing him, as Aurora sent another dozen spider-like tendrils of ice to harden around his arms and legs. The King moaned in pain and aggravation. Aurora hesitated, unsure whether to aid Eleanor in her attack against Zagan or to trap her in ice as well. Choosing the lesser of two evils, Aurora sent another scorch of flame across Zagan's skin and tried not to feel any satisfaction as she watched him convulse in agony.

Eleanor strode up to Zagan with a grim, despising look hardening her features. She watched his flesh pucker and shrivel for a moment before speaking.

"Nothing but a greedy, merciless, tyrant," Eleanor growled, drawing her sword.

"You going to run me through, Eleanor?" Zagan chuckled passed his fury, still struggling to free himself from Aurora's wrathful magic. The Queen's eyes darted to Aurora, back to the King, then back to Aurora.

"There is nothing you can do that I cannot recover from," Zagan growled, clenching his trapped hands into fists beneath the sheet of ice.

"Perhaps physically that is true," the Queen growled. "But look around. Most of your Descendants have deserted you. Soldier and Descendant alike are leaving your ranks to join ours. You will recover to a world where you have no people, no loyalty, no lands. Your cause is lost. You have lost."

"You do not have the guts to kill nor to rule," the King retorted. "Threaten all you want, but this war isn't finished." Aurora's shoulders tightened as the Queen glowered.

"Yes," Eleanor breathed, "yes, it is. Because you are finished."

Eleanor sheathed her sword then lifted a small glass vial from a cord around her neck. Aurora's jaw tightened and her skin paled. Zagan's eyes widened.

"Going to give me a drop of poison, are you?" the King laughed sadistically. "Put it to your lips first, sweetheart, I'd love to taste your tongue before I die."

"You disgust me," Eleanor spat.

In a burst of strength, Zagan wrenched himself free from Aurora's entrapment. Instinctively, Aurora's arms lashed out. Sparks spiraled into snow cyclones that locked the King back into a case of ice before he had a chance to move. "You know my body heals from venoms just the same as wounds!" the King shrieked, furious that two small, docile women had him at their mercy.

"Not if I remove your head from your shoulders!" the Queen retorted. For the first time, there was a glint of fear in Zagan's eyes. The Queen's lips curled into a sinister smile.

Zagan sent a mental order to his soldiers nearby, *Come and murder the fools who dare challenge your King!* Palms to her temples, Aurora's knees buckled at the ferocity of which she heard the message. Zagan startled and stiffly turned his head to stare at her. "You heard that?" he asked. "That was for my soldiers!"

"You screamed it into their skulls!" Aurora snapped. "I heard it because I have mind connections with them! Why do you think your recruited Descendants have been deserting your army?" The Queen grabbed the King by the jaw as Aurora spoke. "I have been encouraging them to! And they have been listening!"

"You wench! I will kill them all!" Zagan jerked away from Eleanor but it only made her grasp more firmly. "Their deaths will be on your head!"

"We have wasted enough time," the Queen said emphatically. She popped the cork out of the vial with her teeth and spat it on the ground. After yanking Zagan's jaws open, she poured the contents of the vial down his throat. Zagan gagged and tried to retch the thick liquid back up. "Swallow it, you bastard," Eleanor swore as she wrapped her hands over his mouth and rubbed her thumbs along his chin and throat forcing the liquid down.

I am here for Zagan not for you! Aurora tried to convince the Sharnin soldiers not to follow the King's order. *I wish you no harm. Ignore his command and I can spare you!* Hooves sounded from the ridge into the woods. Eleanor and Aurora met eyes. With a curt nod, Aurora straightened her shoulders and resignedly turned to meet the approaching swarm of Sharnins.

****

"Would you be so good as to come downstairs, your Highness?" Bridget smiled prettily as she turned away from the two Kings and gestured towards the door.

"Which one are ya talking to?" a bewildered guard whispered.

"Bridget, please, where is my love, the Queen?" the second King begged, taking a few tentative steps after her.

"Your love?" the first King interjected irate. "She is my wife, you bloody fool!"

"Which one do you think is the true King?" another guard whispered. "The King hasn't been in his right mind for quite some time, you know."

"My Lord, please," Bridget bit her lip then gestured for the identical men to leave the room. "Perhaps we could discuss this, and figure the confusion out, over a bite to eat. It is dinner time after all," Bridget curtsied and smiled her sweetest, most innocent smile.

"What are you doing?" the first guard asked in a loud whisper.

"Trust me, please," Bridget murmured back. "A Seer will be able to see through the magic."

"But all the Descendants left for battle."

"All but one," Bridget grinned.

"I don't get it."

239

"The other man is a shifter. He's a Descendant." She gestured with her eyes for the guards to escort her and the Kings out of the room. "That is how we will tell who is who!" The first guard hesitated. Subtly, so only Bridget noticed, he raised his fist in front of him in a sign of loyalty.

"I don't know for sure what you're suggesting. But you've been 'round the Highnesses far more than we have. I will follow your lead." He bowed and led the group out of the Royal Chambers.

"I'll meet you in the dining hall," Bridget said as she scampered the opposite way down the hall, then stairs, then into the kitchens.

"What be the problem?" the cook asked when he saw Bridget barge through the door.

"You knew that magic was latched onto me. That I was up to mischief, yes?" Bridget urged.

"Yeah, I always know when someone ain't tellin' the truth." The cook ignored Bridget's blush of embarrassment and asked grimly, "You got somethin' to do with the Sharnin Shifter?"

"A Shifter was here?" Bridget gulped.

"Yeah. A big, solemn guy with the palest skin I'd 'ver seen. Very skillful, too."

"Where is he?" Bridget replied fearfully.

"Left in a rush, he did. Figure the bad news I tol' him 'bout the scarlet Descendant not being here put him in a bad way with his master."

"He was after Aurora then?" Bridget panted, feeling both relieved and guilty.

"Aye," the cook admitted. "Is that all you was worried 'bout?" he asked, raising his eyebrows. "And no lies, missy, I knows when you tell 'em."

"No. No, no really," Bridget stammered, trying to get her thoughts back in line. "Not about him at all."

"What is it then?" the cook prompted as Bridget faltered.

"There's a shifter—"

"There be another one o' deem?"

"Yes, only probably even better than the one you met."

"You sure 'bout that? That fellow were mighty talented."

"Yes, he-he is one of the best," Bridget gulped. The cook's eyebrows arched even higher. "And that's why I need you to identify him for me," she begged. The cook's expression darkened. Bridget ran her hands through her hair, causing her curls to bounce. She winced and said, "He's in the King's form."

"King Malcolm?" the cook coughed in disbelief, clutching the handle of an oven door to steady himself against his astonishment.

"Yes, sir," Bridget bit her bottom lip.

"And you can't tell no difference between 'em?"

"No, sir. That's why I need your help!"

The cook tugged on his chin thoughtfully, a spark of interest growing in his eyes. "To see the magic?" he guessed, warming to the challenge.

"To see his magic," Bridget nodded.

"Alright, little missy. I like where yer head be at. Where's the Shifter? Take me to 'im."

Bridget tentatively led the cook into the dining hall through the kitchen's side door. "Don't say anything about magic until we're back in the kitchen," Bridget whispered before approaching the table.

In the dining hall, both Malcolms were seated at opposite sides of the table to keep them from bickering over who the honor of sitting at the head belonged to.

241

"Whoa," the cook's eyes bulged when he saw the Kings.

"Your Highnesses," Bridget curtsied, "the cook has offered to prepare something special for you to ease your nerves about the battle." The cook bowed and smiled softly, eyes roving over the identical men at the table. Bridget resisted the temptation to smirk. She half expected the Kings' choices of meal to give the truth away. The cook's eyes closely examined both Kings. Donovan disguise was exact to the tiniest detail, but the cook knew who the imposter was.

"Potato soup," the first King requested. "Though I do not see how I could possibly consume much. I find my appetite is rather diminutive in the presence of this imposter," he added angrily.

"Whatever my sweet Eleanor wants," the second mused. The guards standing behind the Kings looked to Bridget for orders. The cook bowed and left the room. Bridget hesitated a little longer then shrugged at the guards with her eyes.

"I will return shortly. Excuse me," she curtsied again then followed the cook into the kitchen.

"They've both got magic 'n them," the cook said as soon as Bridget had closed the kitchen door behind her.

"What?" Bridget sputtered.

"The second that spoke, he be the Shifter," the cook waved one hand to dissipate Bridget's panic. "But the true King's got sumtin' of a nasty strong magic lingerin' on him."

"He was acting awfully strange earlier," Bridget speculated, scratching her forehead. "Which would be why the guards were thinking the second King was the real one!" Bridget pointed a finger at the cook, "Donovan was betting on that, so he's acting like the King is still under the influence of magic."

242

"Donovan?" The cook gagged and dropped the sauce pan he had just picked up.

"He's the Shifter in the King's form," Bridget nodded despairingly.

"Woah," the cook's breath left him in a whoosh. Bridget knelt and picked the pan up for him.

"He's been after—" Bridget was interrupted by shouts erupting from the dining hall. The cook and Bridget looked at each other fearfully then dashed toward the commotion. Guards were yelling and trying to pull the second King off of the first, who lay on the floor.

"What happened?" the cook asked, kneeling by the unconscious King.

"Insulted my Queen, he did," whimpered the second King. "Imposter."

"He dove at him! Tried to strangle him!" stammered one guard.

"He's not breathing," bleated the guard leaning his ear over the first King's mouth.

Bridget's chest clenched in fear. "Get the doctor," she stammered. "Now!" she shouted.

"Lairson's at war with the troops," the shell-shocked guard in front of her warbled.

"Then get me another," Bridget demanded.

"Yes'm," the guard scampered to his feet and out of the dining hall.

Bridget looked down at the peaceful, bland expression on the King's face and balled her fingers into fists of aggravation. She turned to the second King, took his jaw in her hands, and bore her eyes into his.

"Are you sure he's the Shifter?" whispered one of the men.

"Absolutely," Bridget snorted, patting the second King on the cheek. "You'll have to drag him away there though," Bridget instructed. "I've put a spell on him to stiffen his body so he can't move." The guards' eyebrows shot up. "It's just like being paralyzed," Bridget laughed, sobered, and waved them toward the door.

"I can't get no response outta' him," the cook admitted as Bridget joined him on the floor beside Malcolm. Bridget desperately searched the King's face for movement. If he died now her decision to go after Donovan would have been for nothing.

"Hurry up, lad," called the returning guard as he and a small boy burst into the dining hall. "Go! Go, work your magic," he pushed the boy forward to the King's side.

"You're a Healer?" Bridget was skeptical.

"Yes'm," the boy admitted grudgingly.

"He's the only Healer that we know of in the castle right now. Sorry, Bridget," the guard cringed.

"Do what you can then," Bridget rubbed the youth on the shoulder. "Your King needs you."

"What about the laws? I'm not fully trained," he squeaked.

"It will be alright. I will not let you be punished for your help."

The boy gulped uneasily then leaned forward and set his trembling hands on either side of the King's head. Orange loops of light circled from his hands across the King's skin as he closed his eyes. Tears began to stream down his cheeks from concentration and strain. Bridget and the cook looked at each other, wondering if they should stop him. They waited nervously. Finally, Malcolm sputtered and jerked awake with a wheeze of breath.

"My head!" The King's eyelids fluttered as he tried to sit up.

"I think it's best if ya' stay where you be, Yer Majesty. Just for a bit, no?" The cook gently helped Malcolm lay back again. Bridget swept the young healer up into her arms.

"He was barely even alive," came the faint voice of the exhausted boy. "B- but I helped him." Bridget stroked his cheek, concern creasing her brow.

"You did very well," Bridget bit her lip. "Now we need you to rest. It takes a lot of strength to do what you just did."

"You tend to the King. I'll go find help for the littl'n," the cook frowned and reached out to take the boy from Bridget's arms.

"He's a gifted little hero," Bridget smiled despite her worries.

****

Aurora stood still and watched as everything around her moved. Magic surged through her with a strength she had never experienced before. The Energies of her slain companions pulsed in her veins so strongly her skin vibrated.

The Sharnin soldiers moved in on them quickly. Aurora tried to reach out to them but their minds were clouded with hate and rage. She knew it was Zagan's doing to blind them from all other thoughts. She hated what she was about to do, but something inside of her took over. With one snap of her wrist, fire had erupted in a wall in front of them. One soldier, a Descendant was quick to extinguish her fire. They kept at a full charge. Aurora reached down deep into the ground, her hands shaking as the soil began to move. In one sharp movement, the ground around her, Zagan, and Eleanor shot into the sky. A butte now stood high above the soldiers. Too tall to climb. Slowly she turned to Zagan, still trapped in ice and Eleanor, staggering to her feet with the settling of the earth beneath her.

Aurora shuddered at her own power but grim resolve kept her fighting. Her teachers and fellow pupils had thought her worthy of their lives; they had perished so that she could save Thurnadan and all the Temperate Lands. She refused to let them down.

The elements she claimed control of swept through the battle like angered hornets. Aurora closed her eyes and tilted her head back, her arms outstretched. She could feel the very breath of each person in Layton, the swelling of the earth in reaction to her expanding bubble of magic, and the ripping of life from body as her powers became a gruesome weapon. She threw down another wave of fire to the ground and soldier after Sharnin soldier disintegrated at the touch of her flames. Tears knifed down Aurora's face as she sobbed with guilt. She did not want to take a single life, but she knew if she did not fight for Thurnadan, did not face her magic against theirs, Zagan would corrupt every Descendant and kill every person without magic. Life would be nothing but fear at the hands of Zagan. Aurora had no choice but keep going.

A voice reached out to Aurora that took her by surprise.

Aurora, take this from me. Granthan's voice slid across her confused mind.

What?

Look, he urged her. *A gift. My gift, is now yours.*

Just then her upper right arm burst with light as the coils of the Shape Shifter Inking appeared on her skin. Her arm seared with pain.

Suddenly a light shot from Aurora's Inkings, all of nine of them appeared on her skin and the combined power took over her body and raised it off the ground. She floated there as a sphere of light began to form all around her. Her body flew off the ground. Her words spoke out in a loud booming echo, a voice that was not hers.

"Mercy hath been put aside. There shall be screams of sorrow. The end comes for those who resist." Louder and louder she sang out the words of the Ancients' poetry, words she was not sure how she knew. Her body filled with strength.

The people below stopped to stare up at this glowing figure high above them. The light blinding their eyes.

Aurora conjured lightening to strike the ground and take out only those who were true to Zagan. Their bodies vanished in the fire of the light. Her body quivered from her power but the sphere of light around her stayed strong. Rain began to pound down from the skies above, clearing the battle field below her. Behind Aurora, Eleanor had been struck immobile in amazement. Zagan, however, was becoming consumed with an uncontainable, violent rage.

The King broke his right arm free from Aurora's icy entrapment, shoved the Queen out of his way, then flung his dagger as hard as he could toward Aurora's exposed back. Aurora felt the gleaming blade as it pierced through her sphere of magic, but it was too late. She stumbled as the dagger stabbed into her body with perfect accuracy, piercing her heart. Her muscles tore and her heart writhed. Her eyes darkened to a stony gray, her rosy cheeks paled, and her dark lips parted from the excruciating pain slashing through her chest. She fell to the ground. Her light sphere vanished and the butte came crashing back to earth.

Aurora trembled with dizziness as her magic dulled. She wondered feebly how many times she would be killed before she actually died and how many times she would suffer before she would no longer be able to heal. Aurora's saliva thickened with blood as she tried to bring herself to her knees. The sky lightened as her rain and fire dissolved.

Aurora's eyes went white as a memory of her old Dan'te's voice rang in her mind. *You will be a legend one day, Dram Red One. Just you wait and see. You have love and you have strength. Together those two things will accomplish great feats. You are the Scarlet Prophecy, my child.* Aurora shuddered at the memory of her as a very young student at the Achlese Academy.

"Life through death," Aurora whispered. Her eyes flew wide, then she understood. The only way to be done with death, dying, and killing was for she herself to perish. "Energies given to build anew. Life is the gift, death is the sacrifice." And in one breath she fell to her side as the light left her eyes.

Eleanor got to her feet, unsheathed her sword, grit her teeth and seized the opportunity to thrust her sword through Zagan's throat. "This you will not heal from!" she growled as pulled her sword back. The King gagged in seizure. His blood mixed with the shoots of ice still tangled around his limbs. The Queen staggered a few steps away, her energy drained. Zagan's seemingly lifeless form nauseated her so she turned and fled.

Twenty

Back in the center of Layton Argus held Silvia in his arms, tears streaming down his face.

"Argus?" Silvia coughed as her eyes struggled to open. Her hand raised to the nape of Argus' neck. She stroked his short hair, certain that if she was seeing who she thought she was seeing, she must be dead. Argus gingerly lifted his head and met his shocked eyes with hers.

"Silvia," Argus swallowed hard, his face pale, "I thought? I thought you'd been killed."

"You're dead," Silvia half-laughed, half-cried, growing more confused by the minute. "So I must have been killed." She shivered with pain, not noticing that the rain had soaked them and the ground, mixing oil-like with the fallen soldiers' blood.

"I ain't dead, yet," Argus coughed and doubled over. "Only I don't see no way how ya' could be alive with a gash like the one you was dealt!" Argus' expression flickered between relief, bewilderment, and overwhelming physical agony. "I hurt too much," he spoke slowly, "to be dead." Argus pulled at Silvia's chainmail and tunic to examine her wounds. The deadly strike that had cut through her chest was rapidly knitting closed. Argus shook his head in bafflement then looked to Silvia for an explanation. "What?" he gasped. "Maybe I'm wrong. Maybe we are dead."

"Am I healing?" Silvia brought her hand to her own chest. "Then I'm not dead," she laughed then coughed. "I'm not dead!" She looked excitedly at Argus before clutching both her hands around his face. "Which means neither are you!" She sat up and flung her arms around Argus to hug him. "How?" She gasped between tremors of tears. "How is this possible?" Silvia's excitement faded and her voice filled with concern, "Argus, you're bleeding terribly. Are you alright?"

"How come you ain't dead?" Argus persisted. He winced and pulled out of Silvia's embrace. Silvia bit her lip, wishing she did not have to explain. She simply wanted answers.

"Wade!" Silvia suddenly remembered the fight she had been in before waking in Argus' arms. "What happened to..." She left her sentence unfinished for she had laid eyes on Wade's corpse sprawled soddenly on the ground.

"That's what the bastard's name is, eh?" Argus glared at the dead man.

"You know him?" Silvia questioned, blinking rapidly as she tried to steady her thoughts.

Argus looked back at her, "He tried ta' kill me years ago."

****

The Queen had managed to run back to the edge of Layton before her breath gave out. She limped the rest of the way under the support of a turncoat Sharnin soldier.

"My Lady!" Ryder caught the stumbling Queen as she fell from the assisting arms of the Sharnin. A half dozen Thurnadanian soldiers drew their swords and menacingly glared at the man.

"I mean her no harm," the Sharnin sank to his knees in surrender. "She was disoriented, coming from the woods. She looked like she needed help." Eleanor moaned and sagged forward. The two men carefully lifted her back to her feet.

"That is Queen Eleanor you had in your arms. Why help her?" Ryder asked suspiciously.

"I am Thurnadanian," the man replied, expression distorted with guilt as he revealed the Earth Grounder Inking on his ankle. "I wanted a better life. I trained. Became a captain in Zagan's army." He lowered his eyes, too ashamed to put his emotions into words. "Many of us recruited Thurnadanians have gone renegade or surrendered."

"Take her to Gwendolyn," Ryder ordered the men supporting the Queen as he gently ushered Eleanor toward the Main Hall. "You," Ryder pointed at the captain, "don't leave my sight and perhaps you will be shown mercy."

If you have not already, lay down your arms! The captain mentally shouted. *Let those who truly fight for Zagan be killed! Thurnadanian Descendants need not take this brutality any longer!*

"We won, have we not?" the Queen mused unstably.

"So it would seem," Ryder replied, following them into the hall, cheeks flushed with exertion. "With the magic and all," Ryder pondered. "Which is strange considering the Descendants have vanished from the Sharnin camp. It was Thurnadan Descendants that won the Battle. Where'd that storm come from?" Ryder asked the captain who followed behind him. "I figured it was an enemy attack seeing how you're the ones with the reputation. But it didn't bring us down."

"It didn't bring us down either," the captain half chuckled-half sobbed. "It killed only Zagan's true soldiers. Not recruits. Not those of us who were forced into fighting."

Gwendolyn interrupted as she dropped into a deep curtsy in front of Eleanor, "An honor to finally meet the Ivory Queen." She tried to smile through her exhaustion, "'Tis a pity the meeting has to be under such circumstances. What ails you, My Queen?"

251

"My injuries are minor, just fright I believe. I feel I should not trouble you," Eleanor spoke softly, ruefully eyeing the wounded sprawled across the floor

"The Descendants seem to have joined us! Not a single Descendant is left who fights under Zagan's banner. Nearly a third of the Sharnin troops are laying down arms now, saying they will no longer support Zagan's cause! Many of them have fled," the Healer reassured the Queen. "We will be alright."

"Thank you," Eleanor's cheeks flushed.

"I have a few leaves you could chew on. They will help with the nausea if nothing else," Gwendolyn patted one of the Queen's shaking hands.

"We will tell all souls in all of the lands that the Descendants who were deceived and ensnared have been pardoned in my eyes."

Shock coated the expression of the people surrounding the Queen. "We have to find balance," she explained, sinking onto a stool by the Healer's table. "We have to have peace between Descendants and those who have no magic."

"Your Highness," Lairson whispered from behind her a few minutes later. Eleanor startled. "Forgive me," the doctor sniveled, "I did not mean to frighten you."

"What is it, Lairson?" the Queen snapped.

"The Venom," Lairson wrung his hands together, "did it serve its purpose?" He asked without making eye contact.

"It did," the Queen pursed her lips.

Lairson smiled sharply, relief pouring through him. "Good, good," he nodded, grateful that Donovan had indeed gotten the concoction made and into the Queen's hands instead of keeping it for himself. Aurora's blood had not been wasted.

"Thank you for your assistance," Eleanor said.

252

"Glad to be of service," Lairson smirked.

"Do not gloat too much. You have dying people to attend to, do you not?" Lairson flexed his jaw, bowed, and turned to leave. Eleanor let out a long, slow breath.

He hesitated and turned back to her, "Where might the red-haired witch be?"

"Watch your tongue, Lairson. She saved us all," the Queen growled.

"So, she has managed to brainwash you as well," Lairson sneered. "Once a witch, always a witch."

"She is dead."

"But — ?" the doctor choked. "She's a Healer!"

"I don't think she could heal from what I saw," Eleanor ground her teeth.

"Wha-what?" Lairson stuttered, unable to form a complete thought or question.

"Zagan stabbed her in the back through the heart," the Queen stated flatly. Lairson's eyebrows shot up. "Something you would appreciate, no?" the Queen condescended. "That is why the storm broke. It had been her magic causing it."

"Lairson!" Ryder shouted from beside a sweat-covered man. "This man has got a fever!"

"Excuse me," the doctor bowed again.

Gwendolyn returned to the Queen's side to check on her, "Feeling any better?" Eleanor nodded affirmatively. "Good. Glad to hear it. Your Highness, thank you for the use of your doctor. Lairson has been of great aide to me. I'm certain I would have been overwhelmed without his help," Gwendolyn gestured to Lairson who was bent over a man with an arrow through his chest next to Ryder's concerned figure.

"Happy he has proved himself useful. I admit," the Queen chuckled, "it amuses me and lifts my spirits to see him at a woman's beck and call."

****

The landscape of Layton was worn away, the beautiful green grass had been trampled to mud under the rains. The nearby trees and homes, scorched from the fires. Blood ran thick on the ground. The battle was over. Ryder rode out into the fields to look for survivors.

Zagan's body was slumped down in the dirt. No breath, no life. Suddenly, the huge gash on neck began to mend. Zagan's eyes came to life. His wound was excruciatingly slow to heal. Zagan had been through worse pain, but the nausea, fever, and light-headedness he had now was something he had never experienced. He had never felt so truly terrible in his life. He cursed mentally, still too injured to speak. Trying to pry open his eyes to look around, Zagan was struck with dizziness. Furious that he had not yet healed, he attempted to probe for a mind connection with Aurora or Eleanor but was met only with sludgy, dark, stiflingly silent nothing. He could not feel out, connect to, or even sense anyone's presence. The King began to quake with an impending sense of dread. Growing more and more anxious, Zagan reached up and stripped off his green tunic. He strained to get to his feet once more and look around. Ash swirled across the red-stained floor like dry snow on a windswept night. The scene before him was strangely both gruesome and angelic. Zagan groaned.

Silently, he vowed that he would make Thurnadan suffer and crumble. His mind swirled with plans of revenge as he fought to heal himself.

Zagan saw Aurora lying on her side just a few feet in front of him. He leaned over and grabbed up Aurora's head by her hair. Bruises marred her tan skin and blood had begun to dry along her face from her nostrils and split lip. The King sneered and flipped Aurora over so she was face up. He laid his dagger against her throat.

"You won't," he choked, "be there to stop me next time."

Bright gold spirals of magic laced from Aurora's flesh to the King's and froze the dagger where it rested. Guttural noises of frustration boiled from Zagan's throat as the Energies of Aurora's companions bolted through her motionless figure. The voice of Aurora's master teacher coaxed her from unconsciousness. She grabbed Zagan's wrist and forced his dagger away from her throat as her hand burned Zagan's flesh. Her power surged and her eyes flashed open. Magic sparked from her fingers.

"Yes, I will," she snarled.

"How...?" tshe King stuttered. Aurora felt her companions magic surge inside of her, and she knew that it was not her own strength making her heart beat and her wounds rapidly heal. She shoved Zagan away and watched as he toppled back to the ground. Aurora leaned down and grasped him by his shoulders.

A distance away, Ryder stopped in his tracks as he saw Zagan and Aurora stand and began to circle each other.

"I should kill you," she seethed, her words hot on the King's chapped skin. Aurora lunged forward to plunge a dagger into Zagan. "I should watch you bleed out, watch your eyes as the light fades from them. I should hold you, force you to perish in your enemy's arms, watch as your pride dies right before your final breath. I should," Aurora twisted the dagger, causing Zagan to convulse in pain. "I should kill you. But I

255

think death would be a mercy. And I have no mercy left in my heart for you." Zagan's forehead crinkled with confusion. "You cannot deny it. You must feel it," Aurora continued. "The instant you awoke you knew."

Aurora grimaced at her own pain but kept her focus on the King. She withdrew the warm blade from his abdomen and took a step back. Slowly, fearfully, Zagan looked up, raising his left hand to his throat and his right to his stomach. Congealed blood stuck to his hands. His mouth gaped open in terror.

"How?" The King's eyes filled with self-pity.

"You're defeated, Zagan," Aurora growled. "Sharnin has lost the war. And you," she paused to slowly shake her head, "you have lost control of your magic. Look at the blue hue of your veins! You power is fading as we speak!" One loud, raw sob escaped the King's lips. "I know that being without magic is your worst possible fear." Aurora grimaced, stepping back from Zagan as he sagged to the ground in devastation, "I hope you live a long, terrified, miserable life."

"This is not over!" Zagan coughed. "Even without magic I can make you suffer!"

"But you will always suffer more," Aurora replied. "You will wish that I had killed you." Her body became pure energy and burst with golden light, blinding all those around her. Zagan shielded his face from the glare. When it was over, he looked to where Aurora had stood, but nothing. She was gone.

****

Silvia and Argus knelt in the town square, Wade's lifeless body just a few paces away. Silvia examined Argus, battle weary and covered in blood, as he tried and failed to get to his feet.

"We have to get you to a Healer, Argus! Now," Silvia insisted, knees dug hard into the ground. She pulled herself up the rest of the way to her feet then bent to help Argus. Her body ached, but she knew her wounds were already on the mend. Silvia knelt beside him and yanked off his chainmail.

"Tundra wolf," alarm coated Silvia's face. "There's no way you should have lived this long!" She cried, ardently wedging herself under Argus' arm so she could support his weight and help him to his feet.

"Guess I'm stubborn 'er sumtin'," Argus lisped, blood flecks dotted his lips as he spoke. Silvia stayed quiet, focusing on helping Argus wobble toward the Town Hall. "You're a Healer, ain't you?" Argus groaned.

"Not the type you need," Silvia grunted.

"That's why you be alive, while I be dying," his laugh turned into a violent cough. He tumbled to the left, and nearly knocked Silvia over. Fever-induced delusions filled his mind, his skin became clammy, and his steps became weak.

"Just a little further," Silvia sobbed as they struggled to step over a dead Sharnin. Argus' heavy breathing softened and his weight on Silvia's shoulders doubled as he sank against her. "Argus!" Silvia screamed, turning her body against his to keep from falling. "Help!" She yelled, "Help us!" A couple of Thurnadanian soldiers rushed over to them. "Help him, please," Silvia sobbed.

"It's the High Constable, Argus," one of the soldiers gasped as he slipped his hands under Argus' arms. Both men's mouths dropped open. "hurry up!" He demanded of the other man.

257

"You," the second soldier gestured with his head to Silvia. "Warn the Healer and the doctor that they have a miracle to work!" He grabbed Argus by the legs as Silvia exhaustedly ran ahead to the Hall.

"Help," Silvia shouted, shoving open the hall doors. "Argus! Argus he's dying!" she lamented. Lairson looked up from where he knelt.

"The High Constable?" he questioned.

Silvia's mind raced, "Is he really the High Constable?

"Argus? Yes, of course," the doctor furrowed his brows.

"Just help him, please," she panted. Gwendolyn came rushing to the door.

The two soldiers carrying Argus squeezed through the doorway. They brought him over to a cot near where Gwendolyn stood and laid him down.

"Tundra wolf," Gwendolyn covered her mouth with the back of her hand. She looked at Lairson, their expressions mirroring each other.

"Strike wounds that never heal," Lairson lowered his eyes.

"No, no!" Silvia flung herself across Argus' torso and growled defensively at the doctor, "Don't tell me I've lost him." She looked to Gwendolyn, fury and soul-deep sorrow flooding from her eyes. "Not again! I just got him back," she whispered.

"Can we do something?" Eleanor swept over to the doorway, followed by Ryder coming in from outside. Concern covered both their faces.

"My Lady, please," Gwendolyn winced, "we are tending to him. I think it best you stay where you were." Eleanor sulked as she turned away. Gwendolyn instructed Lairson, "Get me the rest of the selva leaves I have. There's not much left but it's more than nothing,"

"He is as good as dead," Lairson hissed, annoyed that the healer would waste the precious plant on certain failure. "A tundra wolf's strike this deep is poisonous. There is no healing him."

"And the jar of dried frog hearts," Gwendolyn locked eyes with Lairson, ignoring his words. She bit her tongue and waited. Lairson resisted for a moment then got up to get her the root and jar. "Thank you," she murmured, pushing loose strands of hair back behind her ears.

Silvia slipped to Argus' side, she took his hand and laced her fingers through his, her face pressed against his chest. She sang to him sadly as Gwendolyn washed his wounds, crushed the dried flowers into them, stitched them closed, then gently pressed the leaves across his puckered skin.

Silvia now lay next to Argus. Tears running down her face. Suddenly, every fiber in Silvia's body vibrated with her healing magic. Everyone stepped back as her body convulsed.

"What is happening to her?" Ryder urged.

"She's giving her magic to him," Gwendolyn whispered.

"You can do that?"

"Yes, but at a cost. Instead of healing her own wounds, she is forcing her magic out of her body and into Argus. She is in great pain. It is unlikely that she will survive this."

Silvia hugged herself to Argus even more fiercely. With the very essence of her soul, she begged the Ancients to let Argus live.

Gwendolyn laid her hands against Argus' collarbone then stared at Lairson until the doctor relented and set his own hands on Argus' chest. Finally, the gashes on Argus' chest began to mend closed. A feeble smile tugged at one side of Gwendolyn's mouth. Argus' body was consumed by light. Silvia's shaking stopped and she fell limp at this side.

259

Gwendolyn and Lairson sat back and let the lights of their magic fade.

"You think he will heal?" Ryder asked quietly. Gwendolyn ignored his question, leaning forward to gingerly push Silvia's sweat-soaked hair off her face. "And Silvia? Will she be alright?"

"Don't disturb them," Gwendolyn hushed. "Lairson, go back to helping the others."

"What about the woman?" Lairson pestered, a bit worried.

"Shh. Go," Gwendolyn waved him away. Gwendolyn looked down at Argus. "She must love you very much," she cooed, glancing over at Silvia, "to give her magic to you."

****

Donovan screamed, as the rusted, metal door clanged shut.

"Don't think he'll be gettin' out this time," one guard clapped the other on the shoulder. "Let's go."

"Is a pity he caused the ol' man to lose his position."

"True. I still don't think it was the guard's fault."

"Magic, I tell you."

"Must have been involved somehow."

Donovan listened as the men's voices faded down the dungeon hall then let himself tip sideways to rest against the cell wall. Self-pity poured through his veins thicker than his own blood.

Donovan reached out to Eleanor and Aurora, repeating a message over and over: *I was willing to help you! Was willing to help the Descendants. Fools! I will get free once again. I will have both thrones. And I will make you pay for this.*

****

Bridget spoke slowly as she filled Malcolm in on all that had happened in the last few days. Livid tears stung the back of the King's eyes as he realized what his Queen had done to her own country and to him.

"…And now Donovan is back in prison and you have been revived by a Healer," Bridget concluded.

"It was unwise to ignore Aurora's warning," the King chided himself. "I sought her counsel and when I got it, I ignored it."

"Perhaps," Bridget double checked the King's vitals. "But you did not act rashly due to foolishness," she chuckled lightly, "but rather out of love and loyalty."

"I do not know how to react to this! Eleanor is my wife! She is the Queen of Thurnadan," Malcolm shook his head as he gingerly sat up. "Yet she broke a most dangerous prisoner out of our dungeon, and broke many of our laws," he paused and swallowed hard. "Donovan is her half-brother?"

Bridget shrugged slowly and frowned, "I'm sure there is much to the story neither of us know."

"I will have an explanation, that is for sure," Malcolm's jaw tightened. "I cannot believe such family secrets have been kept from me! There's been enough blasphemy within the castle to last an eternity!"

"Though, if I may be bold enough to say," Bridget looked down at her hands, noting that they were not currently glowing but sure that it was just a matter of time before Zagan called again. "We all have our demons, our mistakes, our bad decisions for good reasons. Have we not?"

"Yes, I suppose we do," the King rubbed at his temples. "Though it does not make me all the more pleased." Bridget bit the inside of her cheek to keep from blurting out her guilt and begging for help and forgiveness. "You, however, have acted most honorably. The way you stopped Donovan like you did surely saved my life. I am indebted to you," the King stated as he patted Bridget on the shoulder. With the help of a guard, he shakily rose to his feet.

Pressure built up in the back of Bridget's eyes but she forced herself to keep her demeanor calm. "Got lucky is all," she swallowed and got to her own feet. "Had a suspicion turn out true."

"Highness!" shouted a young, winded soldier as he burst into the room. He snapped into a salute. Malcolm saluted back. "Scout, Sire, from Layton's battle."

"Out with it," the King prompted.

"Thurnadan has been victorious!" the scout grinned then grew solemn. "Many losses, my Lord. Rather gruesome," he gulped loudly. "The whole thing is most strange." The King and Bridget both listened intently. "Pardon me, my Lord, I'm rambling," the scout saluted again.

"At ease, soldier," the King waved. "Now speak straight, what is this about the fight being strange?"

The scout fidgeted. "We were losing. Damn near slaughtered. Er, near slaughtered," he looked at Bridget and bit his lip. "Excuse my language, miss," he frowned.

"Continue," the King bluntly ordered.

"Well, we were so near defeat, then out of nowhere a storm rolls in. Awe inspiring. Pure magic, nothing else it could be though I reckon few will believe it," the scout's eyes became wide at the memory. "Flashes of fire like strikes of lightning came outta' the sky and burnt the Sharnins to a crisp! We watched them disintegrate from the inside out. Some even crumbled like dry bread 'til there weren't nothing left of them!" The soldier's face paled with sudden nausea, "Looked like some of 'em even bled out from invisible wounds. It went on for some time too, then stopped as abruptly as it had started."

"Guess that answers my question," Bridget smiled faintly. "We won."

"Thank you for your report," the King replied. "You are dismissed."

"Thank you, Sire," the scout saluted and pivoted to leave.

"Aurora, you think?" Malcolm pondered aloud.

Bridget's thoughts raced. "Aurora's certainly powerful enough," she nodded as a twinge of guilt tightened in her stomach. "It would definitely make sense."

****

Aurora licked her dry lips. She felt like she had been drug over the mountains and out to sea, to be beaten by the surf, then brought back and buried alive in the sand. A deep breath escaped her lungs that was part relief and part disappointment: she was not dead.

As Aurora stumbled down the hill into the northern wind that would carry her to her people, she could feel her wounds knitting and healing. Her eyes welled with tears for she could also feel the fading of her companion's Energies. She did not know how her companions had done it but, somehow, they had funneled their magic — and in part their own beings — into her. They had sacrificed themselves so that they could save her life. Twice!

Aurora tried to stop her swirl of thoughts for fear of adding a headache to her pains. She rubbed her palms against her eyes and noticed that her wounds were almost healed. She smiled forlornly in wordless thanks to her companions as the last of their magic was depleted from her conscious. She entered the wind and was immediately swept off of her feet with a fully recovered body, and a grave heart.

****

"Will Silvia be alright?" Ryder whispered, squatting down by Gwendolyn and watching as she methodically wrapped a bandage around a wounded villager's upper arm. The Healer looked up at Ryder, a tender, worn-out look on her face.

"I have no reassurances for you," she admitted, then dropped her eyes back to her patient. "Nor for many of the wounded here in the Hall."

"You don't think she will?" Ryder insisted.

"Ryder," Gwendolyn touched the villager's forehead to check for a fever, found none, then rose to her feet. "Ryder, I don't know. I really don't," she repeated, kneeling beside a wounded Thurnadanian soldier.

"But?" Ryder pestered.

"But I've never heard of a transfer of magic," Gwendolyn relented and answered, "where the giver lives."

"She's a Healer and she is giving him all of her magic?" Ryder's mouth dropped open in shock. Gwendolyn remained silent.

"I believe she won't live if she transfers her magic," Gwendolyn bluntly stated.

"You don't know that!"

"Yes," Gwendolyn fought back tears, "I do. To my knowledge that is how it works. Never in our history have both survived a transfer of magic."

"My King?" called a surviving Sharnin soldier from up a tree. His voice echoed strangely in the empty woods. Zagan had been dragging himself forward on his hands and knees but halted his wobbling, strained movements in order to look around for the voice. "We thought you were dead, Sire," the soldier swung down from the tree to stand at attention with his fist on his chest. Zagan tried staggering to his feet and failed. "A little help here, soldier!" Zagan snapped at the young man.

"None of us could hear you," the soldier exclaimed as he helped the wounded man to his feet.

Zagan choked on his own blood. "I am wounded," he struggled to say. "How," Zagan wheezed once his features had solidified again, "how many have survived?"

"Very few," the soldier admitted.

"Lead the way to them," the King held his wounded throat protectively.

"We have not really regrouped, my Lord. Most who lived have fled," the soldier tucked himself under the King's arm to try to support him. "You don't wish to call the others here?"

Zagan did not reply. His body betrayed him; it shook, shifted, convulsed, and wobbled even with every fiber of his concentration focused. He wanted to call his men, but he had no mental magic. No healing magic. No control. The King forced back his feelings of helplessness.

"Just get me to a Healer."

"I hope there is still one to find," the soldier grimaced.

****

"Her body must become accustomed to the change from magic to no magic," Gwendolyn sighed, as Silvia writhed in pain.

"And if her body fails to adapt to the change?" Ryder's question hung ominously in the air.

"She won't live," Gwendolyn wrung her hands.

"And what about my High Constable?" Eleanor asked from behind them.

"If Argus' body accepts the magic he will heal, and in the future, continue healing. If his body rejects the magic — "

"He'll die," Ryder finished. A silence fell over the group as they all observed Silvia and Argus.

"They will both die," Gwendolyn broke the silence with her grim news.

"I will have the soldiers prepare to return to the castle," Eleanor stated before she spun around. "Ryder, I request your help in assembling a return party," she called over her shoulder.

Twenty-One

A long-legged spider crept into the dining hall then callously shifted into human form. "It seems even the best of Descendants can get into trouble," Xenos said as he leaned casually against the dining room table. Malcolm and Bridget sat startled and the remaining guard in the room drew his sword.

"Xenos, so you are the Shifter that the cook was talking about." Bridget realized, protectively edging her way in front of Malcolm. The King gestured for the guard to stay his sword.

"Who are you?" Malcolm demanded of the pale-skinned shifter.

"I am. And you are a traitor whose demise is fast approaching," Xenos answered ignoring the King's question. Bridget paled. "The unfortunate thing about plans going awry is that you usually have to get your hands dirty in order to fix them."

"What are you talking about?" Bridget gulped.

"I demand to know who you are!" the King insisted.

Xenos grinned mirthlessly and focused his gaze on the King. "I am a skilled Shifter of the Snow Lands, though I serve the Sharnin King. Don't even think about it," Xenos warned Malcolm. "Did you really think I wouldn't notice that nod to your soldier? Come now, don't insult me so." The shifter growled, "Besides, Malcolm, I'm not here for you."

"King," Malcolm spat. "King Malcolm. Then why are you here?" he insisted.

"Well, my original duty was to kill Aurora," the Shifter tweaked an eyebrow at Bridget and continued, "but clearly, she is not here. The battle is over. Sharnin has been defeated. Therefore, I cannot fulfill my orders."

"And?" the King pressed.

"I don't feel much inclined to tell you more," Xenos shrugged, pulled out a chair from the table, and sat down. "Though I admit my inquisitiveness is getting the better of me again," he frowned.

"Zagan sent you?" Bridget squeaked.

"You know this man?" Malcolm asked, now even more confused than ever.

"Sharnin has lost, go home with your tail between your legs. Beg Zagan to take you back," Bridget spat.

"Is that what you are doing here?" Xenos guffawed. Bridget flushed with anger and Malcolm's eyes darted between the maid and the shifter with suspicion.

"Bridget, what is he talking about?" the King asked.

"She didn't tell you?" Xenos laughed, his indigo-rimmed eyes glinting with mischief.

"Tell me what?" Malcolm inquired, irritation sharpening the edge of his voice.

"What do you want?" Bridget repeated her question.

Xenos sniffed and rubbed his nose, "Compensation."

"I don't understand," Bridget locked eyes with the Shifter.

"Neither do I. Someone tell me what is going on or I will have you both thrown into the dungeons!" the King roared.

"When I was still in school in the Snow Lands, I heard of a prophecy foretold long ago by the Ancients in their dying days about a red-haired woman who would save the Temperate Lands from ruin," Xenos spoke in a low tone. The King fell silent as he strained to hear the Shifter's soft words. "When I was told to dispose of Aurora," the shifter murmured, "it triggered my recollection of the Scarlet

268

Prophecy. I don't take kindly to being given orders to destroy someone fated with the power to save the lives of my kind. My loyalty resides with Sharnin but my teachings are Snow Land, my knowledge Snow Land, and my sense of honor Snow Land."

"If you did not want to kill her why did you come here?" the King inferred.

"Zagan," Bridget answered for Xenos.

"There is no need to kill her now. Her destiny has been fulfilled," Xenos smiled, smugly avoiding giving the King a straight answer. "However, I know I have fallen from the graces of King Zagan by not completing his task."

"So you wish to lessen his wrath," Bridget lowered her eyes to the floor, "by taking him me."

"Why you?" Malcolm implored.

Bridget lifted her eyes to the King's and grimaced. "I am a traitor," she breathed out hard, "of the worst kind."

"Bridget, what are you talking about?" the King snapped.

"I left out details of the story," she bleated.

"I have a feeling this is going to take a while," Xenos said with a chortle. "Mind if I take a nap?" Bridget rolled her eyes then sobered. The Shifter set his head in the crook of one arm and rested it on the table.

"Queen Eleanor requested my assistance to free Donovan. And I did," Bridget admitted. Xenos raised one hand, and one finger, from the table. Bridget cringed. "But I- I had already been recruited for the Sharnin army long before then." The Shifter held up a second finger. "Donovan trained all the Sharnin recruits," Bridget stuttered. "He made it sound like his father's takeover of Thurnadan would free Descendants like me from fear and judgment by those who do not have magic." Bridget rushed on, "I was a spy for King Zagan."

Xenos held up a third finger. "I reported to him on the plans of the castle, on the Queen, on you. Everything. Whenever he called on me. I knew more than anyone else because- because you and the Queen trusted me." Xenos wiggled his fingers. "Zagan plans became more and more brutal. He deserted his son. He tortured his own soldiers. He had no intention of doing what he had promised."

The King's frown hardened. "I wanted to get away. But I didn't know how. He told me to kill Aurora. Kill her or have my mind wiped by a Handler. But I didn't. I refused his order." Xenos held up a fourth finger. "I thought perhaps Donovan would still make the changes he had long-ago swore to when he'd first started recruiting. But I realized he's not much better than his father. I figured out you were Donovan's next target and stopped him from killing you." Xenos held up his fifth and final finger. Silence fell over the room. The guard closed his gaping mouth and Malcolm pinched the bridge of his nose. The Shifter dropped his hand back to the table.

"That is quite the tale," Malcolm finally replied. "The betrayals just keep mounting today, do they not?" The King wrapped his finger's painfully tightly around Bridget's wrist.

"I deserve whatever death King Zagan gives me," Bridget admitted.

"Yes, quite true. I should certainly have you imprisoned or killed or both. Or maybe I should just let the Shifter take you," he hissed. "Obviously, your pretty words of demons and mistakes were not innocently spoken. You turned traitor, lived a lie, and then you spite me to my face?" His eyes blazed with anger, "The only reason I am not sentencing you to a ruthless death right this instant is because you saved my life." Xenos stretched, sat back up in his chair, and watched Bridget tremble.

"Is one redeeming act enough to cover five betrayals?" Xenos interjected, trying not to sound too smug.

"And you? You think you are in regard high enough to cast judgement on her?" Malcolm turned to Xenos and let go of Bridget's wrist. "You betrayed your homeland by joining Sharnin, did you not?"

"I left," the Shifter replied bluntly. "There's a difference between turning traitor and simply leaving."

"Really?" Bridget brayed.

"If I remember correctly, Aurora was from the Achlese Academy in the Snow Lands, the same as you," the King continued. "Her companions were sadistically slaughtered on their way here to help Thurnadan. And I can only assume that was the handiwork of the Sharnin army," the King straightened his shoulders and glared at Xenos.

"How does that have anything to do with me being a traitor or not?" the Shifter rose defensively from his seat, his eyes growing sinister.

"You were among those soldiers, weren't you?" Bridget replied in an icy monotone. Xenos' pale skin grew even whiter.

"You don't know that," he snarled.

"I think you just confirmed it," Malcolm stated without emotion.

"I had no choice," he growled.

"The magic of the Snow Lands and the build of a trained warrior? I find it hard to believe you had no choice. You are an intimidating man, to be sure."

"Yes, but I let her live." The room fell silent.

"What do you mean you let her live?" Malcolm said.

"After the attack on the Academy, she was there lying in the snow. I could have killed her then. But I left her," Xenos spoke and hung his head.

"To die."

"Yes," Xenos admitted.

Malcolm paused briefly as he surveyed the Shifter in front of him. "You will stay here with us, Xenos," Malcolm stated abruptly.

"No," Xenos shook his head and laughed. "And no one here could make me." The King looked suggestively at Bridget.

Instantly comprehending, Bridget murmured, "Ficar seranda."

"What spell did you just set on me?" Xenos lunged at Bridget.

"You're not harmed!" Bridget squealed, narrowly avoiding his clutches.

"Silence!" the King bellowed.

"I have bonded you to King Malcolm just as Zagan bonded to me. When he calls, you will be compelled to answer."

"So many things need to be sorted out," Malcolm raked his hands through his dark hair. "When the Queen and Aurora return, there will be much to discuss. Until then, I will not have either of you escaping my watch."

"My Lord!" Bridget tried to protest.

"You said there was no reason to kill Aurora now that the Ancients' prophecy has been fulfilled," the King expounded, talking solely to the Shifter. Xenos ground his teeth. "And my conscience keeps me from being willing to give Zagan the satisfaction of killing Bridget. Therefore, a compromise is going to have to be made."

"I am not pleased," Xenos grunted at Malcolm. "Do not expect my cooperation."

"I'm sure you don't want to, but I will get it."

"And I may be bonded to you but that is only while..." Xenos' gaze drilled into Bridget.

"While what? While he lives? Do you seriously think you are going to kill King Malcolm? I do not think that is who you are, Xenos," Bridget taunted.

A flash of a smile crossed Xenos' lips before he shifted to his hawk form and glided out of the room.

"Escort Bridget to her chambers and do not let her leave until you have gotten such instruction from me, and me alone," the King ordered his flabbergasted guard.

"Yes, my Lord," the guard saluted and lead Bridget from the room.

****

As she mounted her horse and looked over the people, Eleanor sighed at what she was sure would be a long, tiresome journey back to the castle where an uncertain welcome awaited her. The troops who were well enough to get into formation had done so. The wounded had been loaded onto wagons. The majority of Layton's population had either been killed or was going on to the castle for medical help. Ryder gently arranged blankets around the still-unconscious Argus and Silvia while Lairson climbed into a wagon of wounded soldiers.

"We're as ready as we'll ever be," saluted the captain as he rode up beside the Queen.

"Thank you," she replied. All of the sudden she could feel someone tugging at her mind. With the war over she decided it was safe to connect.

Your Highness, Aurora's voice tugged at Eleanor's mind. Perplexed, and feeling very guilty, the Queen was reluctant to respond.

You're alive? she hesitantly accepted the mind connection.

I do not feel like you deserve my help, Aurora scolded, causing the Queen to flinch. *But for the sake of the wounded I will help your trip go more quickly.* The Queen raised one fair eyebrow but immediately winced at the pain caused by the wound along her cheek.

What about you?

My whereabouts are not currently of your concern.

"Well then," the Queen said to herself. Mystified, she turned to her captain, "Let us be on our way."

Eleanor felt the breeze pick up and knew Aurora had begun using her Wind Whispering. Her brow creased as she urged her horse forward toward home.

Twenty-Two

Five days had passed since the battle in Layton, and the castle was still in disorder. The troops had returned, border patrols had been set up, but still the Queendom struggled to resume normality. Malcolm summoned his subjects together in the Grand Hall to collectively decide the future of Thurnadan. Despite the beauty of the hall, with its floor to ceiling stained glass windows, and gleaming silver and gold chandeliers, the King's heart lay heavy.

The King spoke solemnly, his words echoing off the Queen's ominously empty throne, "Due to emotional attachment, I feel I may not be able to bestow unbiased judgment upon your Queen," Hundreds of people gathered in the room. Nobles, soldiers, villagers, Descendants, and servants alike were so quiet the King thought they may all be holding their breath. "Battle nearly tore Layton to nothing and an all-out war was narrowly avoided. The scars of intrusion, still raw on our land, will long be a reminder of our mistakes and our fears. I can, however, tell you with confidence that Sharnin has issued no further threats, Donovan, son of King Zagan, has been securely re-imprisoned, and King Zagan's renegade Descendants have remained peacefully quiet. Enemy soldiers have not dared set foot across our border since their defeat. But," Malcolm swallowed and calmed his nerves, "we are not yet at peace. The shadow of deceit has found its way into this Queendom, into this castle, even into my own marriage." The crowd began talking over one another. The King raised his hand for silence. "My Lady?" Malcolm's expression was filled with sadness as Eleanor entered the hall from a side door. Despite her plain attire, out of respect, the gathered people bowed deeply.

"I am Eleanor, the Lady Queen of Thurnadan. Your Ivory Queen," the Queen spoke with her head held high despite the tears that ran from her eyes without end. The wound on her cheek had mostly healed, leaving only a small crescent-shaped scar. "I have not reigned honorably as my mother did and unfortunately, like her, I have stumbled. As a traitor, I betrayed my home and as a wife, I have betrayed my husband. I used my magic against Thurnadanian law. I am a Descendant."

The crowd gasped as angry shouts rose from the back of the room. "A Descendant!?"

Eleanor tried to gather the crowd's attention to move on. She began to shout her confessions.

"The hunger for power corrupted me. I do not deserve your mercy. But I plead for it just the same," she turned and braved the crowd. "My mother bore me, the heiress of Thurnadan, but she also bore another."

"Is this true?" shouted one brave villager. The crowd eyed each other in questioning, wondering who else knew of this secret.

"It is," Malcolm said gravely. "I asked the Queen Mother's nurse maid. It is true she had another child. A son." Mutters of surprise and disbelief threaded through the crowd then faded.

"Donovan, the man you know as the Shifter who wreaked havoc on our lands years ago," the Queen wrung her hands together, "is my half-brother. He is the son of my mother and the son and heir to King Zagan. To keep the scandal a secret, Mind Handlers wiped the memory of many people." Shock shook the crowd so badly they could not respond. "My mother was wrought with self-loathing that she had lain with another man, but she loved Donovan nonetheless. His imprisonment broke her heart. On her deathbed, she blessed my reign and made a request," Eleanor swallowed, the lump in her throat growing. "She made me vow to release my brother. His escape was not an escape. I have covered my Inking, but I am a Handler; I broke Donovan out of prison using my magic." The onlookers erupted in shouts and taunts. The King raised his hand again and the crowd was silenced.

"Everything I did was wrong. Foolish. But I did it out of duty. And to add to it, King Zagan was perfectly satisfied with his son being locked away. Because of his healing abilities, he sees no need for an heir," Eleanor shook her head. "I failed to kill King Zagan in battle. He lives on. However, we are told his magic consumes him: that it has turned against him and is torturing him. He has no control." The crowd erupted into shouts of enthusiasm and disbelief. "I have betrayed you all as Queen," Eleanor restated over the shouting. "A traitor deserves death. It is the law."

The Queen knelt then bowed forward toward the King. When she stood again her posture seemed hollow and sad.

"Have you anything else you wish to say?" Malcolm spoke coldly.

"I beg of you though, spare my life, please. If not for me," Eleanor swallowed hard, "for the sake of our heir." She gently placed her hands over her stomach. Astonishment slammed the crowd into silence. Even the King's mouth dropped open. "Layton's healer, Gwendolyn, can confirm that I am indeed with child," the Queen lowered her eyes to floor, curtsied, and guards started to escort her out of the hall.

"Has the Queen done anything in a short time that would cause us to reduce the punishment from death?" Malcolm forced his voice through the lump in his throat.

"Your Highness," Aurora appeared in the idle of the floor in a swirl of earth, air, fire, and water. The crowd jerked back in awe. Aurora curtsied nonchalantly then rolled up her gown's sleeves and pulled up the hem of her skirt. Her Inkings appeared, shining more brightly than the hall's chandeliers. The crowd gasped when they saw the glow radiating from her limbs, chest, and face. She stood regally in a white gown with a golden cape that flowed delicately behind her. Her red hair was piled and twisted on top of her head.

"Look at me," Aurora's voice trailed through the crowd, undemanding yet prevalent. *Look at me,* she repeated mentally. "You will not find a Descendant stronger than I. Yet, it broke me to my soul to use my magic as a weapon." Having heard the story of Layton's magical victory, the crowd knelt in respect to the one who fulfilled the Scarlet Prophecy. "I believe," Aurora spoke softly making the crowd hush and lean forward to hear her, "that if the Queen will now bear the Inking of her magic it will serve as a permanent reminder of what she has done. She will not soon forget the lesson of mercy we have the opportunity to give her." Aurora stared fiercely into the crowd. She closed her eyes and lifted her hands towards the sky. Red sparks began to fly from her finger tips, and with a flick of her arms she threw the sparks into the Queen's shoulder. The Inking of the Mind Handler was shown brightly on her skin. Eleanor screamed out and fell to the ground in excruciating pain. "I have made it impossible to hide your Inking. If you use your magic, you will feel the pain of the lives you have cost as you do now." Quickly, Aurora sent silver sparks onto the Queen shoulder, instantly dulling the pain. Eleanor rose to her feet. Aurora turned to the crowd. "The Queen has reigned poorly. At one time, I foresaw a dark future for Thurnadan because of her. However, my

Sight makes me believe that, if some changes are made, this country will flourish under the reign of your child," Aurora smiled at the Queen and King, and then in a burst of gold she vanished just as quickly as she had appeared.

"Hear hear," someone from the crowd shouted.

"I second that," called another.

"Only if the laws are put down!" yelled another.

Malcolm raised his hand for silence, "Yes, I agree. Due to our victory, the laws should be put down. A new reign will mean a change from the old ways."

"Long live the King!" the crowd cheered.

****

"Your Highness," Argus and Ryder saluted Malcolm once he had settled in his study. The King motioned for them to sit at the table across from him.

"I have come ta' make a request I never figured I would," Argus began. "I have fought in every battle ya' could think of in the last thirty years. Many an occasion I shoulda' died. I lost my family an' I thought I'd lost my Silvia —" Argus choked up.

"Is she still unconscious?" The King's eyebrows creased together in concern.

"Yes," Ryder answered for Argus. "But she still breathes."

Argus regained his composure and continued speaking, "Silvia were a Clodith military daughter, did a lot of travelin' wit' her family. Picked up proper speech like I ain't never done. We was content wit' each other for years, even got married. I were a soldier though. And she din' like that none since she wanted ta' leave that type a' life. I tried stayin' away from the job but seein' how war ripped people apart, I had ta'

279

keep fighting. Silvia felt betrayed." Argus continued, "I heard after the Battle that my village in Clodith by the river's mouth had been wiped out. I didn't go back. Didn't wanta' see the carnage. My Silvia had lived an I assume she believed I died same as I believed in her fate." Ryder patted Argus on the back in commiseration.

"My Lord," Argus breathed heavily and raised his eyes from the table to meet the King's. "I came to Thurnadan and joined your ranks not wanting nothin' to do wit' home or house. But," Argus paused, "I have finished my warrin' days." Malcolm leaned forward to speak but Argus held up his hands, "Hear me out. I was struck by a tundra wolf. The only reason I ain't dead is 'cause my lady sacrificed herself ta' save me." Argus picked up a letter opener from the table and scratched it across the back of his hand. Blood welled up instantly. The King winced then watched, impressed, as the wounds closed up almost as quickly as they had sprouted. "She gave me 'er Healin' magic. I could go on fightin' for eternity," Argus straightened his shoulders. "But I don't want ta." Argus frowned sternly, "My Lord, I request that you release me from my position as High Constable."

"It saddens me to hear this," Malcolm admitted sincerely.

"Ryder's village was destroyed." Argus cleared his throat, "He ain't got a reason to return home but his skills as a leader would be a shame ta waste. Mighten' I humbly suggest him as my replacement?"

"You have been far more than a soldier to me, Argus," the King inclined his head. "You have been an ally and a friend. I cannot refuse your request. Ryder, at Argus' recommendation, I will gladly appoint you as the new High Constable."

"At your service," Ryder bowed forward in his seat.

"But Argus," Malcolm halted the men as they rose to leave.

"Yes, my Lord?"

"It would be a great comfort to me to still have a friend nearby. There is a courtyard house and small plot on the eastern side of the castle, I would be pleased if you and Silvia, when she wakes..." he smiled sorrowfully, "take up residence there. Perhaps you can still offer counsel when need arises?"

"With honor, thank you, my Lord," Argus bowed, and he and Ryder left the room.

****

As the hills around Thurnadan's castle glowed orange in the evening light, Eleanor stood alone in her bedchambers. The skin of her face was splotchy from crying, her eyesight was blurry, and her nose ran with persistence. Eleanor hummed tunelessly as she laid a gentle hand on her belly. She winced at the pain that the movement caused where the Inking of a peacock feather had been revealed on her upper arm. It glowed mockingly from the reflection in her mirror. Hypnotically, Eleanor traced the top of the feather with the trembling fingers of her opposite hand.

"My Lady?" Bridget cajoled as she entered the room. "Come away from the mirror. It does no good to look at it." The Queen turned to Bridget but said nothing. "Let me rub some of this healing gel on you," Bridget suggested, holding up a bottle. The Queen nodded and sat down on a stool by her dresser. "The pain goes away but the knowledge does not. It was a fair decision." Bridget murmured. "Your husband, he is a good man. He spared both our lives, you know?" She gently massaged the gel into the Queen's new Inking as she spoke, "It feels good to be honest, doesn't it?"

"It does," Eleanor whispered. Bridget smiled, happy that she had gotten the Queen to speak. "Malcolm let you leave your chambers, I see?"

"He did, though only because he had another Descendant set a spell on me to keep me locked within the castle grounds. I do not deserve his trust."

"You're alive though. The Shifter, Xenos, did not take you and Malcolm did not have you beheaded. I see there is mercy yet in your bones."

"I suppose." Silence filled the air between them.

"Eleanor," Malcolm called out as he swung their bedchamber door open. Bridget curtsied then slipped out of the room with a sad smile. The King walked over to the bed and sat down beside his wife.

"Malcolm," Eleanor sighed, her voice tinted with sorrow. She tilted her head. "Will you ever forgive me?" the Queen implored in a hushed voice.

"I cannot honestly say how long it will take me to forgive you. You have betrayed everything we have worked for, everything we have built together. You broke my trust and my heart. These last few days have been the most tortuous thing my soul has ever been put through," the King replied, voice gravelly with emotion. "But it would be a lie for me to say that I do not still love you," the King's stiff posture softened slightly. "I love you, Eleanor. And somehow, love always seems to forgive."

"You may love and forgive me, Malcolm," the Queen whispered. "But what of the people? I fear they will not let me live after the baby is born."

"They may not."

****

In the Western mountains of the Snow Lands, Aurora sat near the fire in her new encampment.

"Thank you again for your kindness," a man said as he turned to Aurora.

"It's the least I can do for saving my life," Aurora smiled at Xenos.

"I should have done more. I will prove myself to you, Aurora."

"Good. Your loyalty is all I ask."

They both looked into the fire as it began to die down. Aurora threw a few sparks to reignite it keep them warm.

"Strange. It is so strange," Aurora set her chin in her hand, baffled. The Descendants hard at work all around them.

"Why did no one tell you about the prophecy?" Xenos questioned.

"I did remember being told once when I was young." Aurora admitted. "However, the memory was buried deep."

"They probably tried to wipe it from your mind. What you must have remembered are the traces if it. You went to the Academy a few years before I left. That place was alight with whispers and rumors about the 'Dram Red One.' But the Dan'tes and the council did not want to burden you with a preordained future. It changes a person," replied Xenos. "They were also very hesitant to proclaim the fulfillment of the Scarlet Prophecy since it meant the coming of a desolating war and indicated the first step toward the end of man's reign."

"If that's truly the reason they kept me ignorant, I can accept it," Aurora stated grimly. "Though I hope it is not true. Stories are all I've ever heard concerning the Ancients, though

I know many people take their prophecies to be the solemn truth."

"My people hold the Ancients in high regard. The prophecies are not just tales, but rather the truths of time," Xenos admitted. "To us, the Ancients are creatures of wing and scale and fire, explosively full of magic and power. They lived and reigned centuries ago," Xenos' voice became melodious as he repeated the legend that had been passed down for generations. "My people believe that every person's fate has been determined by the tide and turn of the seasons and that the Ancients in their wisdom saw our destinies long before we came into existence. However, believing in the Scarlet Prophecy meant believing many great tragedies would take place."

Aurora chewed on her bottom lip as she processed what she had been told. "I wonder if my parents are still alive. My mother I never knew. My father... after he left me at the Academy, I never heard from again," she choked up. "But I assume he's still out there. Why did you leave?" Aurora abruptly changed the subject. She stared at Xenos accusingly.

"The same reason Bridget did," he admitted, ashamed. "After I graduated from the Academy, I was at a loss for what to do with myself. A soldier from Sharnin talked me into joining the army," Xenos scratched the back of his neck.

"Go on," Aurora urged.

"For this you will hate me," Xenos' posture wilted. "I received a mind-message from the master teachers that King Malcolm had traveled to the Snow Lands to plea for Descendants' assistance in the approaching war. Unfortunately, at that exact moment, I was mentally linked to Zagan."

"So he heard the message as well," Aurora whispered, shivers washing across her skin. Xenos bowed his head further over his cup. "Sharnin ambushed us at the Academy because of you?!" Aurora snarled.

"For that I am sorry and will spend the rest of my days atoning," Xenos lifted his gaze to meet Aurora's. "Zagan is a Mind Handler, for I could not otherwise have been so monstrous. I- I killed my own people, left them naked so no one could recognize them, watched as they bled out into the snow. In a tundra bird's form, I stayed through the storm to make sure you were all dead. Well, most of you," Xenos faltered. "After that, I still served him. I even went to Thurnadan to murder you for him!"

Aurora swallowed the vile taste in her mouth, "Zagan has that influence no longer. His powers are gone," Aurora stated bluntly.

"That's true? I thought the Queen was just being delusional."

"Yes, it's true." Aurora contemplatively stoked the flames of her campfire once more. "Donovan came to Achlese Academy a year after I did," Aurora's motions became more animated as realizations flooded her mind. "His father, Zagan, came years later to take him away." Aurora bit her lip in concentration, "He tried to suffocate me using a trick of shifting into mist. I must have formed a mind connection with Zagan then, because he was speaking to Donovan through me!" Aurora rubbed her hand across her face, "that must be why I was able to hear his memories during the battle," she finished. "Queen Eleanor gave Zagan an extremely potent concoction for magic removal. Something thought to be able to completely wipe out his magic," Aurora's voice grew coarse. "She then drove her sword through his throat. Zagan's magic reacted strangely. It was like he had lost his power but the magic had no place else to go, so it turned in on him." Aurora shrugged, a bit baffled. "His mist shifting caused him a horrendous amount of pain and he could not heal his wounds nor connect to another mind." She turned to Xenos, "Bridget says he has not called her again. She came to me to remove the magic between her and Zagan because Donovan," Aurora rolled her eyes, "told her that Seers could do such things. She has not felt a connection to Zagan, just like I have not."

Xenos closed his eyes and frowned. "You are right," he breathed after a moment. He opened his eyes again and sincerely smiled for the first time in a long time. "I can no longer feel my connection to Zagan."

"The strength of his mental connection has died away," Aurora rested her small tan hand on Xenos' pale forearm. "You're free."

"As are you, Aurora," Xenos replied pointedly. "Oh, I have something that belongs to you." He reached into his pocket and gave her a stone. The clear stone, with shards of blackness running through, hung on a silver chain.

"My necklace! I thought I had lost it on the day of the attack. How did you…" Aurora stopped herself. "Thank you for returning it to me."

"I didn't know how precious it was to you. I'm sorry."

"It's an Ancient's Stone. The light and the dark seem to be fighting. It's messy and somehow beautiful," she spoke as she twirled the pendant in her fingers. She smiled up at him.

"Xenos?" Aurora hesitated, tugging at her gown sleeves. "I intend on starting up a new magic academy."

Xenos shook his head, belittling. "And you think another academy can make things better?"

"Yes," Aurora smiled. "We must rebuild," she stated firmly. "I will teach to honor my Dan'te's life." She clutched her hands together.

"I wish you luck, Aurora," Xenos said gravely as he stood to leave.

"I had rather hoped," Aurora sought out his eyes, "that you might join me."

"Me?" Xenos touched one hand to his chest. "I'm a Sharrin soldier!"

"You're a Snow Land Descendant and a former student of the Academy," Aurora pursed her lips, "and I could use the help."

"Even after all that I've done?"

"Because of all that you've done," Aurora bluntly reminded Xenos.

"You trust me?"

"Not particularly," Aurora replied honestly. "Maybe a bit." She smiled. Xenos smiled back at her. "Well?" Aurora pressed for an answer. Xenos snorted as he looked down at Aurora's anxious face.

"Fine," he relented. "But you should not trust me. Not even a bit."

Aurora tilted her head and gave Xenos a little smirk. "I'll be sure to remember that."